PROJECT PROMETHEUS

Also by Aden Polydoros

PROJECT PANDORA
HADES RISING

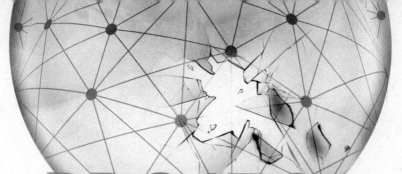

PROJECT PROMETHEUS

AN ASSASSIN FALL NOVEL

ADEN POLYDOROS

Entangled Publishing, LLC
2614 South Timberline Road
Suite 105, PMB 159
Fort Collins, CO 80525
rights@entangledpublishing.com

Entangled Teen is an imprint of Entangled Publishing, LLC.

Visit our website at www.entangledpublishing.com.

Edited by Liz Pelletier
Cover design by Clarissa Yeo
Interior design by Toni Kerr

Cover images by
Ronald Sumners/Shutterstock
lukas_zb/Shutterstock
andersphoto/Shutterstock
zhu difeng/Shutterstock
Netfalls Remy Musser/Shutterstock
Runrun2/Shutterstock
PERFECTO/Shutterstock

ISBN 978-1-64063-189-2
Ebook ISBN 978-1-64063-190-8

Manufactured in the United States of America

First Edition August 2018
10 9 8 7 6 5 4 3 2 1

an imprint of Entangled Publishing LLC

To Barbara Youngs,
Thank you for the last three years of encouragement,
mentoring, writing-related puns, and laughter.

REPORT:

SOLE SURVIVOR OF GEORGETOWN SHOOTING DISAPPEARS UNDER SUSPICIOUS CIRCUMSTANCES

By Priscilla Hines
Posted 10/31 9:10

Chaos broke out in Georgetown yesterday morning, when residents of the affluent D.C. neighborhood reported hearing automatic gunfire coming from a private residence. SWAT teams, police officers, and paramedics immediately rushed to the scene. According to an anonymous source with the Metropolitan Police Department, Senator Hawthorne's daughter, Elizabeth, 17, was among the seven dead. Two of the other victims have been identified as Dr. Dimitri Kosta, 48, a psychiatrist based in Columbia Heights, and rightwing extremist Johnathon Bay, 36. The identities of the four remaining victims have yet to be released.

A young man was admitted to MedStar Georgetown University Hospital in critical condition, only to disappear from the hospital late last night. According to our sources, two men dressed as hospital employees took the sedated victim, who was under police protection at the time, out for a "scheduled operation." In a televised press conference at 8:00 this morning, police spokesman Max Umbridge described the victim as a person of interest in not only the Georgetown shooting but also the vicious assault that occurred at nearby Manderly Preparatory Academy on the 29th. He declined to comment on the possibility that the shooting might be an act of terrorism.

The gunshot victim is described as a Caucasian male between 16 and 20 years of age, with medium-length black hair, blue eyes, and an athletic build. He has "A-02" tattooed on his right wrist, a tally mark tattoo on his left forearm, and heavy scarring on his back. He is believed to be in imminent danger. Anyone with information pertaining to his whereabouts or identity is requested to contact authorities.

CASE NOTES 1:

HADES

Hades awoke inside the sensory deprivation tank, in full dark.

As he struggled to cast off the drugged weakness that enveloped him, he could almost feel the darkness wrapping around him, heavy as wool, smothering. Needles bit into his arms, and the walls collapsed in, closer, closer. Soon they would crush him.

Gasping in terror, he extended his arms to touch the steel walls of his prison, only to discover that his hands were immobilized above his head.

Chains rattled with his panicked movements. Chains. Slim metal bands around his wrists. Handcuffs. Fear mellowed into powerful disorientation. Why was he wearing handcuffs? Was this another one of Dimitri's experiments?

He suddenly became aware that the surface beneath him was not buoyant water, but instead a mattress of some sort. Soft, lumpy cushioning, damp with sweat or blood.

He wasn't in the sensory deprivation tank at the Georgetown safe house, so where was he?

Not a hospital, that's for sure. Hospitals were bright,

noisy places, filled with the cacophony of monitor alarms and intercom chatter. Here, there were no safety lights, and the only sound he could distinguish was his own heavy breathing.

As he pulled at the cuffs, pinpricks raced down his arms. Not needles, just muscle soreness and poor circulation. There might have been an IV tube in the crook of his elbow. It was too dark to tell, but that was what it felt like. With his hands chained to what he assumed was the headboard of a bed and his ankles similarly fettered, his movements were restricted to the minimum.

This was wrong. During those times when his rage became uncontrollable and he lashed out at everything around him, Dimitri had always used soft restraints and sedatives on him. Never handcuffs. Torqued the wrong way, handcuffs could cut off the circulation in his wrists.

His hands were the most valuable part of him.

As Hades shifted on the mattress, his stomach throbbed with a soft, bruised ache. Whatever drug muddled his mind also took the edge off his pain. He had difficulty associating the feeling with himself.

That's right, I was shot, he thought. *So what am I doing here? Where am I?*

As he yanked at the chains, he was distracted by a creaking overhead. Footsteps crossed the ceiling, and from deeper into the room above, hinges squeaked as a door was opened.

Light flooded the room. Concrete floor and brick walls. Boxes along one wall, workout machines along the other. No windows. The far wall opened into an alcove that he assumed led to a stairwell, and he watched a brown-haired man step out from it.

"Oh, you're finally awake," the man said, walking up to

his bed. "I was getting a little worried, kiddo. The doctors really doped you up. I heard you tried to bite them. Like a wild animal."

Though the man's expression was bland, his flushed complexion and narrowed eyes suggested internal turmoil. Caged rage. His voice only confirmed as much.

With a jolt, Hades recognized the man's lean, patrician face. Lawrence Hawthorne, the state senator of Virginia. He had given one twin daughter to Project Pandora and kept the other, only to take the first away again when the latter twin died two years ago.

A low growl escaped Hades's throat. This was the man responsible for the death of the only girl that he had ever loved.

"I know you're a child of Pandora," Hawthorne said, resting his hands on the bed's cast-iron footboard.

He saw no point in responding.

"Tell me your name."

"I don't have one," Hades said.

"Your name."

"Subject Two of Subset A." A-02. Two. They all meant the same thing—a weapon, not a human.

A vein throbbed in Hawthorne's temple. "That's not a name."

"Hades."

"Hades? What's that supposed to mean?"

"It's Hell, and it's the god of Hell."

Hawthorne scoffed. "You're not a god. You're just a sick kid."

"It's the codename Dimitri gave me," he said, allowing his head to fall back against the pillow. "He asked me, isn't it interesting that Hell is both a person and a place? I didn't understand what he meant at first. Then I did."

It surprised him how effortless it was to grasp at that memory. Usually, his memories were scattered and disjointed, like bits of shattered bone that he had to sift through and reorganize. But everything had drifted back into place while he slept, leaving only the smallest gaps. Soon, he sensed, even those empty spaces would mend.

"We're not here to talk about Dr. Kosta," Hawthorne said. "We're here to talk about what you did, and don't try to deny it. I know you were acquainted with Dr. Kosta, but you work for someone higher up in the organization, don't you? Who do you take your orders from? Who in Project Pandora told you to shoot Elizabeth and the others?"

"Subject Nine of Subset A."

Hawthorne wrinkled his brow. "What?"

"That was her name. Not Elizabeth. Nine."

"Don't call her that," Hawthorne growled.

Hades lifted his head. "You're just her cell donor, so why do you care? You sold her before she was even born."

Hawthorne took two small bottles from the counter and carried them over. They were apothecary bottles, darkly tinted. They couldn't hold more than ten milliliters each, but even a fraction of that amount could be lethal, depending on the type of chemical.

"Listen, kid, we can do this the hard way or the easy way," Hawthorne said, then held up one of the bottles. "If you cooperate, I'll give you morphine once we're done talking."

He didn't want morphine. Pain was familiar, easy to work around. Morphine would only dull his senses. But he had a feeling the other chemical would do far worse than that.

"This is sodium thiopental," Hawthorne said, raising the second bottle. "I've heard that it can make subjects quite talkative, that they'll say things they'd never say otherwise. However, at a high enough dose, it can be fatal. And I'm willing to take that risk."

"Oh, I'm perfectly fine with telling you the truth. I don't need drugs for that." Hades lifted his head to look the man in the eye. "But first, just tell me... Does it give you satisfaction to kill your children?"

Hawthorne reeled back like he had been slapped. Huffing, his face red, he rushed to the counter and scrambled among its contents. Plastic crinkled under his searching fingers, and when he found what he was looking for, he turned back to the bed.

"You'll regret that." With a bottle in one hand and a plastic-wrapped syringe in the other, Hawthorne returned to his bedside. "If I can't get the truth out of you, this will."

"Did you know, your daughter and I were part of the same subset? We lived in the same barrack at the Academy, and we were in many of the same classes."

A muscle ticked in the corner of Hawthorne's mouth, and he looked away. In his poor eye contact and bodily tension, Hades saw unease beneath anger. Doubt. He held the syringe without trying to open it.

"Over the years, we came to be very close friends. Well, more than that, actually."

"Shut up," Hawthorne whispered.

"Nine wanted a real life so badly, did you know that?"

"Don't call her that."

"I forgot about it for so long, but I remember it now," he said. "It's all coming back to me. I remember how she talked about it. How you were going to give her a real name and a room of her own. How she was going to convince you and your wife to take me in as well, and I would be like a bodyguard to her."

Hawthorne sputtered for a response. He didn't even try to open the syringe now, just dropped what he held and strode around to the other side of the bed.

"Having a name, having a family, those things meant so much to her. But you just used her as a replacement. You used her like *trash*."

As the man glared down at him, Hades tensed, pulling at the handcuffs. His helplessness frustrated him to no end. There was nothing he could do but yank at the chains, rattling them.

What was Hawthorne going to do?

"You know it's true," he said, hiding his unease behind a mocking smile. It was easy to put on a mask.

"You bastard," Hawthorne growled.

"You know that, and you think you have the right to act resentful? You think you deserve sadness? You think I should feel guilty, when I was the only one who ever truly *loved* her?"

"You little—"

"I wasn't the one who killed her." His muscles flexed in expectation of a punch. "It was you. If not for you, she would never have died. You sacrificed your daughter for your own political gain, you—"

Hades never had a chance to finish, because then Hawthorne reached down and began choking him.

Gasping for breath, he writhed against his restraints. The handcuffs dug into his wrists while Hawthorne's fingers dug into his throat, cutting off all airflow. His shackled feet kicked against the bedframe, rattling it, to no effect.

Dark spots swarmed his vision. The burning in his throat became unbearable. In the distance, he heard hoarse gagging sounds. By the time he realized that the noises were coming from his own mouth, the darkness had already drawn close, closer, waves of lapping ink. His limbs weighed a hundred tons each, and his struggles stilled into the frail twitches of a baby bird fallen from its nest.

Just as he began to black out, the hands released from around his throat. Air rushed into his punished lungs, and the dark spots dissipated.

"N-no," Hawthorne whimpered, backing away. "Can't do it. Not like this."

Then the man made a low, anguished groan, and fled up the stairs without saying another word. The door slammed shut behind him.

Sinking into the mattress, Hades waited for his heartbeat to return to a normal rate. This wasn't his first near-death experience, and the symptoms were expected. Adrenaline left him shaking, consumed with the uncontrollable impulse to break free of his restraints and go in for the kill. His throat felt flayed, and each time he drew in a deep breath, his chest ached. The fact that his movements were limited to the two inches of chain that the handcuffs provided was an aggravation that made him want to howl in rage.

He listened until he couldn't hear the man's footsteps anymore, then stretched his hands out along the metal bars of the bedframe. He felt for any exposed screws or fastenings, and when he had reached as far as he could go on either side, he shifted his attention to the mattress itself. Because his hands were held too high to reach the cushion, he turned his head to the side and pulled back the sheet using his teeth. All it would take to fashion a lock pick was a stiff piece of metal, even something as simple as an upholstery pin.

Nothing. Just a protective rubber cover beneath the

linen, too thick to bite through. Useless.

As he continued his search along the pole, the paint flaked off under his nails. He craned his head back and stared up at the speckles of rust he had exposed.

Maybe his prison wasn't as solidly built as it had first appeared to be.

He cinched his fingers around the bar and twisted it, pulling until sweat stung his eyes and his chest burned.

Hades knew pain. It was like an old friend to him, and it was something Dimitri had taught him how to distance himself from. He closed his eyes and took a deep breath that ached, held the air inside him until he counted to four, then slowly exhaled. He did that twice more before trying again.

Another violent twist of the bar, and the headboard groaned. Particles of rust fell on his hands and face, and he felt the bar move a little. It wasn't welded on after all, and if there were screws, they must have been corroded as well.

Minutes passed as he struggled to twist the bar from its threaded hole. He toiled through the blisters and raw skin, determined to free himself before the senator returned.

When he yanked at the pole, it wiggled in its frame, just barely. Something tinkled to the floor. Probably a loose screw.

Grunting in exertion, he gave one final jerk and wrenched the pipe free. Careful not to let it fall, he drew his hands back over his head and rested the pole next to him. Though hollow, it would make a useful weapon.

As he sat up, he examined his hands. Blood welled from shallow scrapes. His palms were coated with rust and white paint. The handcuffs had cut into his wrists during his breathless struggle, leaving him with rings of welts. In places, the skin was broken.

Small sacrifices. They meant nothing.

Tetanus was no concern of his. Dimitri had treated his body like an expensive weapon, keeping him updated on all his vaccines and bandaging the wounds he acquired.

His mind had not been handled with the same respect.

Hades couldn't reach the IV in his elbow with his hands cuffed, but he leaned over himself and used his teeth to peel off the tape. He bit down on the plastic plug that the tube was attached to and pulled its tip from beneath his skin. It took nearly a full minute to perform a task that would have taken mere seconds if he had the use of his hands.

He transferred the IV tip to his fingers and studied it. Saline solution dribbled from the hollow point. The tip was too short to serve as a lock pick, and if he tried to bend it even the slightest, the rigid plastic would break off in the keyhole. Yet instead of letting the tube drop, he draped it over the mattress cover. Maybe it would serve some use in the future.

His ankles were chained to the footboard by cuffs of their own. Made specifically to restrain a person's legs, the shackles featured a long chain designed for restricted mobility. Useless unless he freed his legs.

Hades scooted forward and tested the pole his feet were attached to. It refused to budge. When he kicked the bar, it shook, sending vibrations through the chain and into his legs. He tried to twist the pole free a second time. Just from the metal's resolute silence as he pulled, he knew it would take even longer to free his ankles than it had his wrists. He went right to work.

Like with the headboard, the decorative bars on the footboard were anchored in place and reinforced with screws, which, unfortunately, were in better condition than those at the headboard. When he realized that his fingernails weren't up to the task, he pulled the plastic port from the IV tube and used the slender tip as a makeshift screwdriver. That didn't work very well either, and he tried the other end with better luck.

The first screw took five minutes to remove, but he was able to extract the second in half that time. He fell into a comfortable rhythm, losing himself in the aches and pains and the monotony of turning the IV port around and around.

By the time the second screw rolled onto the floor, it was a good thing that there weren't any more. Plastic shavings clung to his skin. The port's nub was worn into nothing, absolutely useless.

He freed his feet, swung them over the side of the bed, and stood, only to have his legs collapse beneath him. He dropped to his knees and thrust his hands out in front of him, clenching his teeth as jarring pain traveled from his palms up his arms and deep into the gunshot wound in his stomach.

Hades wormed to his feet again and seized the pipe from the bed. He hobbled forward, staying close to the wall. His legs were weak and trembling, the muscles cramping with each step. There was enough chain between his ankles that he could walk.

Handcuffs. He needed to get rid of these handcuffs.

He searched the cabinets along the wall, then the cardboard boxes. Pool gear, racquetball rackets, dumbbell weights, glassware. Worthless junk. Nothing he could use to pick the locks.

Hades made his way over to the home gym. There, resting beside the treadmill, he spotted a red toolbox. The exercise machine must have been assembled recently.

He eased to his knees and rooted through the box, shoving aside wrenches and screwdrivers until he came across a rat's nest of loose wire, nails, and picture hooks. He found a thin, wire in the mess and pushed it into the keyhole of his handcuffs.

As he maneuvered the wire back and forth into the hole, he listened for footsteps. Nothing yet.

The lock disengaged, and he slipped the band off his right wrist. He didn't bother unlocking the other handcuff. That could wait until after he freed his ankles.

As he inserted the rod into the keyhole of his leg shackle, the floor overhead creaked. He glanced up, then quickly got to work.

The door opened at the top of the stairwell, and the wire kept fumbling, slick with sweat and blood.

The latch clicked open, and he ripped the cuff from his ankle. He dropped the wire and stood. As soon as he climbed to his feet, he was struck by a dizzying wave of vertigo. He kept moving regardless, the loose ankle cuff rattling across the floor.

Once he reached the stairwell, he leaned against the wall and waited, preparing himself. He realized that he had forgotten the pole near the exercise equipment. So much for using it as a club. Oh well, his fists would do the trick. It wouldn't be the first time in the seventeen years of his existence that he had beaten someone into unconsciousness.

The stairs creaked as the person descended them. Heavy footsteps. Was it Hawthorne or someone else?

He didn't trust himself to peer around the corner, so he relied on his hearing to determine how close the person was.

Hawthorne stepped into the room. He took two steps

before noticing the empty bed, and began to turn.

Hades lunged forward, his fist connecting with the man's nose in a gratifying crunch of breaking gristle.

Blood spurted from Hawthorne's nostrils almost instantaneously, and his legs collapsed beneath him. Moaning, he curled over himself, cradling his face.

Seizing a fistful of oily brown hair, Hades wrenched Hawthorne's head downward and slammed his knee into the man's jaw.

He went down like a bag of bones, without so much as a whimper.

Dropping to his knees, Hades rolled the unconscious man onto his back.

Blood coated Hawthorne's face and oozed down his chin. Faint breaths rattled from his open mouth. His thin, narrow nose was a politician's worst nightmare—severely tilted, one nostril crushed into a crimson slit.

In Hades's mind, it was an improvement.

He searched Hawthorne's pockets for the handcuff key. Once he found it, he turned the man onto his side to prevent him from choking on his own blood.

There was still so much they needed to talk about.

After unlocking the dangling cuffs, he used them to bind Hawthorne's hands and ankles together. He wasn't worried about the man finding a way to escape. Not in his condition.

He considered stuffing a sock into the man's mouth, but decided to take his chances leaving him ungagged.

Crossing the room, he took the stairs one at a time, his hand on the railing, worried about a fall. Pain radiated from the balls of his feet upward, nesting in his hip and knee joints like lit matchheads. His tendons felt as dry and inflexible as strips of beef jerky, ready to snap at the slightest extension. He paused at the landing to massage his calves, waiting for the tingling to subside before going into the hallway beyond.

Sunlight spilled through the windows. So, it was daytime. But what day?

With his senses still muddled by the sedatives, he used the wall for support until he was certain he had regained complete coordination. He searched through empty, unlit rooms, straining to detect the noises of other occupants. No chatter, no footsteps but his own. If the senator had regained consciousness, the thick walls muffled his shouts.

One of the first doors he came across led into the garage. The room was large enough to accommodate four cars, but only three of those spaces were occupied. Two of the vehicles had their keys on the dashboards.

Going back inside, he explored the first floor in its entirety, passing through rooms that had no apparent purpose to him. There were flat-screen televisions on many of the walls, alongside luxuries of more antiquated origin: Chinese vases and Victorian furniture, art nouveau statues and the works of dead painters.

Hades stopped when he came to a gallery of family photographs, perplexed. The joyous scenes depicted in the photos felt as carefully designed as the rest of the home's decor, as if they were still shots taken from a movie. Staged and unrealistic.

Sometimes he wondered if people really went to bed at night. It always seemed a bit implausible to him that people living in the same household actually felt attached to each other, and that each day children were kissed good night by their parents, and spouses woke entangled in their lovers' arms.

It just wasn't right. It didn't make any sense to him.

As he stared at the images of the happy family, his chest suddenly tightened. He felt choked a second time and had the sudden urge to tear down the frames and smash them. The smiling faces mocked him. They represented something he would never have, but that he could not think of the precise word for.

CASE NOTES 2:

APOLLO

In a Colorado rest stop over a thousand miles away, Tyler Bennett stared at the streams of rainwater coursing down the windshield of an SUV with stolen plates, calculating the time that had elapsed since his life had officially ended.

Two days, fifteen hours, and counting.

To think, less than a week ago he had been attending high school in Washington, D.C., looking forward to graduation. Now, it was doubtful he would survive until autumn's end.

Two days and fifteen hours ago, Tyler had awakened in a stranger's home, heavily disoriented, armed only with a loaded pistol and the explicit instructions to execute a man in cold blood. Instead of carrying out his mission—a mission that he hadn't consciously been aware of until that very moment—he had fled.

That single act of awareness had been the beginning of the end for him, the catalyst that brought back his repressed memories of other assassinations performed while brainwashed. Those same memories had led him to Shannon Evans and "Hades," two other teens who were also subjects of the mysterious Project Pandora. From there, Tyler had found Dr. Kosta, the psychiatrist responsible for brainwashing them in the first place. Now, Dr. Kosta was dead, and Hades, too, but Project Pandora was still very much alive.

Two days, fifteen hours, and counting. How many days did he have left until the organization behind the Project found Shannon and him? Or the police, for that matter?

He didn't want to think about it.

"Shannon," he murmured, looking into the backseat.

She lay curled under a blanket, sound asleep. Tomorrow night, it would be her turn to sit in the front, but that was no consolation to him. Sooner or later, they would have to find real shelter. Preferably not a jail cell or shallow grave.

He stared at her for the longest time. The blanket had slipped down to reveal one slim shoulder and the elegant curve of her collarbone. Rain water drizzled down the windows, casting trickling reflections across her delicate face. In the soft ambient glow of the streetlights, her skin was as smooth and white as fresh milk, her full lips slightly parted. She had dyed her hair brown, but in the right light, if he looked closely, he could perceive a trace of auburn still remaining, like a fire softly smoldering. Beautiful.

Over the last couple days, they had spent endless hours talking about each other. To avoid ruminating on their crimes, they had filled the empty hours of driving with gallows humor and light flirting. Anything to forget for a moment that the threat of death loomed like a guillotine blade above their heads.

Turning away from her, he took his pistol from the car door compartment. The gun weighed all of two pounds, but it felt heavier than that, as if its inner mechanisms were gummed with the innocent blood he had spilled.

He thought about how the gun had lurched in his hand when he had pointed it at Dr. Kosta's head and pulled the trigger. It had been the first murder he had performed while conscious of his actions, and yet, he felt only the slightest regret. Dr. Kosta had to die. There was no other alternative.

But even though Dr. Kosta had been the one to brainwash them, the Project hadn't ended with him. If what the psychiatrist had said was true, then there were teenagers like Shannon and him scattered all over the country, living fake lives with fake names, their true memories repressed.

The place of their upbringing, the Academy, was within this very state, located somewhere in the San Juan mountain range. How many more children would continue to be born and raised in that secret place, trained to become future military and political leaders? No doubt, some would be deemed failures, unsuitable for leadership roles, and would be used to assassinate people the organization considered problematic.

Unless he ended the Project, this cycle of violence and lost innocence would go on forever.

Tyler unzipped his jacket and slid the handgun into the shoulder rig he wore over his shirt. To distract himself, he retrieved Dr. Kosta's research files from the footwell of the front passenger seat.

He leafed to the page he had stopped at the night before, too sickened to continue. A grainy image of his own face stared back at him. Vacant amber-brown eyes, bordered by thick, gold lashes. Burnished blond hair sheared close to the scalp. The photograph was eight months old, and his hair had grown out since, but there was no mistaking it. That boy was once him.

Typed over the top of the photo were the words:
SUBJECT 10 OF SUBSET B (B-10)
CODENAMED APOLLO

B-10. The person he had been before, he was given the name Tyler Bennett. And the worst part was, he could not remember anything from his time at the Academy. Not a single thing. Dr. Kosta had seen to that.

The life he knew was a lie. His name was a lie. His memories of a happy childhood had been falsified, like a nice painting placed over a deep, dark, empty hole. Nothing on the other side.

Tyler sighed and turned the page, reading the transcripts of the interviews that Dr. Dimitri Kosta had initiated with him when he had first come into the man's care.

DK: Tell me about yourself, B-10.

B-10: That's not my name.

DK: Would you prefer to be called Ten?

B-10: That's not my name.

DK: Lean forward. Talk directly into the recorder.

B-10: I'm scared.

DK: Why are you afraid?

B-10: I don't like it here. Where's Dr. Finch?

DK: Who's that? Is he a doctor at the Academy?

B-10: Where are the others?

DK: I will be the one asking questions. You will answer them. If you continue to behave disobediently, there will be consequences. Do I make myself clear?

B-10: Did you cut them open?

DK: Pardon me?

B-10: Did you kill them?* No. Get away from me. Get away!

*Let the record show that at 00:04:38 subject B-10 forcibly removed his intravenous feed and was subsequently restrained. Scan showed increased activity in amygdala, blood pressure increased from 118/65 to 140/91. Consider increasing dosage from 5mg to 10mg in future interviews.

The paper crumpled in Tyler's hands. He couldn't remember ever being subjected to such an interrogation, and that only made it worse somehow. It was like reading a story about a prisoner's torture, only to realize that person was yourself.

He took a deep breath, loosening his clenched fingers. That was the past. It didn't matter now. He couldn't go back and change what had already happened; he could only live with what he had done and ensure that it happened to no one else.

He flipped through the packet until he found Shannon's file. Subject Five of Subset D, codenamed Artemis. He wanted to read her transcripts, but at the same time, it felt like a violation.

Next.

Subject Two of Subset A, codenamed Hades. The dark-haired teen smirked boldly at the camera, but it was just an expression. Nothing genuine behind it. Cold eyes that were gray in the photo, but searing blue in real life. No emotion.

Looking at the photograph, Tyler thought about how he and Shannon had left Hades to die back at the Georgetown mansion where the Project had set up its East Coast headquarters. There had been no way to stop the gushing blood, and time was running out.

"Just leave," Hades had said, but Tyler regretted it even now. Maybe they could have saved him somehow. Or maybe death was a mercy for someone like Hades, like putting a rabid dog out of its misery.

Tyler sighed and flipped past Hades's file, turning to the next one.

Subject Nine of Subset A, codenamed Persephone. The blond girl who had died in Hades's arms, after taking the bullet meant for him.

Staring at A-09's picture, he swore to himself that he would never let Shannon die in such a way. He would protect her, even if it meant sacrificing his own body.

Frustrated, he picked up a second stack of papers and continued sorting through them. Dr. Kosta had been incredibly meticulous about his records, but he had also been cautious. Nowhere in the files did he mention the full names of the people he had forced his brainwashed subjects to assassinate. All references to Project Pandora were veiled behind euphemisms and vagueness.

To a court, these files would be useless. Dismissed as an elaborate hoax.

A rustling from the backseat drew his attention away from the documents. He glanced over his shoulder just in time to see Shannon sit up and yawn.

"Are you looking at those again?" she asked, brushing her hair out of her face.

"Yeah," he said, taking in the sight of her velvety, brown eyes and small, distracted smile.

She blinked. "Uh, do I have something on my face?"

"Just a beautiful smile." He moved the documents aside to allow her to crawl into the front passenger seat.

"Oh, that's a good one," she said, plopping down on the worn cushion.

"It's true."

"I'll remember that when the people from Project Pandora come for us," she said. "If I can't smile them to death, maybe my gross morning breath will kill them. Because my mouth tastes like something died in it while I was asleep."

"I'm sure it doesn't."

"It most certainly does." She cupped a hand over her mouth and breathed into it, then grimaced at the apparent odor. "Ugh. You could fumigate houses with this."

"Want me to check?" Tyler asked. "The taste, I mean. Not the smell."

"You're unbelievable." Chuckling helplessly, Shannon rooted through the glovebox until she removed the plastic grocery bag where she kept her toothbrush and things. "I'm going to the bathroom."

"Okay. I'll go, too." He retrieved his own toiletries bag from the center console box and stepped into the rain.

Before he got out of the car, he checked that his jacket was zipped. The shoulder rig created a slight bulge, but there was nothing he could do about it. No one would notice. The important thing was to act natural, act like he had nothing to hide. Keep smiling.

The weight of the gun should have comforted him, but instead, he loathed it. He knew the destructive power that the weapon contained. How easily it could take a life.

At night, the rest stop had been a jungle of big rigs, and in the early morning, it was almost as crowded. The massive parking lot was fringed by a scatter of cement and stucco buildings.

"Hey, Tyler," Shannon said as they crossed the parking lot.

He glanced over. "Yeah?"

"Do you think the Project got rid of our foster parents?"

"I don't know." He didn't really want to think about it. He had spent the last several months in a household that wasn't his own, led to believe that he belonged. Why would his foster parents take him in, just to keep track of him for the Project? What had Project Pandora given them for it?

"I miss mine, but I don't really feel surprised anymore, you know?" she sighed. "I think I've always known, deep down, that something just wasn't right."

"Yeah, I know what you mean."

"And I'm beginning to remember everything now," she continued. "My real memories are starting to come back."

He wished that he could say the same, but at the same time, he was terrified by the thought of recalling his past. He sensed that something terrible lurked deep in the darkness of his repressed memories. Something that might destroy him if he uncovered it.

While Shannon waited for the line in front of the women's restroom to shorten, he went into the men's restroom. Even though both urinals and one stall were occupied, the row of sinks went unused.

He washed his hands and face with soap from the dispenser, then took a mass of wet paper towels and his toiletries bag into the empty stall. In the privacy of the stall, he rubbed the paper towel wad under his armpits and between his legs. He had purchased deodorant and body spray at a convenience store, and now he applied them liberally.

Once he had finished cleaning himself up, he returned to the sink counter.

While brushing his teeth, Tyler stared at his face in the mirror. Although he recognized himself as both the terrified boy called B-10, and the detached assassin codenamed Apollo, he struggled to accept it. It would have been easy to dismiss those facets of himself as split personalities, fabrications created by a troubled mind, but they weren't. They were him, one and the same. He just couldn't understand how.

As he rinsed his mouth out, a stocky, brown-haired man came out of the other stall and went to the sink next to him.

"Some nasty weather we're having, huh?" the guy said. He dropped his rolled-up newspaper on the counter and ran his hands under the water, neglecting to use soap.

"I guess." Tyler looked down to avoid meeting the man's eyes in the mirror. Lately, he found it increasingly difficult to make eye contact with people. Sometimes, he wondered if they could see the guilt in his face.

The police might not be looking for Shannon, but because his would-be victim had seen his face, they were definitely searching for him. Not to mention that the DNA evidence he had left at the scene might tie him to other actual murders. Even though this was the last place on earth where someone might recognize him, he didn't want to take any chances by letting his guard down.

As he wiped his mouth with the back of his hand, he glanced at the man's newspaper by chance—and froze. Without reason, he began trembling. His hands shuddered so badly, when he picked up the newspaper, he could barely hold it.

The trucker frowned. "That's mine."

The page's headline proclaimed: "AWARD-WINNING

GENETECIST CELEBRATED AT DENVER CEREMONY."

He stared at the photograph that had caught his attention. The man in the photo appeared to be in his late seventies. With his bald head, hooked nose, and heavy black overcoat, he resembled a vulture.

"Give that back," the trucker said, grabbing his wrist.

"Don't touch me!" he snapped and shoved the man away.

"Hey, easy, kid." The trucker lifted his hands. "You want it so much? Fine, take it."

He left the restroom, holding the newspaper against himself to protect it from the rain. It was only when he sat down in the car that he realized he had forgotten his toiletries back at the restroom. Didn't matter. The only thing that mattered was the wad of damp pages he clutched in his hands. The ink had smeared in places, but he could still make out the individual letters.

Shannon returned to the car, her jacket pockets crammed full of food from the vending machine.

"I got your favorite," she said, tossing a Snickers bar into his lap. "Hey, what's the matter?"

"The man in this article," Tyler said. "Doctor Belmont. I recognize him. There's a picture of him in the files. He's standing right next to Kosta."

CASE NOTES 3:

ARTEMIS

"**I**t says here that Dr. Belmont works at an IVF clinic. Ponderosa Fertility Center." Shannon spread the newspaper across her knees, avoiding the small brown stain on the corner of the page. She prayed that the newspaper's original owner had only used it for entertainment, not as an alternative to toilet paper.

"Shannon, do you realize what this means?" Tyler smiled. "This might be a way to find out who our real parents are."

"That's going to be one hell of a family reunion," she said, frowning. Unlike Tyler, she wasn't thrilled at the thought of learning more about the Project. She just wanted to get the hell out of Dodge, maybe go up to Canada. She had heard that Calgary was nice. They could start new lives for themselves there.

Tyler ignored her pessimism. "If the Project used spare donor embryos like Dr. Kosta said, maybe there's some record of it at his office."

"What are you suggesting now? Breaking and entering?"

"This is the only lead we've got."

"Maybe we should just run away. Never look back.

Live off in the woods somewhere. Come on, Tyler, let's just go to Canada."

"No, this can't happen to anyone else," Tyler said. "I refuse to just hide away and hope someone else deals with this problem. It's ours. Running away won't make it go away. We're always going to have to live with what we've done."

Shannon sighed and looked into his dark, gold-flecked eyes. Another individual might have thought Tyler had dangerous eyes, but all she saw in his gaze was despair wrestling with stubborn tenacity. Not for the first time, she sensed that a part of him wanted to succumb to a dark urge he would never admit to.

She worried about him. Last night, she had woken to find him just sitting in the front seat in the dark, looking at the gun in his hand. She tried not to think about the expression on his face when she caught him, or the way he had been stroking the trigger guard, his finger so close to the trigger.

"You can't save everyone, Tyler," she said.

"I know, but I can't pretend the Project doesn't exist, either. They can't just keep getting away with this."

For the first time, Shannon wondered if his eagerness to stop Project Pandora was just a different kind of self-destruction. He knew what he was up against. Why didn't he want to run away?

"What exactly do you hope to achieve from this?" she asked.

A flash of irritation raced across his handsome features. His narrowed eyes caught the glow of passing headlights and glinted like chunks of Baltic amber. "These people need to be brought to justice."

That doesn't mean we have to be the ones to do it, Shannon thought.

Project Pandora had taken her childhood, her peace of mind, and the theater performance she had called a foster family. She wasn't ready to give the Project her future as well, and although she hated the thought of spending the rest of her life as a fugitive, at least she would be alive. Confronting the organization, fighting it head-on—that was a death wish. This whole thing was way more than what the two of them could handle. If they searched for trouble, they'd just end up like Hades—bleeding out in a stairwell, alone and hopeless.

"I know you don't want to do this," Tyler said, "but please, don't run away from this."

He reached over the center console and took her hand in his. His fingers were long and slim. Hardly the hands of a killer. He was too kind for the rotten lot that life had given him. And too damn stubborn.

"We need to expose the Project, Shannon, and the way I look at it, there's only one way we can do it. We need to find the Academy, and we need to liberate it. Our testimony won't mean anything alone, but if we have fifty other teens who can corroborate our story, they won't just be able to cover this up. Then we'll be free."

She sighed again.

He said it like it was so simple, but it wasn't. The San Juan mountain range covered hundreds of miles, and nothing in Dr. Kosta's records had shed light on the exact location of the facility. Then there was a matter of actually "liberating" it. As if that would do any good. They would die before they could get past the gates, and even if they did somehow manage to get inside, it's not like the children at the Academy were prisoners, at least not in the traditional sense. They had spent their whole lives there, raised and taught to become political proxies and killers.

Why couldn't Tyler see that? Why was he so dead set on sacrificing himself for a lost cause?

"Okay," she said, hating herself for being so compliant. "Fine."

He smiled and leaned over the center console, brushing a strand of hair out of her face and resting his palm against her cheek. He leaned in for a quick kiss. "Thanks. I really don't want to do this alone."

Shannon riffled through the papers at her feet, pushing aside the loose documents until she found a crumpled road map. She spread the map out across her knees, consulted it, and then glanced at the street signs. "Okay. The town where he works can't be more than fifteen miles from here."

Even though the clinic was only a short distance from the rest stop, it took them almost an hour to find it. Twice, they had to stop to ask for directions.

"I miss the internet," Tyler said as he pulled away from the curb, after asking the third person in a row.

"Tell me about it."

"You think they had internet at the Academy?"

Shannon shrugged. She still remembered very little of her time there. During the last two nights, as she had lingered at the edge of sleep, vague memories had returned to her. She recalled a large mess hall and having to cook for other teens. She recalled the forest and the smooth coldness of a paintball gun in her hands—a toy compared to the pistol hidden in her purse. But her most recurring flashback wasn't of any set situation, just her own voice:

"I am Subject Five of Subset D."

She had woken once in the night to hear herself whispering it.

Shannon, she thought. *I'm Shannon now. I'm never going to be called by that other name again.*

The Ponderosa Fertility Center was located in an attractive stucco complex, between the businesses of a plastic surgeon and an orthodontist. Tyler drove past the building once, taking note of its exits and entrances, then swung around to find a parking spot.

"I just realized something," Shannon said as he parked.

"What?"

"We might have siblings. Like real, normal siblings."

"Real, normal siblings. Are you saying we're abnormal?" His smile was like watching the sun emerge from behind storm clouds. A fading bruise discolored his cheek, but the sight of him still took her breath away.

Nobody should be this gorgeous, she thought.

"Just think about it, Tyler," she said. "Somewhere out there, you might have a preppy *Mean Girls* sister."

"I'd rather be kicked to death... Wait, is that because I'm blond?"

"What?"

"The *Mean Girls* reference."

"Don't worry, the stereotype doesn't apply to you," Shannon said, grinning in spite of her apprehension.

"Thank God for that." He turned his attention back to the front of the building. "You think we should get out?"

"I'll go, just to see if it's even open. I don't think we should approach Dr. Belmont just yet."

As Tyler unbuckled his seatbelt, she grabbed ahold of his arm and felt his hard bicep flex beneath the sleeve of his windbreaker. He looked back at her, surprised.

"Stay here," she said. "You're a guy, so you'll attract more attention."

He sighed. "Fine. I'll keep watch."

"Don't look so disappointed," she said, getting out of the car. "I'll be right back."

As she hurried through the parking lot, she struggled against the driving wind. Rain slammed into her face, stinging her eyes. Just as she reached the front of the building, she misjudged the depth of a puddle and drenched her feet up to the ankles.

Shannon's only consolation was that if a cop was making his rounds, he probably wouldn't be on the lookout for a car with stolen plates in this kind of weather. They were safe for now, but soon she and Tyler would have to switch vehicles.

Her shoes squelched as she stepped under the shelter of the eaves. She wanted to take them off and shake the water out, but she didn't like lingering out front, where she could easily be spotted by a patrolling officer. She kept her eyes directed downward as she approached the clinic's door, slightly paranoid about the security cameras mounted overhead. It was a stupid thing to worry about, considering she wasn't going to try anything, but it made her feel better to take preventative measures, no matter how small.

She sighed as she read the sign in the window. Closed on Mondays. Just her luck. She returned to the car and sat in the passenger seat. "They're closed today."

"Good," Tyler said, unbuckling his seatbelt.

As they walked around to the back of the building, her unease heightened into dread. She felt like a chicken running around with its head cut off, using sheer physical instinct to avoid the obstacles that surrounded it. Dangers lurked everywhere.

"I love breaking and entering," Shannon said.

"Sure beats murder."

"We should do this more often."

"Make a date out of it," he said.

"You mean we aren't already on one?"

"If we are, I forgot the wine and cheese."

"Who eats wine and cheese on a date?" she asked.

"Just about everyone in every romantic movie ever made."

"Wait, you watch romances?"

"Well, no, but it's common knowledge," Tyler said. "Can't have a romantic date without wine and cheese."

"I'll pass on the wine, but I'd kill for a bacon-cheeseburger and some mozzarella sticks right now."

"Simple tastes. I like that."

Their conversation petered off as Tyler tried to open the backdoor, to no avail. Looking around, Shannon noticed a high window further down the wall.

"Think you can crawl through that?" he asked as she walked over to it.

"If I can reach it." She set her purse on the ground and shoved her gun into her jeans' waistband after detaching the weapon's magazine and stowing it in her pocket.

"Here, I'll give you a leg up." He turned to her and bent down, cupping his hands to provide a foothold.

"Can't believe I'm doing this," she muttered under her breath, stepping onto his knitted fingers and holding onto the wall for support.

He grunted as he helped elevate her.

"I'm not that heavy, am I?" she asked, trying to calm her apprehension with a little bit of humor.

"Not at all. I'm just enjoying the view." He must have

caught onto her unease, because when she glanced down, she found him smiling with the same fearful tension she felt contort her own features.

She reached the window and tested it. The pane yielded with a rusty squeaking sound, providing her with an opening large enough to crawl through if she did some contorting.

"I'm probably going to break my neck," she said, hoisting herself through the open window, pushing aside the louvered metal blinds. Her hips briefly became trapped in the frame, but by then, she'd already found a sturdy foundation in the high cabinets that hugged the wall of the dark inner room.

Resting on her knees, she regarded her surroundings, taking in the unlit lamps and examination table. Peering back through the window, she called, "I'm going to look around. Just go back to the car."

He frowned, clearly worried about leaving her alone. "Sure you'll be all right?"

"I'll be fine. Don't worry."

She jumped down from the cabinets and landed lithely on the vinyl-tiled floor. Removing her gun from her waistband, she reattached the magazine and checked to make sure the safety was engaged. Striding into the hall, she blinked in the gloom, struggling to make out her surroundings. Closed doors proliferated, and even mundane objects like the anatomical pelvis model on the counter took on a morbid light.

As she tried doors, she thought about the patients that must frequent this place. Hopeful couples, dreaming about families. Men and women who were unaware that some of their children would end up in a place best described as Hell on earth.

What kind of doctor could bring joy in one hand, while simultaneously swindling his patients with the other?

She wondered if she had a brother or sister out there somewhere. Then it occurred to her that she might have more than one sibling, and for all she knew, they could have ended up at the Academy, too. Maybe Tyler was right. They were the only children of Project Pandora who knew the truth of the outside world. Maybe it was their duty to finish this.

Entering a small office, she went straight to the filing cabinets arranged along the adjacent wall. She tugged at the drawer. Locked.

Going to the desk, she set the gun on the blotter pad and searched the various drawers and cubby holes, hoping that Dr. Belmont had hidden the key in one of them. She found old papers, used tissues, and a hoard of other miscellaneous objects, but no keys.

With a sigh, she snatched the letter opener from the desktop and returned to the filing cabinet. She inserted the letter opener into the gap between the door and inner box and wrenched the blade around until she felt the lock give way. Throwing the tool aside, she yanked open the drawer and turned her attention to the manila folders stored within.

Keeping one ear cocked to the door, listening for any fellow intruders, Shannon examined the documents. Patient records, test results, and bills. Her eyes glazed over as she sorted through them.

Near the back of the third drawer, she encountered a folder unlike the others. The cardstock was aged to a wrinkled brown and crammed full of papers. As she retrieved the folder from the cabinet, a cassette tape fell into her lap.

Remembering having seen a recorder in the desk, she carried the folder and cassette over there and set them next to the keyboard. She inserted the tape into the recorder and turned it on.

The soft chirr of wheeling film was loud compared to the silence that surrounded her.

"My name is Dr. Belmont." A man's deep, aged voice crackled from the speakers. "And this is a confession. If you are listening to this, detectives, then I am either dead or have disappeared for at least thirty consecutive days. If it is the former, my autopsy report might accredit my death to natural causes, but I can assure you that is not the case. I did not commit suicide. I did not die of a heart attack, stroke, blood clot, or brain aneurysm. I was murdered."

As she listened to the tape, she opened the folder. This time, the faces that confronted her didn't belong to patients, but men and women dressed in white lab coats.

"In the folder, you should find documents pertaining to Project Pandora, a eugenics experiment conceived two decades ago as a way to bring forth a new world order. My role was to find suitable genetic material for the Project's children, and it was one I performed well."

Shannon skimmed through the pages, before pausing at the photograph of a dark-haired woman. There was something terribly familiar about the woman's sharp, pale beauty, but Shannon couldn't pinpoint the exact quality that drew her gaze. Had she seen this woman somewhere before?

"Dr. Francine Miller," she whispered, scanning over the name printed on the top of the page. The woman's address and phone number were listed on the form, along with various numbers that Shannon suspected pertained to other documents in the folders.

"This is only a small amount of the actual research data," Dr. Belmont's voice said. "The rest is hidden at my home at 50300 West Mayflower Street, under a loose floorboard in the master bedroom. In the event that my house is destroyed or the files are otherwise unobtainable—"

A clatter from down the hall stole her attention. Shannon turned off the recorder and reached for her gun. Just as she disengaged the pistol's safety, Tyler burst through the door.

"Don't shoot," he said, lifting his arms.

"How did you get inside?" she asked, lowering the gun.

"I used a trash can." He walked over to the desk. "What did you find?"

"Some stuff about Pandora, I think. If what this tape says is true, the rest is at his house."

A brilliant smile spread across his lips. "Well, what are we waiting for? Let's go over there."

"One moment." Using the Google Maps function on Belmont's computer, Shannon found out how to get to his house from the clinic. As soon as the printer spat out the directions, she stowed them in the folder and stuck the recorder in her pocket. "All right, let's go."

CASE NOTES 4:

HADES

Upstairs, down the hall, past the powder room and library, Hades reached the master bedroom of Senator Hawthorne's home. Though it was the grandest of all the bedrooms, there was a jarring divide between one half of the room and the other.

On the side facing the window, the dresser and nightstand were adorned with picture frames and decorative baubles. Everything was clean and orderly. The other side of the room was covered in dirty menswear, and a spilled bottle of scotch formed a puddle on the floor. Clothing spewed from the open doors of the wardrobe.

Hearing the rumble of an approaching vehicle, he went to the window and parted the drapes an inch, peering into the street that was visible beyond the decorative hedge. He watched a minivan drive by and waited until it had turned the corner before dropping the curtain.

It surprised him that Hawthorne had been stupid enough to bring a fugitive to his own home. The man might be good at politics, but when it came to kidnapping, he was a complete moron. Then again, desperation and loss made people do crazy things, as Hades knew from experience. The possibility that the police could have the house under surveillance might've never even occurred to Mr. Hawthorne.

Hades fished a few pairs of pants from among the suits and polo shirts in the tall armoire. He sorted through the trousers and Levis, searching for a pair in his size. He loathed the idea of wearing the man's clothes, but he had no other choice.

After he selected a suitable pair of pants, he retrieved a white, button-up shirt from the drawer. Nice quality, but nothing too flashy that would draw attention to himself.

Normally, he preferred dressing in all black. The color made him feel secure, like he was wearing armor, and reminded him of the uniform he had worn at the Academy for the first fifteen years of his life. The best years of his life. But blending in trumped personal preference. The sooner he changed his appearance, the better.

Just as he considered going commando, he came across an unopened bag of boxer-briefs shoved in the back of the dresser and took the entire package.

He stepped back into the hall and retraced his steps to the bedroom at the other end of the house. As he stepped inside, he wondered if Elizabeth—no, *Subject Nine of Subset A*—had picked out the gold brocade bedspread and the posters on the walls, or if her room's decor had been just another decision made for her.

He set his clean clothes on her bed and undressed before her full-length mirror.

His muscles hadn't had time to atrophy during his imprisonment, and he'd lost little if any weight, but when he looked at his reflection, he had the unsettling impression of staring at a stranger. His ink-black hair hung in unwashed, matted clumps over his face, and the skin under his eyes was smudged with dark shadows. He wore a necklace of angry welts around his neck; by tomorrow, they would become bruises.

The bandages on his stomach were fouled. A tube snaked out from beneath the gauze, taped against his skin and attached to a transparent rubber bulb.

Hades stepped closer to the mirror and peeled off the bloodied bandages. Underneath, his pale skin was mottled black and blue, but he found none of the swelling or striated rashes that would signify infection. A small incision had been made next to the bullet hole to accommodate the drainage tube.

He despised the feeling of having a foreign object inside of him, and wanted nothing more than to tear the drainage tube out from beneath his skin. He resisted that impulse. It wasn't a bad thing. It was there for a reason.

Looking at the injuries alone, he couldn't tell how long he had been down. He had vague memories of lying in a hospital bed, of writhing against the hands of orderlies as he tried to tear the tubes out of his arms. Drawing blood with his teeth. Padded restraints around his wrists and ankles. A police detective standing at his bedside, asking him questions he refused to answer. Lying on a moving stretcher, the night sky above his head. Voices without words. A dreamless, drug-induced sleep. Insubstantial things.

It felt like a dream. Sometimes, he wondered if that's all life was, just a painful dream.

When he parted his hair, he touched cold steel where a laceration on the back of his scalp had been stapled shut. The hair around the immediate area was short and bristly with new growth. Maybe a few days' worth at most.

Why hadn't the organization killed him?

Turning away from the mirror, Hades caught a brief glimpse of his back. Jagged scars tore from his broad shoulders to just above his buttocks.

They were meant to be a reminder that he was not a person.

He took a framed photo of Nine from the wall and carried it into the bathroom, setting it on the counter as he emptied the rubber drainage bottle into the sink. The liquid that had gathered in the bulb was a translucent red, too thin to be pus. He sniffed the contents to smell for infection, but the only odor he detected was that of his own stale sweat.

After resealing the collection bottle, he went to the luxurious walk-in shower and twisted the faucet, turning it as hot as it would go. He hated lukewarm showers because they reminded him of the sensory deprivation tank, whose water had been heated to skin-temperature. Even bathtubs were intolerable, and if he had any choice in the matter, he would never step foot in a pool or Jacuzzi. He could only tolerate extreme heat and extreme cold.

As he waited for the water to heat, he searched through the sink counter and medicine cabinet. Prescription bottles lined the shelves of the medicine cabinet. He picked up a few and read the labels.

Some of the drug names stood out to him. Uppers, downers, antipsychotics. Just a few of the ingredients in the chemical cocktail that Dimitri had tested on him. Little things to keep her sated. Obedient. Unaware of who she truly was.

He wanted to pour the pills down Hawthorne's throat.

The drawers were filled with makeup, cosmetics, brushes, and perfume. These items held little interest to him, but he searched until he found the forget-me-not perfume Nine had favored.

He uncapped the bottle and breathed in its fumes. Closing his eyes, he could almost pretend that she was still there with him. The floral aroma brought a tide of memories with it.

After Nine had been taken from the Academy and inherited the name of Elizabeth Hawthorne, she had been sent to Dr. Dimitri Kosta, a Project-affiliated doctor who had repressed her memories of the Academy. But unlike with her, Dimitri hadn't just repressed Hades's memories. Dimitri had crushed them.

For so long, he had forgotten who he was. He had forgotten about Nine. Then he had found her again, only to lose her once more.

He had loved her, and he had failed her. He had lied to himself over and over, insisting that he was still in control, not programmed, *not like them*, when he was just another trained dog. When the lies weren't enough, he lashed out at everyone else around him, everyone but the one person who deserved his anger the most, Dimitri.

She had paid for his weakness in blood.

With a howl of rage and anguish, Hades threw the bottle against the wall. It disintegrated on impact, shattering into a sunburst of blue glass.

He swept the jars of cosmetics off the counter, slammed his fists against the sink top. He wanted to destroy everything in sight. He wanted to feel pain and share it.

Spotting the framed photo, he picked it up to hurl it. Instead, he clutched the frame against his chest and crumpled over, raked by tearless sobs. He slid into a fetal position and pressed his forehead against the cool tile.

Damn her! Nine never should have died. With her

death, he felt like a lifeline to his past had snapped, like just another part of himself had broken off and drifted away. She had been the only one who had ever truly loved him.

Now, there was no one left in the world.

CASE NOTES 5:

APOLLO

Belmont lived in a neighborhood of quaint older houses. Flags sailed in some yards; plastic flamingos and garden gnomes occupied others. Tyler spent the first ten minutes of the stakeout studying the impressive Halloween display at one of the neighboring houses. As they approached the fifteen-minute mark and there was still no sign of life at the Belmont house, his impatience flared.

Shannon must have sensed that he was growing annoyed, because she set aside the documents she was reading and laid her hand over his. A small smile touched her lips as she rubbed her thumb across the back of his hand. "Aren't stakeouts great?"

"Screw this." He unbuckled his seatbelt. As much as he enjoyed her company, he wasn't going to sit around and wait for the doctor to leave so that they could break in and steal the documents. Belmont didn't deserve to get away with this. The doctor needed to be confronted with the brutality of what he had done.

"Tyler, wait." Shannon grabbed ahold of his arm.

"No, I'm not just going to sit here, hoping he leaves.

I'm done waiting. This is our problem, and we need to confront it head-on." Pulling his arm away, he touched his shoulder rig, driven by an anxious need to make sure the gun was still there. "We can't just turn away from this."

"I'm not suggesting that! I just think it's too dangerous to barge in there like this."

"Look, just keep guard," he said, opening the car door. "I'll go in alone."

"Tyler!"

He closed the car door and set off across the lawn at a quick walk. Shannon got out of the car and hurried after him. She caught up just as he reached the front step.

The door hung slightly ajar.

He exchanged a look with her and reached into his jacket. As he withdrew his gun from its holster, she did the same.

Easing open the door, Tyler stepped into a poorly lit foyer. The green wallpaper and unlit lamps made the room seem smaller than it truly was, like a cage meant to entrap him. He cleared the room in seconds, covering the blind spots, then advanced into the hall with Shannon right beside him.

They didn't speak as they moved through the house. In the living room, he found a wooden coffee table overturned and magazines spilling from a wicker basket next to the couch. Several droplets of blood marred the armchair's velvet upholstery. He glanced at the stains. Still wet.

A trail of larger stains led into the kitchen, where he found Dr. Belmont tied to a chair.

Dressed in white pajamas, with a dishtowel tied around his eyes and blood oozing from his hawkish nose, Belmont hardly resembled the imposing figure captured by the reporter's camera. At the sound of their approach, he strained against the ropes that restrained him. Duct tape muffled his voice to the point of inaudibility, reducing his words to the pathetic whimpers of an animal caught in a trap.

At the sight of the man's face, Tyler felt an immediate violent loathing. His fingers curled around his pistol's handle, and he had the sudden urge to point the gun at Belmont's head and pull the trigger.

The murderous rage that flared up inside of him was so strong and unexpected, it took him aback. He was forced to remove his finger from the trigger guard, afraid of what he might do. The feeling went beyond mere anger. It was intimate. Personal. Deep down, he sensed that Belmont, like Dr. Kosta, had done something reprehensible to him.

Forcing down his hatred, Tyler turned away from Dr. Belmont. It wasn't like the man was going anywhere.

"Whoever did this might still be here," he whispered to Shannon and nodded toward the archway at the other end of the kitchen that led deeper into the house.

She nodded and advanced forward. He followed behind her, resisting the urge to turn back around and look at the man responsible for so much death.

Doctors, he thought. *These aren't doctors. They're a bunch of insane sadists. Monsters.*

Edging down the hall, he listened for any footsteps aside from their own. The rain beat against the roof above their heads like a distant drumming meant to signal some approaching enemy. As he reached the end of the hall, a sudden crack of thunder sent shivers racing down his spine, and his finger curled around the trigger in reflex. If not for his light touch, he might have fired off a shot.

Just thunder. Not a gunshot. Nothing to worry about.

The real danger didn't linger overhead. It lurked somewhere within this very house.

He reached the stairs. Like the rest of the house, the staircase was antiquated and overbearing in its dark wood construction and ornate railing. The whole decor reeked like a Dickens novel. He could just imagine Dr. Belmont sitting by the living room fireplace on a rainy nights, sipping spiced wine as he plotted how to ruin more kids' lives and advance his fascist agenda.

If not for the threat of another armed intruder, Tyler might have laughed. Instead, he crept up the stairs, staring at the unlit passage above.

As he entered the hallway to find it empty, he searched for puddles that would suggest someone had been up here. A patterned rug concealed any water stains. Damn it.

They covered the rooms one at a time, searching under beds and in closets. In the master bedroom, he found one of the floorboards removed. Nothing waited in the space below.

Shannon groaned at the sight of the opened cache. "No, they took them."

"It's fine," he said, hiding his own disappointment behind a thin smile. "Let's check his study. I saw some papers there. Maybe he removed them from the floor."

They walked back downstairs. In the study, they searched the desk drawers and file cabinets. The top of the desk was covered in loose pages and envelopes. Tyler gathered the papers into a pile and leafed through them, keeping one eye on the door in case the intruder returned.

Some were bills or advertisements, but in the stack he also came across documents with the same scientific jargon that he had noticed in Kosta's files. It made no sense to him at all.

"Hey, Tyler, does the name 'Dr. Francine Miller' ring a bell?" Shannon asked.

"No." He glanced over his shoulder to look at her. "Why?"

"Her name keeps showing up in these files, and I remember seeing something about her in the stuff in the car. From the sound of it, she's some sort of scientist or something."

"Maybe there's more about her on his computer."

While Shannon sat in front of the ancient PC, Tyler searched the recycling bin next to the desk, in case Belmont had disposed of any important papers.

"There has to be at least a hundred pages worth of shredded documents in here," Tyler said, poking through the bin.

"His computer is password protected." Shannon sighed, rising from the desk chair.

"Not for long," Tyler said.

They returned to the kitchen. Dr. Belmont was where they had left him, struggling futilely against the ropes.

Tyler ripped off the duct tape that encircled the old man's mouth and removed the blindfold.

One of Dr. Belmont's eyes was swollen shut, but the other widened at the sight of him.

"No, how are you here?" Dr. Belmont cried in a hoarse, wavering voice. "We *killed* you."

CASE NOTES 6:

ARTEMIS

Shannon wrinkled her forehead at Belmont's bizarre statement. As she opened her mouth to ask what the doctor meant, she sensed movement in the corner of her vision. She swiveled around in time to spot a flash of dark clothes emerging from the archway and see the kitchen light glint off a steel silencer screwed onto a pistol's barrel.

"He's still here!" she shouted, darting toward the granite-topped island.

Over the echo of the rain pounding into the roof above, she didn't hear the suppressed gunshots, only the clatter of breaking glass and the sharp *twang* of a bullet ricocheting off the counter's corner. Shards of granite speckled the air inches from her face, and then she was behind cover.

She emerged only long enough to fire at the person dressed in black, who retreated deeper into the house before she could verify if her bullets hit. In the kitchen's close confines, the gunshots were deafening.

Shooting to her feet, she took off after the figure.

"Stop!" she yelled, skidding into the hallway. Down the

corridor, she spotted an oozing trail of blood that hadn't been there before, and lying in the mess, a small pile of documents.

By the time she reached the end of the hall, all she found was the back door hanging open. Rain rushed in from outside, and the screen door rattled in the wind. Deciding not to pursue the shooter, she shut the door and locked it, then returned to the papers in the hall.

"Tyler, he's gone for real now," she called, leaning down to pick up the letters and folded pages. As she crammed the documents in her purse, she was suddenly struck by the silence that greeted her.

"Tyler?" She returned to the kitchen—and froze in the doorway.

He leaned on the counter, clutching one hand against his shoulder, where the fabric was already beginning to darken with blood.

Shattering scenes flashed through her head: her first kill, wet blood on her hands, a knife clenched in her quivering fingers; Hades, bleeding out on the stairwell, holding a dead girl in his arms. So much blood. So much death. When would it ever end?

"No," she heard herself say, and as she stepped into the room, she barely felt the floor beneath her. Approaching the counter, she vaguely took in the sight of Dr. Belmont hanging lifelessly against the ropes that restrained him, but he fell from her mind as she reached Tyler's side.

"I'm okay," he said. "I'm fine. We need to go. Before the police arrive."

He took three steps forward before gravity conspired to drag him to the ground. She lunged toward him just as his knees gave out and grasped him in her arms before he could fall. His body sank heavily against her, his jacket damp with rainwater and blood. His chest rose and fell with harsh, gasping breaths, and the pistol slipped from his limp fingers.

When she pulled back after stabilizing him, her stomach lurched at the sight of the growing ooze of blood streaming down his sleeve, dripping to the floor. His eyes focused distantly on her; they no longer resembled Baltic amber, but smog or dust. Dissipating.

"I'm okay. I'm okay." He leaned down to pick up the handgun, swayed a bit, but retrieved it without needing her assistance. Still, as they returned to the front door, she kept one arm hooked around him, worried about the way he struggled to move. This couldn't be happening. Was he going into shock?

By the time she reached the car, he could barely walk. He needed her help to climb into the passenger seat. She put her gun in her purse and lowered him onto the seat. He collapsed against the upholstery the moment she let go.

His eyes fluttered shut, and he cursed softly under his breath. His teeth chattered, his body shook.

No, it couldn't be. Not him.

She wanted nothing more than to press her own hands over his wound and try to hold back the blood, but there was no time for that. The deluge wasn't loud enough to drown out the crack of her gunshots, and any moment now, she knew the police would arrive.

She grabbed the seatbelt and leaned over him, struggling to find the clasp. As she pulled away, he grabbed her hand. His own fingers were so cold.

Just from the rain. Just the rain.

"I'm okay," he whispered, his lips cracking in a painful smile. "Just drive."

She shut the door and raced around to the other side

of the car. Getting inside, she threw her purse into the backseat and rammed the key into the ignition.

As she shot down the street, she glanced over at him. He regarded her through half-closed eyes. Even in anguish, his fair features were wrenchingly beautiful, like the face of a martyr. An angel becoming.

I won't let him die. Not him. Never him.

"Shannon, I can't feel my arm anymore."

"Hang in there," she said, her voice almost as thick as his was. A hard lump formed in her throat, and she couldn't seem to dislodge it.

"I don't think it's there."

"Just hang in there."

"It's gone, isn't it?"

"Take deep breaths. You're going to be fine." She forced her gaze back to the road ahead. Water dripped down her forehead and into her eyes. She took her hand off the wheel only long enough to brush her wet hair out of her face. When she curled her fingers around the leather again, she was disturbed to find fresh blood streaked across her fingertips. Blood that must be in her hair now. Blood that she saw in the corner of her eye, staining the pale upholstery of Tyler's seat.

As she sped down the street, a white car fell into place behind her, close enough that its front bumper was almost touching her car's back one. The windshield was tinted black, but she had a sinking suspicion that the tailgater was the same person who she had encountered in the Belmont household.

She pressed down on the gas pedal. Even after turning the corner, she couldn't shake the white car from her trail.

"Damn it." Shannon clenched her teeth, restraining even worse swearwords in the back of her throat. Talking wouldn't help her now. She needed to keep her full attention on the road. It wouldn't help Tyler if they got into an accident.

Through the curtains of pounding rain, the white vehicle drifted in and out of view. Every time she spotted it in her rearview mirror, it appeared to be a little bit closer. Closer. Closer.

Thunder roared, and in the distance, a siren grew louder.

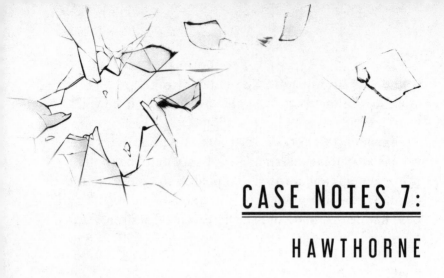

CASE NOTES 7:

HAWTHORNE

Senator Lawrence Hawthorne awoke to find himself in a world of hurt. His mouth felt swollen into a bloody pulp, and even the gentlest motions drove needles of pain into his sinuses and the surrounding tissue, bringing tears to his eyes.

He couldn't see his own face, but from the agony alone knew that his nose must be broken. Crushed, even. When his tongue probed the empty hole where one molar should have been, he sobbed in pain and anger. That only made it worse.

He tried to scream for help, but it did no good. The brick-and-concrete foundation smothered noises, transforming the basement into a soundproofed chamber. He had sent away the help and his security team, and his wife had been staying with her sister ever since Elizabeth's death. Aside from himself, the only people who knew that the boy was here were the thugs hired to retrieve him.

As he listened to the boy move around above, he struggled into a sitting position. His wrists and ankles were secured behind his back with the same handcuffs he had used on the boy. Hawthorne tested them. Tight. How the hell did the kid break free?

His eyes landed on the counter. Maybe he could find something up there to unlock them. For all he knew, the boy had left the handcuff key there after using it.

He tried to rise to his feet, but with his coordination unbalanced and his ankles chained together, he rolled onto his side. Before he could reattempt standing, the basement door opened. He squeezed his eyes shut and went limp, hoping that if he feigned unconsciousness, the kid would leave him alone.

The stairs creaked. Footsteps tapped across the floor.

"Mr. Hawthorne? Can you hear me?" Even hoarse, the boy's voice had a low, smoky resonance to it. But it was also strangely lacking in inflection and emotion, as if he were reciting from a script.

Hawthorne sensed a presence leaning over him and willed himself not to move. He took measured breaths through his mouth. A hand brushed over his cheek before lowering to his throat. Two fingers pressed into the skin below his swollen jaw, hard enough to make him swallow back a groan.

"Your pulse is racing," the boy murmured. "You're awake, and you're terrified."

Convinced that the boy was calling a bluff, Hawthorne remained still. He feared that if he moved even the slightest, the boy would take that as initiative to beat him back into unconsciousness. Or worse.

"Do you think I'm going to strangle you?" the boy asked, his voice warm with amusement. "I wouldn't, even if I wanted to kill you. Asphyxiation is quick. Merciful. And we have so much to talk about still."

Even with his nose plugged by blood, Hawthorne detected the faint aromas of flowers and vanilla. The fragrances soured in his nostrils. The boy must have gone up to Elizabeth's room. Had he washed his hair with her vanilla-scented shampoo? Or maybe he had rutted through her hamper and rubbed her dirty clothes against himself.

"You have good reason to be afraid," the boy said, returning his hand to Hawthorne's chin. This time, his grip was stronger, his fingers grinding into Hawthorne's jawbone, and Hawthorne flinched. "Look at me."

Groaning, Hawthorne peeled open one eye.

The boy's face blurred, then came into sharp focus. He had an exquisite bone structure and remarkable blue eyes. In sleep, the boy had been ethereally beautiful, but now, awake and alert, with his face alive and constantly in motion, there was a cruel, feral quality that Hawthorne hadn't noticed before. His smile was cold, and he maintained eye contact longer than was necessary.

"That's better," the boy said, drawing his hand away once more. He kept his other hand lowered, resting out of Hawthorne's range of vision. "I like it when people look at me when I'm talking to them. Otherwise, it's like they don't even know I'm there. I hate that. Feeling like I don't exist. So, sometimes I need to prove it. To see my effect on others."

Hawthorne prided himself as an excellent public speaker, but try as he might, he couldn't come up with a way to pacify the boy. He decided that it would be safer to remain silent.

"Can you understand me?" the boy asked, sounding a touch concerned. "Or are you just ignoring me?"

"Go away, kid," Hawthorne mumbled, trying to sit up. A single light shove was all it took to push him down again, and the boy rested one hand on his chest, holding him in place.

"Oh. Good. I thought I might've hit you too hard." The boy paused. "I have a tendency to do that."

"Please, just leave." Hawthorne's stomach rolled queasily. He tasted blood in the back of his throat and, twisting his head to the side, spat onto the floor.

Shifting out of a squatting position, the boy rested one knee on the floor. "I like your kitchen. Nice cappuccino maker. That's what it is, isn't it? I tried to make one for myself, but I couldn't figure out how the machine worked."

Now, Hawthorne recognized that faint, sweet fragrance on the boy's breath as cinnamon and pecan praline. The boy must have sampled the desserts left by sympathetic friends and neighbors. Probably tracked crumbs all over the kitchen floor.

Hawthorne was sickened and enraged at the thought of the kid digging through his fridge, eating from the open containers and touching all the clean dishware. It felt like a violation. Then he saw that the boy wore his clothes, too, and that only made him angrier.

This was no way a man of his status deserved to be treated. Especially in his own home! This boy couldn't be any older than seventeen, and underneath the creepy vibe the little brat was going for, Hawthorne was confident that he'd find a scared kid, just waiting to take orders from an authority figure. After all, that was what this boy had been born to do. Take orders. Obey without question.

Among his peers, Hawthorne was renowned for his boldness. Now, he imagined himself at Capitol Hill, in his own hunting ground.

"I'm ordering you to leave, now!" Hawthorne bellowed, even though it hurt to elevate his voice above a whisper. "I'm a state senator, goddammit, and I won't be ordered around by the likes of you!"

The boy blinked. "You're a what?"

"A senator!" he roared in righteous fury.

"Sorry, I don't know what that is." The boy glanced around at the brick walls, smiling to himself. "Yeah, it's a real nice house. I bet she loved it here. You treated her well, didn't you? You didn't bully her?"

Hawthorne dreaded this sudden change in conversation, and his confidence deflated like a pricked balloon. Deep down, he had known that the boy was telling the truth about not having killed Elizabeth. He had known all along who was responsible, from the moment the police showed up, but he had been in such denial that he hired men—the same men who had taken care of some potential scandals of his—to kidnap the boy from the hospital. Then, once he'd gotten a good look at the kid's face, an even worse truth had come to light. He had realized just who in the Project this boy belonged to, and what the ramifications of kidnapping him would be.

"My wife and I loved Elizabeth," Hawthorne said plaintively. "She was our world. We gave her everything she wanted."

The boy sighed, and an almost regretful smile came across his lips.

"Wrong answer," he said and brought his other hand into Hawthorne's range of vision. He held an unusual object that, through Hawthorne's blurry eyes, vaguely resembled a nose hair shaver. Except, instead of a razor attachment at the end, it featured a small steel nozzle.

No, not a shaver. A sickening tremor lurched through Hawthorne's body, and his heart raced faster than he could stand it. Icy sweat broke out on his back, and he began trembling uncontrollably. Not a shaver at all.

A crème brûlée torch.

"That wasn't her name," the boy said, pressing a button on the side of the torch. A long blue flame hissed from the nozzle. "She was Subject Nine of Subset A."

Many evenings, Hawthorne had come home from work to find his wife whipping up one of her delicious creations. Baking was a hobby of hers, and she used the torch to caramelize crème brûlée and flan, toast meringue, and melt marshmallows. When she had purchased the device, she had boasted about how hot it could get: 2,500 degrees Fahrenheit. Now, that number flashed in his head, over and over like a road hazard sign.

"Wait, I didn't mean that," Hawthorne said quickly, and tried to sit up. This time, the boy allowed him to.

"Is that so?" the boy asked, regarding the blowtorch. Twin flames reflected in his irises, which were the same intense shade of blue as the fire.

"We loved both of them," Hawthorne said. "Both Elizabeth and…and Nine. They were our daughters."

"Then why did you give her up?"

"We made an arrangement when Project Pandora first started. My wife had trouble getting pregnant, so we decided to try in vitro fertilization. I was campaigning for governor at the time, so we didn't have much money to spare. The organization funded the whole thing and even provided a surrogate for us."

"You mean a glorified pressure cooker," the boy said, clearly referring to the artificial wombs where all of the Project's children had been gestated. "A lifeless, unloving machine."

"Genetically and racially, my wife and I were the ideal candidates for the Project," Hawthorne said, ignoring the boy's foolish comments. "We matched the donor profile perfectly. All they wanted in return was one of the children."

And in return for his contribution, he had received several generous campaign donations. Just a sample of what the Project would one day yield.

"The ideal candidates, huh?" The boy favored him with a bright smile. "You should use that as a campaign slogan. Who knows? You might even become President."

"It's not like Elizabeth had a bad life there—"

"Subject Nine of Subset A."

"She was raised to become the perfect political diplomat."

"You mean a puppet."

"An ambassador or politician—"

"A slave."

"Goddammit, it's not like that!" Hawthorne snapped, and instantly regretted it. The boy brought the torch close enough to Hawthorne's face that sweat beaded on his cheek. "Wait! Wait, you're right. I'm sorry. You're absolutely right. We just didn't see it that way at the time. We thought we were giving her a good childhood, where she could be raised by capable teachers, all her needs met."

"Why her?"

"What do you mean?"

"Why Nine instead of that other girl? Didn't they let you choose which one you wanted to keep? Did they give you some sort of trial period?"

Hawthorne swallowed hard. A blockage of blood and mucus pressed against the back of his throat, and he couldn't seem to dislodge it. "She had colic and refused to nurse, amongst other things."

Thinking back, the reasons seemed so petty, but how could he describe the sleepless nights, the worry, the shrill and persistent wailing? Elizabeth had been an angel, but that *other* baby—that scrunched-up, red, shrieking thing—

had been more like a wretched demon. Twice, he had to keep himself from shaking the infant just to get her to shut up. More than once, after an exhausting night spent rocking the little beast, he had imagined smothering her in her cradle. It was as though that infant had wanted to spite him and drive him insane. As if she wanted to make him lose his election, and just when his political career was getting started. She had been better off with professionals who would cater to her needs 24/7.

The boy stared at him, evidently digesting his excuses. Then he asked: "What's colic?"

"It's—"

"Actually, never mind. I don't care. It's a bad reason anyway."

Hawthorne decided that it would be best not to disagree.

"How many times did you visit the Academy?" the boy asked.

The Academy was the name of the Colorado facility where all the children of Project Pandora had been reared. Located high in the mountains, the Academy existed in perfect isolation, gated and secluded. Out of sight, with no external influences that might impact the children's upbringing. Because the children were destined to infiltrate both political parties and various military posts, their education had been completely neutral, without religious or political bias. Or so he had been told.

Moistening his lips, Hawthorne considered the answer carefully. If he told the boy the truth—that in the last seventeen years, he had visited the facility all of three times—the boy might see him as irresponsible. The truth was, he couldn't bear to go there, and it wasn't just because of the long flight. He hated being reminded of what he had done, but he had seen no way to rectify his mistake.

Only after the real Elizabeth had died of an illegal drug overdose following a night of drunken, cocaine-fueled partying, a campaigning politician's worst nightmare, was he able to bring A-09 back to the home where she belonged. He had staged a car accident to explain "Elizabeth's" month-long absence, the time it took to wipe the girl's memories and perform minor cosmetic surgeries to make her better resemble her dead twin sister. Now, both sisters would share an urn in the family mausoleum.

"I went there many times," Hawthorne said, feigning confidence. "I always made sure that she was being well cared for."

"Is that so?"

"Yes!"

The boy lowered the torch. "Then you must have seen me with her. We were together all the time. During meals. Between classes and practice. After lights out."

"I…"

"We were each other's first time." The boy sighed. "She had a small birthmark on her thigh, right here." He gestured with the blow torch toward Hawthorne's crotch. "It was shaped like a teardrop. I loved to kiss it."

"Enough," Hawthorne mumbled, sickened by this sudden development. He dreaded to think how a child born of such perversion would have turned out.

"You know, I've always been curious about that," the boy said thoughtfully.

"Huh?" His blood went cold. Had he spoken aloud without even realizing it?

"Oh, I was just talking to myself," the boy said, cocking his head. "Of all the things I've done, I've never actually set someone's balls on fire before. I was just wondering, do you think they'll burst like microwaved eggs?"

"Oh, God, no. P-please don't." Hawthorne shifted back, hyperaware of the heat of the flame through his pants. His bladder suddenly felt overwhelmingly full, and sweat poured down his back. The torch wasn't close enough to singe the fabric. Not yet.

"I'm just kidding." The boy chuckled and turned off the torch. "I'm sure it won't come to that. But you see, Mr. Hawthorne, this is the way I was trained to think. With some people, it takes a little pain to get them to cooperate. Nine might have been trained to be the perfect diplomat, but I was trained to be the perfect soldier."

"I'll cooperate, I p-p-promise," Hawthorne babbled, straining against his handcuffs. "Whatever you want. Just tell me, and I swear to God, I'll do it."

"Morality is subjective. Murder is collateral damage. Violence is necessary. Those were the lessons that they taught me in that place."

"Whatever you w-want, you must believe me. I'll give you whatever you want. There's no need for violence."

"Not that I ever hurt her," the boy continued. "But I hurt people for her. Kids who were jealous of her. The boys who bullied her. A grown man who wanted to do bad things to her. That last one was my first, too. The first time I realized that killing people can actually feel *good*."

"Please, you d-d-don't want to do this," Hawthorne said, his voice shrill with hysteria. "I'm not a b-bad man. I didn't do anything to her. I just wanted to give her a good home, the home she deserved!"

"You took her from me, sir. You made me *suffer*. It's because of you that I'm here right now, instead of where I belong. If you hadn't gotten selfish and tried to steal her away, I never would have tried to escape from the

Academy with her. I never would have ended up with Dimitri, and she wouldn't be dead right now." He paused, and his full lips rose in a pensive smile. "I was meant for something, you know. I was going to be a great leader. That's what they always told me."

As the boy spoke, he played with the blowtorch, turning it on and off again. Each time the flame gleamed in those intense blue eyes, swallowing the pupils, Hawthorne had an unsettling impression of staring into the depths of hell. There was nothing left in those eyes at all.

"But enough about that," the boy said, at last. "The past is past. Let's talk about the present. You're a very wealthy man. You have a beautiful house and nice things. Where do you keep your money?"

"I have a savings account—"

"Please don't condescend to me," the boy said and brought the torch closer.

Weeping like a child, Hawthorne tried to turn his head away, but the boy grabbed his chin and held it.

"I'm not in the mood to play around," he said, clenching down on Hawthorne's aching jawbone and digging his nails in. "I'll give you a choice. Torch or morphine."

Hawthorne's stomach twisted into knots. He had thirty grand in his bedroom safe, the result of a certain unorthodox business transaction. Deciding that the money wasn't worth his fertility, much less his life, he said, "Bedroom. Safe. In closet. Combination is 53615."

The boy's grip eased. "Can you repeat that?"

"53615!"

"That's better," the boy said, rewarding him with an empty smile. "Now, if you've given me the wrong combination, like maybe the one that sends out a signal to the cops, you should know that you will be dead by the time they get here."

"It's the right one."

"A lot of pain can happen in three minutes."

"I swear."

"We can find out if they really *do* explode."

"I promise, I'm not lying!" Hawthorne cried, feeling very close to soiling himself. "Wait! Where are you going? What about the morphine? You promised!"

"Here's another lesson from the Academy, sir: suffering is a good thing." The boy set the torch on the counter, before leaving Hawthorne to dwell in agony.

CASE NOTES 8:

ARTEMIS

As Shannon cleared an intersection, she glanced over at Tyler. His jacket was too dark to show blood, but the pine-green fabric appeared slick.

Her stomach knotted at the coppery odor of blood. Gnawing her lip in worry, she turned her attention back to the road, just in time to narrowly avoid trading paint with a Porsche.

A police cruiser appeared in the lane behind her, lights blazing. The siren howled like a banshee's shriek over the downpour.

As the cop car drew closer, Shannon exhausted every swear word in her vocabulary and began arranging them in creative combinations. Swearing allowed her to convert her fear into anger, but it also made her feel like the world hadn't entirely gone off the deep end and that some things remained the same even when madness claimed the rest.

The white car slowed down, keeping its distance now. Other motorists moved out of the way of the cop car, providing the officer with a clear path to her.

She pressed down on the accelerator and watched the needle climb. As the speedometer dial ticked forward, she felt her own heart began to beat faster and faster until she was certain it would explode. She gripped the steering wheel so tightly her nails sunk into the pleather cover and her fingers began to ache.

Her old driving instructor would have had an aneurysm if he saw her speeding in this kind of weather, but she didn't have a choice in the matter. If the car didn't hydroplane and spiral out of control or roll into a fiery implosion, then she would die soon after being detained. The police couldn't protect her from the organization behind Project Pandora. The official story would be something like she hung herself in her cell or succumbed to a heart defect, while the truth would be far grimmer. She doubted she'd even have the chance to speak to a lawyer.

"You with me, Tyler?"

Tyler mumbled under his breath. She did not ask him to repeat himself.

"You're going to be all right," she said, resisting the compulsion to look at him. At this speed and in these weather conditions, keeping her eyes on the street was paramount. If she lost control of the vehicle, striking any one of the small trees lining the blacktop would be like driving straight into a brick wall. Other cars made even deadlier obstacles, with there being little room to maneuver past them. A single wrong move could result in a massive pileup.

Worrying would do no good. It would only distract her. But she couldn't stop thinking about Tyler, and instead of formulating a plan of escape, she found herself racking her brain for a way to help him.

"We're going to get you to a doctor," she said. "Just keep pressure on the wound. Can you hear me? Just keep pressure on it."

"No one's going to help us, Shannon." His voice was so faint, fading by the moment.

"Don't speak. Save your strength."

On either side of the road, smokestacks and steel girding emerged from the mist like the skeletons of monsters washed ashore. She had passed down this same stretch of highway on her way into town and had been staggered by the mazelike expanse of the industrial area. She and Tyler had discussed it briefly. At the time, she had thought that the smokestacks belonged to a brewery, but now the factory's product was less important than the shelter it could provide.

From memory, she knew that the next exit after this one was miles down the road. It might as well not be there at all, for they would never reach it in time. While the rain and violent wind might prevent the highway patrol from utilizing a helicopter, the weather wouldn't deter a search completely. Soon cruisers would be swarming this highway. Checkpoints would cut off main roads, blockades would be erected, and an all-notice bulletin would be put out for an SUV matching their car's description. Even changing the license plates wouldn't suffice, not anymore.

Shannon pulled off at the next exit, trying to gauge the pursuing cruiser's distance by the sound of its dwindling sirens. The rearview mirror revealed only mist and asphalt. Visibility was reduced to sixty feet, if even that.

With each minute, the weather worsened. Rain struck the windshield, obscuring her view. She eased off the gas pedal, and the speedometer returned to a manageable, although still risky number.

"We've done so much," Tyler mumbled. "We don't deserve help."

"Ty..."

"I can't stand it."

"You deserve to live, Tyler," she said, blinking back tears. "You can't die. If you die, I don't know what I'll do without you. I need you, so you can't die. Okay? I need you. You *saved* me."

Through the curtains of rain, the smokestacks now resembled the bars of a cage more than anything else. She was glad to leave them behind her for busy streets and smaller complexes. She could no longer hear police sirens and decided that because of the dangerous driving situations, the search must have been delayed for the time being. Still, she continuously glanced into the rearview mirror, expecting to see flashing lights.

Tyler stopped talking, and she forced herself not to look at him, afraid of what she might find. At the thought of him lying there, dead and staring, her hands tightened around the steering wheel.

"You still with me?" she asked.

He laughed, or maybe he cried. She couldn't tell.

"It's all hopeless," he said. "It doesn't mean anything, does it?"

"What doesn't?" she asked, half-listening and afraid that if he stopped talking, he would never speak again.

"Everything we've done. We'll never defeat them. You were right, Shannon. I should have listened to you. We should have just run and never looked back. I thought I could stop this from happening to anyone else, but I can't even save myself."

"You can't give up." She felt her blood turn to ice water as a faint siren pierced through the pounding rain. Then another. And they were growing louder.

"We'll do it," she continued. "I promise. We'll liberate the Academy, just like you wanted. So, you can't give up.

You can't expect me to do it on my own."

Seeing no better choice, Shannon made a last-second decision to pull through the gate of a large brick building whose parking lot was crowded to capacity. As she took her place behind a van, her heart sank.

Her view from the road had been obstructed by a row of hedges. She hadn't noticed the small cubicle in the median between the incoming and outgoing lanes, or the narrow guard-operated barrier blocking off the parking lot. The cars were being checked.

Before she could back out, another car boxed her in. While she didn't doubt that she could ram the minicar into submission with her SUV, it would only attract more attention.

The gate opened, permitting the van in front of her to enter.

Smiling through gritted teeth, she rolled up to the guard cubicle, praying she wasn't about to come face-to-face with an actual officer. If she was lucky, it would just be a rent-a-cop.

Instead, she found herself confronted by a giant stuffed bear.

"Good morning," the woman in the mascot suit said. "Welcome to Ravenscrag Chocolate Factory. Are you two here for the tour?"

A crazed giggle threatened to spill from Shannon's mouth as she struggled to come to terms with what she was seeing. In the distance, the sirens grew louder.

"Yeah, we are," she said and for the life of her, couldn't hold back her laughter.

Bearsuit mistook her near-hysteria for mirth. "Fantastic! That will be ten dollars per person."

Twenty dollars was a small price to pay for temporary

refuge. Getting her laughter under control, she fumbled around for her wallet. A car honked behind her as she searched for the correct bill.

"Just a minute," she said. "Sorry. I thought it was just five per person. Let me find a twenty."

"Hey, is he okay?" Bearsuit asked, leaning through the open window. "You look a little pale there, broski."

"Fine," Tyler croaked. "Just carsickness."

"There are refreshments for sale in the gift shop," Bearsuit said. "And there's a lovely little café, where you two can eat homemade pastries and sip on some of our world-famous hot cocoa. The next tour isn't until noon, so you should have plenty of time to get a snack. Just save your appetite for some of our complimentary chocolate samples at the end of the tour!"

Shannon passed two tens through the window, took two tickets in return, and waited for the partition to rise. Once the barrier was up, she resisted the urge to stomp down on the gas pedal. She drove to a far corner of the parking lot, under the shelter of the steel awning, and parked between two pickups. The high fence ensured that she wouldn't be seen from the road. After plucking the keys from the ignition, she allowed herself time for the trembling in her limbs to subside before reaching into the backseat for her purse.

Months ago, her purse had held makeup, spare change, candy, tissues, and jewelry. Those were the privileges of a past life. Now, hers contained only three items: in the main pocket, the loaded handgun; in the outer pouch, her burner cell and a pocketknife.

Slinging her purse over her shoulder, she got out of the car, walked around to the other side of the vehicle, and opened the front passenger door. The reek of blood hit her like a sledgehammer. Until now, she had grown desensitized to it.

"Tyler, I'm going to take a look at your wound," she said, steeling herself for the horror of what she might find beneath his clothes.

He didn't answer, he didn't even look at her. Blood darkened his jeans and dripped down the upholstery.

She tried not to look at the mess and assured herself that whatever blood there was, it hadn't come from his mouth. Bloody vomit meant a punctured lung, that maybe the bullet had shattered bone or torn a helter-skelter path through his internal organs. You didn't just recover from that.

"Tyler?"

He slowly looked up, his gaze clouded and distant. "Hurts. It hurts so much."

"I know," she said, blinking to clear her vision. "I'm sorry."

She would do anything to take away his pain, even if it meant taking it upon herself.

"Is this what she felt?" he mumbled.

"What do you mean?"

"I don't know anymore." His eyes focused on something past the windshield, but all she saw when she turned in that direction was the brick wall. His chest rose with shallow breaths, and a maroon splotch stained the corner of his mouth.

She unzipped his jacket and peeled back the sodden fabric. Goose down clung to his shirt, which was light enough that she could see the thick ooze of blood discoloring it.

She took a deep breath and told herself not to freak out. If she panicked, she wouldn't be able to calm herself.

If she began screaming, she might not stop.

She told herself it was only a little blood.

With infinite care, she cut through the sleeve of his shirt. As the fabric fell away, she grimaced at the leaking hole in his upper shoulder. It shouldn't have bothered her. She had seen worse. She had inflicted worse, she was sure. And yet, at the sight of the wound, her stomach seized.

"It doesn't look too bad," Shannon said, hating the lack of confidence in her voice. It was a lie, and they both knew it.

Tyler looked down and closed his eyes. He muttered a single word under his breath. It sounded like a curse, but his voice was so soft, it might just as well have been a prayer.

"You're going to be okay," she said. "You would have bled out by now if the bullet had hit a major artery. We need to get you to a doctor, but I'm going to try to bandage this first."

She searched through the glove box, cursing herself for not buying a first aid kit when she had the chance. At first, all she found were loose mints, old coupons, and grimy papers left by the vehicle's previous owner. Then she came across her stash of sanitary pads.

She sighed. They were better than nothing.

She laid out two napkins over the frontal wound and instructed him to hold them in place while she ripped long strips of fabric from the bottom of her shirt. As she pressed her last pad against the entry wound, she wrapped the torn cloth around his shoulder.

"I know it hurts, but just keep applying pressure," she said.

"Shannon."

"What is it?"

"I remember. I actually remember being there. It's vague, but…it's all starting to come back to me. I think I get it now. Why these bad things just keep happening to me. I think I finally understand the reason for it."

"There's no reason for it, and it's not going to continue."

"This is all happening because I should have died with all the others."

"I promise someday everything will get better."

"I was supposed to. I'm not like you. I wasn't born right."

"Don't say that!"

"There were thirty. I watched them go. One by one, they went to the white ward and never came back. And then I found out why. I found out, and I ended it." He looked down at his left hand and curled it into a weak fist. "I did it. With my own hand. And when it was over, I kept thinking, it should have been me there. Me on that table. Not her."

The white ward? The table? What was he talking about?

"That doesn't mean anything," she insisted, wondering if he was becoming delirious. "Listen to me, Tyler, there's nothing wrong with us. What we did, we didn't have a choice. We aren't responsible, and we don't deserve any of this."

His eyes began to close, and his hand slipped from his shoulder. Each time he breathed, it sounded like some integral part of him had come loose and was rattling around deep inside his lungs.

"You're a good person, I know you are. You didn't hurt anyone on purpose. It wasn't your fault." Shannon couldn't stop talking. She thought that if she left his side, he would give up on himself.

"Just leave me," he muttered.

"What?" She didn't think she had heard him correctly.
"In my condition, I'll only drag you down. I'll get us
both killed. Just go."

"Like hell I will." She snapped shut the blade of her
pocketknife and slipped it into her pocket. Even though
she loathed letting him out of her sight, she couldn't stay
here. "I'm going to see if I can find a car."

"I love you. I don't want to be the death of you."

"Then don't give up! You can't give up on the ones you
love." She forced herself to take a deep breath. "Wait here
for me, okay? Just wait for me. I love you, too. I'll be right
back. I promise."

She took his gun from the footwell and placed it on
the seat next to him. Then she pulled his jacket back on
and zipped it up. When she pressed her lips against his
forehead to test his temperature, she found his skin cold
and clammy. It frightened her how chilly he was, and she
turned on the heater full blast before leaving him.

Shannon shut the door. She pulled up her hood as
she stepped out from under the awning and entered the
downpour.

She went up and down the rows of cars, keeping an eye
out for older models and peering into windows. Without
the proper tools, she could only test the door handles.
Breaking a window would be a last resort, but when she
found a chunk of loose cement beside the chain link fence,
she slipped it into her jacket pocket just in case.

Five of the cars she tested were unlocked, but she
couldn't find their keys in them.

At the back of the parking lot, an enclosed area housed
company vehicles. During off hours, the gate must have
been padlocked, but with workers in the process of loading
and unloading crates and pallets, the doors were left open.

Against her better judgement, she walked into the loading bay. She clutched her purse, hyperaware of the weight of the handgun inside. She could remember its weight in her hand and the way it kicked when she pulled the trigger. If she had to kill again, she would.

Her eyes roamed across the lot. As she contemplated the dangers of hiding in the back of a transport truck, she spotted a repair van parked off to the side. It was your typical white van, clean and inconspicuous, with a sign on either door featuring the company's logo. As she drew closer, she realized that the signs were stickers or magnetics, not actually painted on. Easily removable. Maybe she wouldn't have to risk being crushed beneath two tons of chocolate after all.

When she tried the driver's door, she found it unlocked. She leaned inside like she had every right to do so and pulled back the floor mat to see if the spare keys were underneath it. When she found only dust and fossilized french fries, she opened the sun visor. She reached under the seat and felt around for a magnetic strip. Just as she was prepared to move on, a glint of metal caught her eye.

The driver had left his keys in the center console. He would be coming back soon, no doubt. By then, they would be gone.

When Shannon drove up to the main parking lot, she didn't even bother finding a parking spot, she just stopped next to their SUV. Time was of the essence here, and before she stepped out of the van, she had already formulated a plan.

"You should have just left," Tyler said as she opened his door. He looked a little better. Maybe it was just her imagination.

"Come on, let's go," she said, reaching for his hand.

"We need to hurry. Can you walk?"

When he got down from the car, his legs almost gave out beneath him. She caught him at the last minute and helped walk him to the van. He climbed inside with her assistance and buckled his seatbelt on his own, though he struggled to do it with only one hand.

"Not much of a James Bond, am I?" he mumbled as she stripped off her jacket and draped it over him as an extra layer to warm him. "Can hardly even buckle my seatbelt."

"It's just shock," Shannon said, although at that point she wasn't sure whether it was shock, blood loss, or what. Instead of wasting time contemplating it, she returned to the SUV to retrieve the backpack containing the Project files. They had purchased clothes as well, but she thought better of dragging out the suitcase into the rain. As for the pillows and blankets, they would only be unnecessary bulk. She left the keys in the ignition and returned to the repair van.

Shannon peeled off the van's magnetic signs with ease and dropped them into the passenger seat's footwell after she climbed into the car. She couldn't do anything about the license plate yet, but she hoped that the cops would be less concerned with investigating a car theft than searching for two fugitives, at least until she switched plates.

By the time they reached the gate, no more than four minutes had passed since she had stolen the van. The automatic exit gate opened the moment they approached it. They left without incident, ignored by two cop cruisers they passed on the interstate.

Once on the highway, Shannon gave herself permission to relax. She eased off the gas and dropped her speed to match that of the other motorists. Already, her focus had shifted from escaping detection to finding a doctor who would treat Tyler.

The way she looked at it, she really only had three choices. She could take him to an actual hospital, force a private practitioner to perform surgery at gunpoint, or do nothing at all. The first and third options were out, which left her with the task of finding a doctor who, for all she knew, might refuse to cooperate even with the barrel of a gun pressed against his head. But where could she even begin her search in the first place?

Damn it! She felt so helpless. If she took Tyler to a hospital, he would die. If she did nothing, he would die!

As a bolt of lightning seared the sky, Shannon thought of an idea that, although safer than holding an entire medical clinic hostage, could mean Tyler's death as well as her own.

They needed to go to the doctor that Belmont had been communicating with before his death.

Dr. Francine Miller.

CASE NOTES 9:

HADES

Hades found the safe in the closet of the master bedroom and opened it with ease. Cash, expensive jewelry, and papers crowded the small space. On the top shelf, there was a revolver in a tooled leather holster, beside two boxes of ammunition.

He took a backpack from the luggage storage space above the racks of clothes. The bag was of a simple design, with a waterproofed liner. Like many of the items in the closet, it still had its price tags.

He transferred all the cash to the backpack's main pocket. Even without counting the money, he knew that there must be at least twenty grand, and probably closer to thirty. More than enough to keep him going for a while.

He leafed through the papers, expecting to find deeds and personal documents, and was surprised when he came across interview transcripts. With only a cursory glance, he realized that the files were research data, and sorted through them. On the fifth page, he noticed two words that gave him pause:

PROJECT PROMETHEUS.

The page was covered in strings of numbers and

letters. He was no scientist, but he had spent enough time organizing Dr. Kosta's paperwork to realize that the numbers must be lab results of some sort.

After reading through a few more pages, which offered even more intriguing information, he shoved the papers into his backpack. His gaze flickered to the jewelry, but he decided against taking it. Although his involvement in Project Pandora had familiarized him with certain parts of the American underworld, he didn't want to waste time finding a fence. The sooner he got out of D.C. the better.

After Hades loaded the revolver's cylinder, he placed both boxes of spare ammunition in a different pouch. While he doubted that he would have the opportunity to use 200 extra bullets, he liked being prepared. He wouldn't be able to acquire more. The same went for medical supplies; before he left, he needed to raid the senator's medicine cabinet for useful pharmaceuticals.

Hades didn't care much for revolvers, but the weapon was better than nothing. At least the holster was designed for concealed carry, to be worn inside the waistband.

Once he clipped the holster to his belt and stowed the loaded gun safely inside, he found a quilted navy jacket in his size. The garment fit tight around his broad shoulders and loose around his waist. He practiced drawing and holstering the revolver until he was comfortable with its placement.

He tried on shoes from the rack, searching for a pair that fit. He missed his military jump boots, broken-in and creased as they were, but he would have to make do with the senator's Italian oxfords.

As he passed through the bathroom, he glanced at his reflection. Even with his long, unkempt hair, the conservative clothes transformed him.

I look like a prep school student, he thought, surprised by the difference a buttoned shirt and designer jeans could make. He brushed his hair out of his face, wondering if he should cut it as well while he was here. No, that could wait until later.

When he returned to the basement, he found the senator worming against the cabinets, evidently trying to reach the countertop.

Hawthorne fumbled among the bottles and medical supplies with his bound hands, but stopped the moment Hades reached the bottom of the stairs.

"What were you trying to get?" he asked, walking over.

Hawthorne tried to back up and, misjudging the length of chain between his ankles, tripped over his own feet. He landed hard on his ass but wasted no time in scooting away.

"You want this?" He picked up the torch and held it out. "Go on. Take it."

Hawthorne shook his head, then groaned at the motion. "No. I was just—the morphine."

"Oh. Are you in pain? I've gotten good at tolerating it. It never really goes away, but you can find ways to separate yourself from it. It's all a matter of mindset. You need to tell yourself it's happening to someone else."

"Look, you've got the money. What's keeping you here? I promise I won't tell anyone you were here."

"That's funny, considering how you tried to strangle me earlier."

"I didn't want to kill you. I just wanted answers."

"So do I."

"I'll tell you whatever you want to know, just don't hurt me."

"Let's start with your friends in the Project," Hades said.

"They're who you should be after!" Hawthorne said. "Not me. I'm not even involved in it. Your mother. She's the one you should blame for Elizabeth's death. Not me."

"What did you just say?" he asked, certain he had heard wrong. "My mother?"

"Francine Miller. You're her son, aren't you? You look just like her."

Hades stared, for once without words.

"My god," Hawthorne said, giving a clotted, mirthless laugh. "You don't even know who I'm talking about, do you?"

Francine Miller. Why did that name sound so familiar? He was certain that he had heard it somewhere before, but where? When?

"She's the whole reason the Project began in the first place," the senator said quickly. "She invented the artificial womb you were born in. You're mad at me for giving up Nine, when your own mother abandoned you. So why don't you hurt her, not me? I'm not to blame for whatever happened to you. She is."

The words tore away at Hades like scalpel blades. He felt a powerful urge to punch the man's teeth in, then keep punching. Rather than act on that urge, he just returned the torch to the counter.

For too long, he had allowed his anger to go unchecked. His hatred had raged like a wildfire, uncontrollable and indiscriminately destructive, and during his darkest moments, only blood had been able to extinguish it. Those days were over. He needed to direct that chaotic energy toward a goal, a purpose.

When Hades put his foot on the first stair, Hawthorne cried out, "Wait, where are you going?"

"If I stay here any longer, sir, I think I might hurt you very badly."

"You can't leave me down here!"

He reached the landing and stepped into the ground-floor hallway. He shut the door, muffling Hawthorne's shouts.

In the kitchen, he drew a glass of water from the tap. As he drank it, he thought about his life as a child at the Academy, those forest wargames he had put all his time and effort into.

Back then, winning had been the only thing that mattered. He had spent exhaustive hours drawing up plans and formulating new strategies. To win meant better food and fewer chores. To lose meant nothing but water and stale bread at meals, repetitive training exercises, and being awoken by shrill alarms during odd hours in the night. Yet the petty rewards were only the icing on the cake. His real motivation came from the knowledge that in spite of what everyone else thought, those paintball games truly meant something. The scientists and overseers who operated the facility were studying them, and by winning, he would show them that he was destined for greatness.

In the end, it had been all for naught. He hadn't risen to greatness; he had fallen into hellish despair. But those mock battles weren't worthless. They had taught him about patience and thoroughness, and how important it was to weigh the pros and cons of every possible choice.

When he thought about it like that, he realized that this was another game, though one with far higher stakes.

It was essential to proceed slowly and with caution, and think things through before he acted. He needed to detach himself emotionally from this situation, regardless of who Hawthorne was to him.

Now, the tactics. Whichever way he looked at it, killing Hawthorne would achieve nothing. The corpse would be discovered within mere hours, and DNA evidence left at the scene of the crime would implicate him in the murder. Worst case scenario, he would be hunted by both the police and Project Pandora, which would severely lower his own odds of survival. Best case scenario, the Project would realize he was on the run, without any support, and utilize every resource they had to find him.

On the other hand, allowing the senator to live could only benefit him. The man would keep silent about his whereabouts as an act of self-preservation. While the organization might eventually discover who was responsible for his disappearance from the hospital, it could be days or weeks until that happened.

He was still alive, and he had no intention of committing suicide. What were his goals, and how would he achieve them with the limited resources he now possessed?

Abruptly, he put down the water glass. The truth hit him like a hammer blow.

Revenge was the only thing in the world. The people who had created him had taken everything else.

They must be punished.

Hades returned to the basement to find Hawthorne crawling across the floor on his belly in a futile attempt to reach the counter again. Noticing him, the man stopped squirming and struggled to elevate himself off his stomach.

"I'm going to remove the cuffs around your ankles, and we're going to go into the kitchen," Hades said, walking up to him. "Don't bother trying to kick me in the face. It won't do you any good."

"Wait, you're not going to…"

"You're not my enemy. Besides, if Nine was still alive, I think she would want you to live. I'm doing this for her." He paused, choosing his next words carefully in an attempt to repair the damage his blowtorch demonstration had caused. He needed to make the senator believe that it was safer to keep quiet about his involvement, at least for the time being. "I know you're probably thinking about crawling back to Mr. Warren as soon as I go, but I wouldn't if I were you. They'll kill you, you know, once they find out that you were harboring me. You're already a liability. If I were you, I'd just run and not look back. That's what I'm going to do."

The man said nothing as Hades leaned down and unlocked the cuffs. He tossed the shackles aside and helped the man to his feet, walking him up the stairs.

"Before I leave, I have a few more questions," he said, pushing Hawthorne into a kitchen chair.

"Morphine."

"I'm not familiar with the drug, and I don't know the proper dosage, sir. The paramedics will give you morphine. You can call them as soon as I go, but I have some questions for you first." He sat down in the other chair. "Is Dr. Kosta dead?"

The senator nodded. "Shot to death with the others."

Hades wondered if Shannon or Tyler had been the one to kill Dimitri. He wished that he had been the one to pull the trigger, but that was just one more thing in life that he could not change.

"And what was the story that the organization told you?"

"They told me that Dr. Kosta was becoming paranoid. Unstable. He thought that the authorities had learned about Project Pandora, and to save his own skin, he tried destroying all evidence related to the Project. Including Elizabeth and you. The other men got in the way, trying to stop him, and were shot to death as well."

"But you thought the Project was covering for me?"

"Yes."

"I've heard enough." Hades rose to his feet. "I'm going to borrow one of your cars. It's a small sacrifice, and I think you're smart enough to realize what will happen if it's found in my possession. A week or two from now, you can report it stolen. By then, I'll probably be in Canada."

"I won't. Now, please, just leave."

"I have one last question," Hades said.

"What?"

"All those years ago, when the Project first began, did the thought of failure ever occur to you? Did you ever envision this same exact outcome?"

When Hawthorne didn't respond, Hades set the handcuff key on the table, within the senator's reach.

"You should know, Nine meant everything to me. So, at least one person in the world loved her for who she truly was." He paused. "She could have changed me, you know. But now it's too late for that."

CASE NOTES 10:

ARTEMIS

Shannon pulled over along the side of the road and retrieved Dr. Belmont's folder from her purse, searching for the paper with Dr. Miller's address. From the door compartment, she took the Colorado road map she had purchased at a service station and consulted it.

When she pinpointed their current location and compared it to the address on the form, she was relieved to find that her escape hadn't taken them in the wrong direction. Indeed, they were actually closer to Miller's office than they had been before.

"Tyler, you okay?" Shannon asked, shoving the paper into the center console.

He didn't answer. When she glanced at him, she was sickened to see him slumped against the seat, head down, eyes closed. His golden tan was reduced to a sickly jaundice, and even his lips were drained of color.

Unconscious. Please just be unconscious.

"Please, don't die on me." She blinked back tears, dismayed by how her voice trembled. Irrationally, she believed that if she sobbed, he would die. She must not cry.

"Tyler," she repeated, louder now. "Just hang in there.

We're almost there."

Dead silence. Blood dripped down the upholstery, and sooty shadows gathered under his eyes and sunken cheeks. His lips were parted ever so slightly, but she couldn't tell if he was still breathing.

The rain tapped against the windows. It sounded almost like cruel laughter.

She turned back onto the highway. There was no time to recover from her wrecked nerves, and any delay could mean death.

As she drove, she was possessed by a sudden unsettling idea that the entire world conspired to kill him. The storm, the newspaper, the opportune shooter. The universe wanted him dead, and it wouldn't stop until it had succeeded.

"Just hold on, goddammit!"

Rain and blood. Drip, drip.

As Shannon neared the address, she was surprised to find herself in a residential area. She had thought that her search would take her to a clinic well equipped to serve an injured patient.

Dr. Miller lived in an attractive neighborhood where the mansions were set far apart and trees bordered the street. Even in the midst of a storm, the entire community appeared so tidy that it reminded her of a hobbyist's diorama of a perfect village. A lie built to look pretty.

As she turned onto Juniper Street, her impression of the neighborhood became distorted. All she saw were dark windows, stone walls, and empty lawns. No life.

She felt as though they were the last two people alive in the husk of a ruined world. The crash of thunder and pounding sheets of rain only added to that grim impression.

She would have liked to park a few blocks away, but she didn't have that luxury. Not when the only thing keeping

Tyler from falling over was his seatbelt. Not when he wouldn't respond to her frantic attempts at reassurances, no matter how loudly she spoke.

She squinted through the rain, reading the house numbers. She paused in front of a luxurious Georgian mansion set apart from the rest, on several acres of land. A low fieldstone wall bordered it, with hedges providing the privacy that the wall didn't.

Shannon drove down Miller's driveway and stopped behind the car already parked there. As she got out of the van, she craned her head upward, staring at the drawn blinds. If the lights were on inside, she couldn't tell.

She pressed a hand to Tyler's neck, searching for a pulse. Then she sighed. Weak, but present.

His skin was so cold.

"Stay here," Shannon murmured, doubting that he could hear her anymore. She unbuckled her seatbelt and took the gun from the center console. Her hands trembled as she slipped the pistol into her waistband and pulled her shirt down over it.

She hated carrying the gun like that, but she had no other alternative. Her jacket was now bloodstained, too.

Shannon knocked on the front door and waited for the drapes to open, for a wary face to peer out at them. She told herself that when the door opened, she would pull out her handgun, point it at Miller's face, and demand the woman to treat him.

"Coming!" The voice was feminine, all right, but much too high for it to belong to a teenager, let alone a grown woman. The door swung open, and standing on the other side was a little girl with short black hair.

Shannon's heart sank.

"Who are you?" the girl asked, looking up at her. She

couldn't be older than seven or eight.

"Is Doctor Miller home?" Shannon asked, forcing a smile. The expression felt carved out of her tissue and sinew, a gash cut deep.

"You mean Mom?"

"That's right, sweetheart. Is she here?" She was hyperaware of the chill of the gun against her flank but didn't remove it from her waistband. Not yet.

"Mom!"

As the girl turned around, Shannon stepped through the doorway. She shut the door behind her and turned the bolt, feeling out of place and shrunken down, reduced to a terrified child herself.

Calm down. Take deep breaths.

Hollow footsteps.

A tall woman appeared from down the hall and strode toward them. "Caroline, what did I tell you about answering the door?"

Dr. Miller had the same ink-black hair as her daughter, but her eyes were blue instead of brown. Her photo in Belmont's file had done her no justice; she was of such stunning beauty that Shannon half-expected to find paparazzi crews detailing her every movement. Yet, as Shannon took a closer look, she noticed an unusual sharpness in Miller's facial structure, a rather lupine quality in her high cheekbones and deep-set eyes that was inexplicably disturbing.

Miller narrowed her eyes. "Caroline, go to your room."

"But—"

"I said go to your room and stay there," Miller repeated in a low, commanding voice, sounding less like a mother than a military commander.

Caroline sighed and disappeared deeper into the house.

"I know who you are," Miller said quietly. "I'm not armed."

"Is there anyone else here?" Shannon asked, hearing a coldness in herself that she hadn't realized existed until now.

"No, it's just me and Caroline."

"This is all happening because of people like you," Shannon said, pulling the pistol from her waistband. "It's all because of you that Tyler was shot, and you're going to save him. If you don't help him, I'll shoot you. I swear to God, I'll do it. I'm not joking around here. I've done it before, and I'm not afraid to do it again."

Dr. Miller's blue eyes flickered to the gun then to her face. Her own features remained placid, unwrinkled by worry or fear. "I understand."

"W-what?" Shannon stammered, taken aback by the doctor's calmness.

"I don't wish to fight you. When a patient's life is in danger, time is everything. Take me to him."

Shannon led the doctor outside at gunpoint, the pistol held only inches from her back.

"You can put the gun down," Dr. Miller said. "I won't try anything."

"That's not happening. Open the door," Shannon demanded, blinking rain from her eyes. Terror clawed at her, turning her guts to ribbons and clenching her lungs in a jagged chokehold.

Tyler lay where she had left him, unconscious and bloodied.

"We need to get him inside," Dr. Miller said, backing away. "I have a wheelchair in the garage."

As the doctor typed the combination into the keypad mounted on the garage, Shannon kept the gun trained on her. She was hyperaware of the growl of nearby traffic, and twice she mistook the crack of thunder for gunshots.

She half-expected the wheelchair to be a lie, a tactic to buy time. But it was there all right, sitting in the corner alongside crutches and a dismantled examining table covered in dust. The rubber treads of the wheels were cracked with age, and as Dr. Miller pulled the chair out into the rain, it creaked and groaned like it would fall apart at any moment.

"It would be better if you could drive the car into the garage," Dr. Miller said. "He shouldn't be exposed to this kind of weather."

Shannon shook her head, knowing that the moment she sat down in the driver's seat, Dr. Miller would flee back inside. The van could wait. No one would look for it here. Not yet.

Dr. Miller opened the car door, leaned inside, and unbuckled Tyler's seatbelt. She glanced back. "Put that gun down and help me get him into the wheelchair."

Shannon hesitated, but shoved the gun into the waistband of her jeans and joined Dr. Miller beside him. Tyler weighed more than she expected, and it took their combined strength to lift him.

As Shannon lowered him, her grip faltered. Her fingers slipped across Tyler's drenched skin, and she grabbed onto his belt to keep from dropping him. A twanging ache travelled from her wrist to her shoulder as his dead weight tried to drag her down.

As soon as Tyler was securely seated, she stepped back and withdrew the gun. The last thing she needed right now was a bullet to the hip.

"My daughter isn't a part of this," Dr. Miller said, wheeling Tyler inside. "Don't involve her."

"I don't plan to unless I have to."

Dr. Miller pushed Tyler into the kitchen. A single lamp illuminated the stove's tile backsplash, but she turned on all the kitchen lights as she entered.

She turned to Shannon. "How long has it been since he was shot?"

"Two hours, I think. Maybe a little less. An hour and a half. An hour. I don't know." Her nerves were frazzled, and she recalled the escape as if it had taken place over mere seconds.

"Help me get him onto the table," Dr. Miller said, before brushing the placemats onto the floor. Her voice was all authority now. "Hurry. I can't do this on my own."

Shannon shoved the pistol into her waistband once more and joined the doctor at the table. She wrapped her arms around his waist, stabilizing him, while Dr. Miller lifted his legs. Once more, she was struck by how heavy Tyler was. It was like dragging a corpse.

As she gently set him down, his head lolled to the side. She pressed a hand against his cold, smooth cheek.

"I won't let you die, Tyler," she murmured, stroking his face. "Not now, not ever. Do you hear me?"

"I'm going to wash my hands," Dr. Miller said, going to the sink. She scrubbed her hands under hot water, dried them on clean paper towels, and then bent down.

"Don't try anything." Shannon took the gun from her waistband and followed. She didn't lower the pistol or let her guard down.

"Calm down," Dr. Miller said, lifting her hands. "I'm just getting the first aid kit. It's under the sink."

Shannon stepped around the table, keeping the handgun trained on Dr. Miller's back as she reached into the cupboard. Cleaning supplies waited there as well.

Bleach that could be hurled in the eyes, and solvents that ate away at the skin. She mustn't underestimate this woman.

Dr. Miller retrieved the kit from among the many bottles and carried it back to the kitchen table. She opened the plastic container and donned a pair of latex gloves.

Shannon stepped closer to take a look at the kit's contents.

As large as a fisherman's tackle box, the first aid kit didn't just contain gauze and disinfectant wipes, but a vast array of vials, syringes, wound dressings, and pill bottles. The bottommost shelf held three plastic sacks filled with what Shannon assumed was saline solution.

"I like to be prepared," Dr. Miller said, catching her gaze.

"For the apocalypse?"

"This is a good neighborhood, but we're more isolated than I would like, and sometimes there are delays. In an emergency, five minutes can mean the difference between life and death for a patient. I don't take chances."

Miller unzipped Tyler's jacket and pulled it off, then rolled him onto his side. From the kit, she took a pair of scissors and cut open his shirt. The damp fabric fell away in sections. Underneath, blood gathered in the hard lines of his abdominal muscles and darkened the makeshift bandages.

As Shannon stepped closer, the sight of his bare back made her head swim. A choked moan escaped her lips, and the hardwood floor turned mushy beneath her feet. The weight of the gun in her hand was the only thing anchoring her to reality.

Blood oozed from a hole several inches below his left shoulder blade.

He had been shot twice.

As she stared at the two bullet holes that devastated Tyler's back, her ears rang with a shrill hazard sound. She took a step back and barely felt the floor beneath her.

"I didn't notice," she mumbled, feeling at the edge of a faint. "Didn't see it."

How was he even still alive?

"We need to put pressure on this," Miller said brusquely. "Put some gloves on. I need your help."

As Shannon returned her gun to her waistband and retrieved a pair of gloves from the box, Miller placed a sterile gauze pad over the entry hole.

"Just hold it in place," Dr. Miller said and removed an assortment of supplies from the box. Wrapped needles, tubes, a rubber strap, and one of the fluid-filled sacks. She laid everything out on a paper she'd taken from a plastic-wrapped package. She worked quickly and methodically, as if she had performed emergency surgeries a hundred times before. Once she had established an IV line, she hung the bag of saline solution from the latticework chandelier.

Shannon pressed her hands against the wound. Even through the thin latex of her gloves, she felt the hot, pulsing warmth of the escaping blood. The gauze soon turned spongy beneath her fingers. She couldn't maintain her calm as easily as Dr. Miller, and each time blood throbbed against her palm, the floor seemed to tilt beneath her. Whimpering breaths pushed through her teeth. She clenched her jaws so tightly, they ached.

"You're doing well," Dr. Miller said, unwrapping a large syringe with a blunt tip. "Now, I'm going to irrigate the hole in his shoulder."

"What's that?" she asked as the doctor drew liquid from a tinted bottle.

"Just saline. If you don't trust me, you're welcome to read the label on the bottle."

Shannon shook her head, deciding that the last thing Dr. Miller would do was keep poison mixed in with her medicine. Her paranoia was getting ahead of her. Fear had been a useful motivator before, but now it would only get in her way.

Calm down, she thought. *Just calm down.*

She couldn't lose hope. The moment she told herself that there was no way to save him, he would perish. She just knew he would.

"Will he be all right?" she asked as Dr. Miller cleaned the wound.

He couldn't die. Not now. After everything that had happened, after he had struggled to stay alive for so long, he just couldn't die. She wouldn't let him.

"Don't talk. If I'm going to do this, I need my full concentration."

Shannon maintained pressure. She wanted nothing more than to hold Tyler's hand and whisper soft reassurances to him, but he wouldn't hear them, and she would only get in the way. This was her part. She must be strong. For the both of them.

"Do you know what blood type he is?" Miller asked.

"No, but I'm O negative," Shannon said. In January, she had taken part in a blood drive at her school. The woman who had drawn her blood congratulated her for having nice veins and told her that O negative blood was in high demand because it could be used by people with other blood types.

"Are you sure?" Dr. Miller asked.

"Positive."

"Good. Once I get this taken care of, I'll get you set

up. He's lost a lot of blood, and it's important that we act quickly."

After the wound was cleaned and the congealing blood wiped from his skin, Dr. Miller examined the entry and exit holes.

"The bullet passed through cleanly. Just a few more centimeters, and it would have hit his brachial artery. He would have bled out in minutes. We're dealing mainly with soft tissue damage here. Now, his other wound is going to be a bit trickier. The bullet's still inside of him." She glanced over her shoulder. "Have you ever assisted in surgery?"

Shannon shook her head.

Dr. Miller smiled wryly. "Well, there's a first for everything."

CASE NOTES 11:

HADES

Instead of heading north toward Canada, as he had told the senator that he would do, Hades traveled west along Interstate 68. As he drove, his thoughts returned repeatedly to the papers he had taken from Hawthorne's study. He had only scanned through them briefly. There weren't just interview transcripts, but entire books worth of gene sequences. And some of the pages had referenced something called "Project Prometheus."

Although Project Pandora had been a eugenics experiment, as far as he was aware, its purpose had never involved genetically altering embryos, as the documents seemed to suggest. He had heard the name Prometheus before, mentioned during poker games and meetings at the Georgetown safehouse. However, he had always assumed it was a codename for another subject or a Project overseer and had never given it much thought.

The fact that there might be another Project didn't surprise him, but it disturbed him. It suggested that there were even deeper layers to the organization as a whole. Things still waiting to be discovered.

Within time, he arrived in Morgantown, West Virginia.

It had been only a month since he had last visited the city. Although he suffered from an unreliable memory, eroded from electroconvulsive therapy and long sessions of sensory deprivation, he was able to find his way easily enough. After gaining his bearings, he stopped in the parking lot of a strip mall.

He locked up the car, though he did not intend to return to it. Before exiting the vehicle, he made sure that he was facing away from the stores, where there might be cameras directed at the parking lot. He kept his head bowed as he crossed onto the sidewalk, his backpack slung over his shoulder.

As he walked down the street, he fought against the throbbing pain that radiated from his stomach. He had stolen painkillers from the senator's medicine cabinet, but he decided not to take them yet. He already felt slightly confused and under the weather, as if recovering from a high fever. The last thing he needed was a clouded head.

He walked until he arrived at a bus stop and sat down next to an old woman with a bagful of groceries. She glanced at him, looked back ahead, and then did a double-take.

"Are you feeling okay?" she asked. She wore a string of gaudy fake pearls around her reedy throat, and crusty clots of makeup clung to her wrinkled face.

"I'm fine, ma'am. Just recovering from the flu." His throat was still raw, and it hurt to speak. "Can you tell me which bus I need to take to get to Memorial Drive, please?"

She blinked, narrowing her eyes at his designer clothes. "What business do you have over there?"

"I'm going to see a friend."

She pointed down the street, to a bus trundling toward them. "That's the one you'll want to take."

"Thank you," Hades said, standing. Even the slight motion aggravated his stomach wound, and he pressed a hand over it, gently. He slid his other hand into his pocket, searching for the grimy dimes and quarters he had taken from the car's cup holder.

In the corner of his eye, he watched the old woman rise as well. Could the strange look she gave him have anything to do with the news reports that were surely circulating about his disappearance? His most distinguishable features—his scars, tattoos, and bright-blue eyes—were hidden, but he still had a memorable face. What if she recognized him?

The thought made him uneasy, and his apprehension only intensified as she stepped into the bus behind him. Before he even paid for a day fare, he glanced around at the other occupants, searching for a threat. As soon as the driver handed him his ticket, he found a seat in the middle of the bus, where he would have a clear view of everyone coming and going.

The old woman sat across from him. Why was she sitting so close to him? Why couldn't she move to the back of the bus and just leave him alone?

Hades reached to his waist and rested his hand upon the bulge formed by the concealed revolver. It made him feel a little better to be armed. He liked knowing that he had the means to defend himself, even though his fists would suffice plenty in most combat situations.

He turned his attention to the front of the bus, where a mirror provided him with a hazy view of himself. His hair had dried in a tangled jungle, his lips were chapped and pale, and even the sunglasses couldn't conceal the unhealthy bruises under his eyes. No wonder the old woman had asked him if he was okay.

With a sigh, he leaned against the plastic seat, thinking about the Rottweilers that had guarded the Georgetown safe house. He had trained the dogs from puppies, fed and cared for them. Four of them had perished trying to protect him from Charles Warren's guards, but what had happened to the other two? Had the police shot them or did they manage to escape through the open gate?

Now I have no one, he thought as the bus lurched forward. *I am alone.*

Knowing that he had nowhere to return to bothered him far more than it should have. He had spent the last two years more or less in solitude and servitude, so why should this be any worse? So what if he had no one to turn to? At least he wasn't a trained dog kept on Dimitri's leash anymore.

A trained dog. He scoffed at the comparison, thinking back to all the times Dimitri had called him a dog. Something that was once wild, only to be broken down and domesticated.

But dogs had teeth, and soon Charles Warren and Francine Miller would learn his bite. He would destroy the Project, even if it meant his own death.

"You were my light," he murmured, remembering the four words that Nine had whispered after she had taken the bullet meant for him, as her life faded fast. He still wasn't sure if she had said "light" or "life." He wished he knew.

Either way, one thing was for certain: what had once been light in him had been eclipsed. The boy he once was, A-02, had died and rotted in the darkness of the sensory deprivation tank.

He would never be the same.

As he shifted in his seat, a piercing pain twisted in his gut like a cruel knife. He clenched his teeth and lowered his hand to the wound. Through his jacket, he felt the thick pad of bandages and the drainage jar.

It's happening to someone else, Hades thought, and the throbbing agony in his stomach faded into a low, steady burning. *This is all happening to someone else.*

It was a mantra he used when the bad things happened. If he repeated it often enough, it became true. The world would wash away, and the darkness would flow in again, darkness like that of the sensory deprivation tank but better, warmer, calming. And then he would cease to care about this worthless carcass he called a body and the things that were being done to it because *it was not him.*

The old woman disembarked at the next stop. He took his hand off the concealed revolver and looked down at his palms. Scar tissue darkened the skin below his first knuckles, left from lifting barbells for hours at a time.

The safe house's extensive home gym would be just another thing that he'd never see again, but that was all right. He had already honed his body into a weapon. Now, he would have a chance to put it to good use against the men and women who had once wielded it.

Excitement swelled inside of him at the thought. In the past, he had gotten the most pleasure out of killing people formerly affiliated with the Project, but this time he wouldn't be acting upon Dimitri's orders. He could do whatever he wanted to his targets. No need to stage suicides or lethal accidents.

They would suffer just as he had suffered.

Three stops later, Hades disembarked the bus and stepped onto a sidewalk spider-webbed with cracks. He surveyed the street, taking in boarded-up windows and crumbling brick edifices. The old woman had been right about one thing. This wasn't the kind of neighborhood to be wearing nice clothes in.

Nonetheless, he felt comfortable in the urban decay. High society would never interest him; he had gotten enough of that as Dimitri's lapdog, living in splendor but entirely apart from it. At least here there was a glimpse of what the world would eventually become—dilapidation and beautiful ruin.

He hoped that it would happen one day soon.

Walking down the street, he kept alert and aware of his surroundings at all times. His gaze shifted back and forth across the street, searching for any sign of a potential threat.

Half a mile down the road, he arrived at a familiar sprawl of decaying, one-story bungalows. Wedged between two other homes of similar design, Randy's house looked dim and of little interest. Security grates covered the windows, providing a narrow view of spotted curtains.

He walked up to the front step and rang the doorbell. Fifteen seconds later, the sound of clattering locks notified him to a presence on the other side. He took off his sunglasses and tucked them into his jacket pocket.

Randy opened the door. He was a skinny man with a scruffy beard and a T-shirt speckled with orange dust. He widened his eyes at the sight of him.

"What are you doing here? You're all over the news!"

"I know," Hades said drily. "I've come to collect what I ordered."

Randy sighed, gave a furtive glance around the street, then ushered him inside. The inside of the house looked like a mix between a man-cave and a hoarder's den, overflowing with boxes of junk and aging appliances.

"There's a problem," Randy said, after locking the door again. "This is too hot for me."

"I've already given you the deposit." Three weeks ago, Dimitri had ordered new IDs for him, including a forged passport and birth certificate. Apparently, one of the Project's dissidents was believed to have fled to Canada, and Dimitri had wanted Hades to be ready to cross the border as soon as the man was located. Neither of them had expected it to end like this.

"I need more. Now that I know you're a fugitive, I'm putting my life on the line here, doing this."

"How much more?"

Randy's eyes flickered nervously across the room as he nibbled on his fingernails like a rodent. "Five, no, six hundred more. So, eleven hundred total."

"Fine," Hades said, feeling a stir of irritation. "Can I see the documents?"

"Do you have enough money with you?"

"Yes." Hades slid his backpack off his shoulders, set it on a side table, and opened it. Making sure that Randy couldn't see how much money the bag actually contained, he peeled off four one hundred-dollar bills from one of the stacks and passed them over. "You'll get the rest once you give me the IDs."

"Okay, follow me," Randy said and, after taking the cash, retreated deeper into the house. Hades zipped up the backpack, slung it over his shoulder, and followed.

Most of the house was in disarray, but other portions had been preserved like a shrine to the departed. A handmade quilt lay folded over the living room's sofa, and a blond woman smiled from photographs on the wall. Until today, Hades hadn't paid much attention to the decor, but now he found his gaze drawn to the woman in the portraits.

He wondered if the woman was Randy's mother. It seemed wrong that this gross slob should have a family, when Hades didn't.

Randy took him down to the basement. The wooden walls bulged with pink pads of insulation fluff. A damp, skunky musk hung in the air.

The hairs prickled on his neck. The odor of weed aggravated him almost as much as the photographs had. For a second time that day, he had the disturbing notion that his perceptions had changed somehow in the time he was asleep. Little details stood out to him, like the posters on the walls, the faint buzz of machines, and the clammy atmosphere. He picked up on things he would normally mute out and sensed they were important somehow.

Forging machinery crowded the small room at the bottom of the stairs. A desk, TV stand, and saggy chair were the only articles of furniture in the space.

Randy put the cash in a drawer, then rifled through his desk. From another drawer, he took a manila envelope like so many others. He opened the envelope and leafed through its contents before setting it on the desktop. "It's all in there."

Hades picked up the envelope and removed the bundle of papers. The passport, state ID, Maine driver's and motorcycle licenses, and birth certificate were all made out to a certain Connor Stone, aged 21.

He placed the envelope in his backpack, after removing the driver's license and sticking it into his jacket pocket.

"So, what exactly are the news articles saying?" Hades asked, zipping up his pack.

"Just for anyone to call if they've seen you or have any information."

"What I want to know is if I'm a suspect."

"All they're saying is that you're wanted in connection with some shooting that happened."

"I see."

Randy reached down to close the desk drawer. The moment his back was turned, Hades lunged forward and wrapped his arm around the man's throat. With one hand, he pressed down on the external carotid artery. With the other, he held Randy steady.

"This isn't personal," he said, applying more pressure to cut off the blood flow. Thin, feeble fingers grasped at his sleeve, then slid off. Within seconds, the man slumped against him. He wrinkled his nose at the pungent musk of sweat and bubblegum that clung to Randy's clothes and lowered him onto the concrete.

Randy wouldn't stay out for long. Acting quickly, Hades unzipped his backpack and removed the first aid kit he had taken from Senator Hawthorne's home. He pulled on a pair of latex gloves and found the bottle of morphine and syringe from among a mess of other medical supplies. He had taken the drug, suspecting his pain might become unbearable at some point, but now it would serve a different purpose altogether.

Kneeling at Randy's side, he inserted the hypodermic needle into the bottle's rubber stopper and drew out enough morphine to reach the topmost line on the syringe. Through other kills, he had familiarized himself with the lethal dosages of common street drugs. Even a hardcore addict wouldn't be able to handle such a large amount.

Hades had watched Randy carefully while he had rutted through the desk drawers and determined that the man was left-handed. Hades was used to receiving injections and giving them, so he had no difficulty finding the vein in Randy's right arm, even without the use of a tourniquet.

Once he inserted the needle beneath the skin, he

aspirated the syringe. Blood oozed into the chamber, confirming he had struck a vein. He pressed down the syringe's plunger. Watching the liquid flow from the plastic chamber, he felt no regret or doubt, not when he had performed assassinations over a dozen times before. If anything, he felt almost righteous.

Randy might not have been personally involved in Project Pandora, but by providing forged documents, he had unknowingly aided the program and become a part of it.

This was not murder. This was collateral damage.

After administering the full dose, Hades pulled out the needle and carefully wrapped Randy's limp fingers around the syringe. Then he stood and set the syringe on the desk, before dragging Randy into the rolling chair.

Searching through the drawers, he came across blank ID cards and birth certificate templates amid fossilized Cheetos and gum wrappers. Another drawer contained a false bottom, partially open, with a mess of loose cash overflowing from the opening. He took only the cash he had given Randy and left the rest behind, wary that the forger's bookkeeping might be tidier than his office.

Turning his attention to the fourth drawer, he sifted through a pile of magazines and touched smooth glass. He set aside the magazines to find a bottle of vodka and a couple small baggies of pills. Just from looking at the capsules, he couldn't tell what they were. Not that it really mattered.

Randy stirred in the chair, groaning softly.

"Can you hear me?" Hades asked, taking the pills.

No response.

He grasped Randy's chin. After a moment, the man turned his head away, moaning.

"You need to take these," Hades said, lifting a handful of pills to the Randy's mouth. With some coaxing, he managed to get the man to swallow.

Hades set the bag of pills on the desktop and dropped a few on the carpet. He returned the morphine to his backpack, concerned that a serial number on the injection bottle might link together seemingly unrelated crimes and make the authorities question whether Randy's death had been an overdose or a homicide. Let them wonder where the morphine had gone. He figured that if the cops did eventually decide that Randy was murdered, they would look to his most recent clients, not a backlisted order. That is, if Randy even had a safeguard in place to notify the police in the event of his untimely death.

He waited for a couple of minutes, testing Randy's pulse. A quick glance around the ductwork and insulator pads reassured him that there were no hidden cameras. On his way out, he wiped down all the doors he had touched.

As he arrived at the bus stop, he experienced the disconcerting sense of being watched and turned to find a pair of skinheads staring at him from down the street. As they approached, he coolly observed them.

Their swaggering walks hinted toward arrogance, but not tactical training. Judging by the bulge underneath one man's acid-washed denim jacket, he was likely armed. Maybe a knife. More likely, a gun.

Even as they stopped in front of him, Hades maintained his calm, confident demeanor. He refused to be intimidated by a couple of lowlife scum.

"You lost or something, man?" the guy in the denim jacket asked, eying him up and down.

"No, I know exactly where I am," he said, meeting the man's pale eyes. They reminded him of Dimitri's eyes—as flat and gray as concrete discs. It would be easy to pretend that this man was someone else. By hurting him, he could pretend that he was hurting Dimitri, too.

As if sensing his train of thought, Denim Jacket's cocky smile faded. He exchanged a look with his friend.

"I know exactly where I am," Hades repeated softly, and perhaps there was a certain quality in his voice or expression, because Denim Jacket nodded and took a step away.

"Whatever you say, man," the other guy said. The two set off again, presumably in search of easier prey.

Watching the men go, it occurred to him that just days ago, he might have seen the men's unease as proof of his evolution. But he knew better now. He was not exceeding humanity at the top of the apex. He *was* human, capable of being shot down and broken, and helpless to save the only person he had ever loved.

For the first time since he had conceived the theory, he realized that his evolution had been a way to distance himself from his current self. Two years ago, he had ceased to be Subject Two of Subset A and has become Hades, but that hadn't been good enough.

He looked down at his scarred palms and the swollen bruises that cuffed his wrists. In a way, it came as a crushing disappointment to realize that he was the same person today as he was yesterday, and tomorrow he would still be stuck with himself. He would never be able to escape from this body that others found beautiful but that he detested for its weakness and mortality. He would never become someone else, no matter how many times he tried convincing himself.

I am not evolving, he thought, curling his fingers into fists. *I just am.*

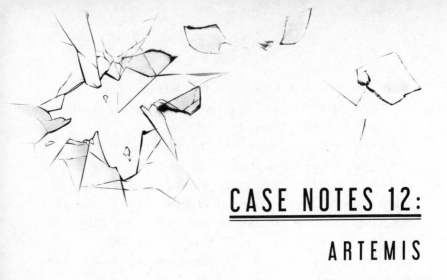

CASE NOTES 12:

ARTEMIS

As Dr. Miller disinfected the kitchen table and cleaned the spilled blood from the floor, Shannon sat at the wet bar, watching her. She felt lightheaded from the blood draw, but hadn't complained when Dr. Miller had decided to take another quarter of a pint. She avoided looking at the collection bag, afraid that the sight of her own blood would make her even dizzier. To tame her nausea, she sipped the apple juice that the doctor had given her.

"You don't keep all that stuff around just for emergencies, do you?" Shannon asked. She highly doubted that an ambulance would be delayed long enough to allow Dr. Miller to draw blood and perform a transfusion. It had taken her almost ten minutes to draw the first pint alone, not to mention the additional time spent transfusing it.

"Caroline and I share the same blood type. If she were to get hurt, I'd want to be prepared to help her."

"But I thought you were worried about ambulances running late." Shannon closed her eyes and groaned aloud. The first pint had been bad enough, but she felt more nauseous by the moment.

"I am, but I'm also concerned with them not being

available at all," Miller said. "Such as what would occur with a natural disaster or a total collapse in societal infrastructure."

"I thought you guys were going to rule the world," she said drily.

"I have a tendency to prepare for the worst."

She felt a strong bitterness toward the woman. To Dr. Miller, "the worst" was a distant future, a threat that would never happen in this life. But for her, "the worst" was happening right this very moment, and there was nothing she could do to change it. She didn't have an arsenal of medical equipment, let alone a roof above her head. All she had was a loaded gun on the counter beside her and the boy she loved lying unconscious in the other room. To put it lightly, the shit had already hit the fan.

"You can put your gun away now," Miller said, stuffing soiled paper towels into a garbage bag. "To tell you the truth, I'm glad you two showed up."

"Yeah, right."

"No, I mean it. I think…I've done a lot of things in my life that I regret, and none more than getting myself involved in Project Pandora. For years now, I've wanted to escape from the organization, but I haven't been able to. This is a way to make atonement."

"Do you think he'll be all right?"

Dr. Miller paused in her bloody task. "There's no guarantee. He'd stand a much better chance at an actual hospital, with staff equipped to deal with severe trauma."

"That would be like a death sentence," Shannon said. The police would have found the stolen SUV by now, complete with blood and DNA evidence. They would be checking every hospital in Colorado for an anonymous boy suffering from a gunshot wound. Even using the stolen van was too dangerous.

"I'm going to be frank with you. He might not wake up." A strange look passed over Dr. Miller's face, and her eyes clouded with thought. "I did my best, but the second bullet did a lot of damage."

Shannon's stomach clenched. She had figured as much, but it was another thing to get confirmation from an actual doctor.

"He'll live," Shannon said.

After everything was cleaned up, Dr. Miller washed her hands and returned to the counter. She disconnected the blood sack from the tube and removed the needle from Shannon's arm.

"Just sit tight," Miller said. "Don't get up yet. I'll be right back. I'm going to check on him."

"No. I'm coming, too." Shannon forced herself to climb to her feet. Her head swam with nausea, and her legs felt liquefied, but she found the strength inside her to follow Dr. Miller into the living room.

"How's he doing?" she asked as Dr. Miller replaced the depleted IV sack with the new one.

"The same, which isn't a bad thing." Dr. Miller turned to her. "I need to wash up and check on Caroline. You look like you could use some new clothes, too. The pants will be a little long on you, but you should be able to fit into mine."

"I'm sorry, but I'm not letting you out of my sight. And I need you to give me your cell phone."

"Is that really necessary? All right, fine. It's in my bedroom. Follow me."

Together, they went upstairs. Miller paused halfway down the hall to knock on Caroline's door and remind the girl to stay in her room.

"I love that girl, Shannon," Dr. Miller said as they stepped into the master bedroom. "I really do. After I had her, my whole worldview changed. It was like a revelation."

To avoid focusing on the possibility of Tyler's death, Shannon refined her worry into anger. "Oh, I get it. So you had to have your own child before you realized you shouldn't ruin the lives of other kids?"

The doctor winced. "It's not like that."

"It's exactly like that. Did you think that by telling me this, I would trust you? Just because you have a daughter doesn't mean you're suddenly a new woman. You're a part of this!"

"I know." Doctor Miller took her cell phone from the dresser top and handed it over. "I've done things that are unforgivable. I am aware of that, and I know that I can never take them back."

Shannon stuck the phone in her pocket. "You ruined lives."

"We can discuss this further after we wash up," Dr. Miller said. As she retrieved a set of clean clothes from the dresser, Shannon watched her carefully, afraid she would extract a gun from the rows of neatly-folded garments.

Even when her fear proved false, Shannon still couldn't help but feel on edge and anxious. Every instinct cried out at her to do something other than just stand there.

"If Caroline comes in here, please don't go waving that thing around in front of her," Dr. Miller added, going to the walk-in shower. "I'd like to think that I've gained at the very least a modicum of your trust."

As Dr. Miller showered, Shannon cleaned her face and hands in the sink. She found traces of Tyler's blood engrained under her nails and drying on her arms, and she scrubbed at it until her skin was raw and red.

After changing into Miller's spare clothes, Shannon began to feel a little better. Her hands had stopped shaking. Even so, she kept her gun close by as she followed Miller into the hall again. She put the weapon behind her back when Miller opened the door to Caroline's room to check on the little girl.

Caroline had a room fit for a princess, with a lacy canopy bed and a whole menagerie of stuffed animals. Cartoon animals raced across the TV on the dresser.

As Shannon looked around the room, jealousy gnawed away at her. She couldn't remember much about her past. Dr. Kosta had made certain of that. However, she recalled enough that she was sure her childhood bedroom—shared with a dozen other girls—had not featured any teddy bears or frills.

"This is Shannon," Dr. Miller said. "She and her friend will be staying with us for a while."

"Hi!" Caroline said, without looking away from the television screen. She sat cross-legged on the floor, surrounded by a scattering of dolls and Legos.

Shannon muttered a greeting, then stepped back into the hall. As they walked downstairs again, she paused in the living room to check on Tyler. His complexion was white and waxy against the cranberry-red blanket she'd wrapped him in. Even with the blood transfusion, he hadn't regained much color. He looked like a corpse prepared for embalmment.

"Hovering over him won't help," Dr. Miller said, ushering her back into the kitchen. "You've done enough, and you can't do anything else for him now."

"I hate just standing around. I feel so helpless."

"You don't have a choice." Miller went to the cupboard and took a lighter and an unopened pack of cigarettes down from the top shelf. From a lower shelf, she retrieved a bag of cookies, which she handed to Shannon. "Eat, and leave the rest to me."

She sat down, rested her pistol on the counter beside her, and opened the bag. After the first few cookies, the taste of chocolate became cloying like gore.

"Do you mind?" Miller asked, tearing off the cellophane wrapper of the cigarette pack.

"No."

Dr. Miller propped a cigarette between her lips. She lit it and took a drag, closing her eyes like there was nothing better in the world. "Now, how did you find me?"

Shannon decided not to tell her about Dr. Belmont. It wouldn't help Tyler if Miller suspected that they had any involvement in Belmont's death. However, since the woman knew who she was, it was likely she also knew about what had happened to Dr. Kosta.

"Dr. Kosta had a file on you.

"That rat bastard."

"Since you were a doctor—"

"Are a doctor," Miller corrected her, going to the window.

"—I thought that you could help Tyler."

"So you didn't come to Colorado specifically to find me?"

"No," Shannon said.

"You're here to find the organization?"

"Yes."

"Why?"

"Tyler wants to expose it, but I'm still trying to figure out what I want."

"If I were you, I would run as far away from here as you could possibly go," Dr. Miller said, regarding the dull glow of her cigarette. She tapped the tip against the rim of the terracotta planter on the windowsill, losing ashes. "You can put the past behind you. Make a new name for yourself."

"It's too late for that," Shannon said. "We're already being hunted."

This was one thing she couldn't run from. They had already passed the point of no return. It was a straight road from here, no exits, just a long way down.

The cigarette was almost all filter now. Miller took another drag before using the cigarette's smoldering tip to light a new one. "Now, here's the really important question. Does anyone know that you two are here? Did you mention me to anyone in passing, or visit any of the clinics where I used to work?"

"No."

"You just found me in his files."

"That's right. Your name and address were in there."

"Lovely. Just lovely. Damn Dimitri. I hope that pig rots in hell."

"It's not our fault!"

"I'm not saying it is. But soon enough I'll have Charles Warren breathing down my neck, wondering if you two might've made contact."

"Who's Charles Warren?"

"The operator of the entire Project, and a man whose bad side I don't want to get on. You need to understand, you two can't stay here. I'll let you stay for the next few days, just until Tyler's condition stabilizes, but then you're gone."

"You say it like this has nothing to do with you. We're only in this mess because of people like you!"

"After Caroline's birth, I cut ties with the Project," Dr.

Miller said. "I'm not a part of it anymore."

"But you were."

"That's irrelevant. I can't do anything else for you. I've already helped you in every way that I can, and I promise that no one will ever know you two came here. What more do you want from me?"

Shannon glared down at the floor.

"I realize now that what I did was wrong, and I wish I could take it back. I really do. I wish that I had never met Charles Warren and never became a part of this, but I did. Now, I must live the rest of my life with the consequences of my actions."

Consequences? Compared to what she and Tyler were dealing with, Dr. Miller's suffering was a drop in a bucket. Miller had years to make amends for her mistakes, but they had days, if that. How could the doctor twist this conversation around and make it about herself?

A facial tic must have betrayed her, because Dr. Miller said, "You must find me detestable."

"I don't," Shannon said, then countered her lie with a truth. "I pity you."

Miller chuckled. "Pity, huh?"

"If I were you, I wouldn't be able to live with myself."

"We all have to live with ourselves." Smoke wafted from her lips as she sighed. "There's only one other alternative."

CASE NOTES 13:

APOLLO

Lost in a haze of sleep, Tyler entered the white ward.

The floor and walls were fitted with glossy white tile. A steel sink sat in one corner, while a computer on a desk occupied the other. File cabinets and metal racks lined the space. The shelves contained jars filled with yellowish liquid the color of diluted urine.

Strange contents floated in the formaldehyde. Once, the specimens were living flesh, but their time in storage had loosened the tissue into bizarre, organic drifts like pale algae or lake scum. Eyes. Organs. Coils of intestines. A tiny, deformed fetus that seemed more larva than human.

Go away, a voice whispered in his head. *Just go back to bed. You don't belong here again.*

The tile was cold and slippery beneath his bare feet. The room reeked of chemicals, as if it had been cleaned recently. A frigid draft blew in from the vents. He rubbed his arms and ran his fingers over the goose bumps stippling his shoulders.

At the back of the room, there was a steel door with a small window. The door was closed, but grinding noises filtered through. Quiet voices.

"I am now removing the calvarium…"

Dragged by reckless curiosity, he pressed his face against the window, trying to see through the thin wire embedded under the glass.

There were two people in the room, their features obscured by the paper masks covering their mouths and noses. Even so, from their voices alone, Tyler recognized them as Dr. Finch and Dr. Belmont.

The two men faced a raised metal platform that was partially concealed by a plastic curtain mounted on a wheeled frame. Dr. Belmont's body blocked Tyler's view of the sheet-shrouded form on the surgical table, but not completely.

Tyler's mouth went dry. That tented shape. Were those limbs under there? Was that a slim, white hand cradled in the tubes and wires, strapped to an arm-board?

"No tumors or lesions on the meninges."

Dr. Belmont shifted, just enough that Tyler was able to make out the object of the doctors' interest. A girl.

Not just any girl.

No. God, please, no.

Bile rose in the back of Tyler's throat, bringing with it a low moan that he barely recognized as his own. Nausea was a slimy, writhing snake, squeezing his stomach in a python's stranglehold. His hands flew over his mouth as he fought down the burning flood of vomit that pressed against the roof of his mouth.

Tyler backed away from the window. It felt like his esophagus had been knotted shut at both ends, sealed as tightly as a sausage casing, trapping the foul bile inside.

Along with the nausea came a graying of the senses, blurring the edges of Tyler's vision.

As he retreated to the desk, a shrill siren pierced his

ears and the safety lamp on the wall flashed red. The door to the operating room began to open, and Tyler barely had enough time to duck into the desk's footwell before Dr. Finch and Dr. Belmont walked into view.

"It's probably another false alarm," Dr. Belmont said, stripping off his bloodstained latex gloves. "Let's continue the vivisection."

"It's protocol, Richard," Dr. Finch replied. "It will only be a few minutes. She will keep until we come back."

Tyler waited until they entered the corridor before crawling out from under the desk. Heart pounding, he approached the door to the operating room.

The knob was smeared with fresh blood. Tyler didn't want to touch it, but he had no choice. He couldn't leave without first confirming that what he had seen through the window was real. If he didn't look, he would never forgive himself.

The door released with a soft groan, and Tyler stepped inside the room. The air was thick and cold, flavored with the odors of antiseptic, blood, and the contents of the bowels. Life-sustaining machines beeped, fluorescent lights hummed. Blood pulsed noisily through his ears.

As Tyler walked up to the surgical table, he barely felt his own legs beneath him. His entire body trembled uncontrollably at the sight of the bloody, motionless girl stretched out on the black vinyl cushions. IV tubes and electrode wires snaked around her, and an oxygen tube retreated down her throat.

Her stomach. Her stomach open and exposed. Don't look! Her head. Her head. No. Her brain. Her brain. Oh, God. Her brain. Her brain. Her brain, and she was still breathing!

Tyler woke screaming. The entire world was a blur,

whirling around him. As he tried to sit up, he lost his balance and tilted forward. Hands grabbed him, held him. No, they were going to cut him open!

"Dr. Finch," he gasped. "Dr. Finch. Don't hurt me. Dr. Finch, please. Don't. Dr. Belmont. Don't do this."

"Tyler, it's me," a familiar voice said. "Tyler, calm down. I've got you. You're okay."

His vision cleared, and he found himself staring into the face of a different girl than the one from his dream. Velvety brown eyes instead of gray. No gore.

Shuddering uncontrollably, he collapsed against Shannon.

"I'm scared," he choked. "I'm scared. I'm scared."

"You're safe, Tyler," Shannon said, easing her arms around him. "There's nothing to be afraid of."

"I'm scared."

"It's okay," she said. "I'm here with you."

"I'm so scared."

"You were having a nightmare."

"I did it. I ended it."

"Shh, don't speak."

"I picked up the scalpel." They didn't feel like his own words, but he couldn't stop himself from saying them.

"Just a dream," she said, stroking his hair.

"My best friend. I killed her."

CASE NOTES 14:

HADES

Hades's next stop was a used car dealership that he had frequented many times before. It took him twenty minutes longer to reach the business than it would have if he had the use of a car, but he didn't want to continue using the senator's vehicle. He didn't trust the senator to keep to his word, and besides, he despised confined spaces.

Sitting in cars for long periods of time reminded him of being in the sensory deprivation tank. Sometimes, it also brought to mind another car ride long ago, when he had left the Academy in a sedated daze, feverish and with his back in agony.

Hades hated thinking about that time of his life. He felt like so much time had passed since then, but at the same time, it was like everything had grinded to a halt the moment he had left the Academy's gates. Two years had been swallowed by the void. Call it life or call it Hell, it was all just the same.

Rows of cars lined the lot. Another section of the dealership was devoted to motorcycles.

He stepped inside the building at the far corner of the lot and approached the counter, where a man sat reading a magazine.

"I need to speak to Sebastian," Hades said.

"No one here by that name," the man said, narrowing his eyes.

"Tell him that Hades is here."

"The hell kind of name is that?"

"It isn't one." He sat down on one of the plastic chairs and rested his backpack at his feet, gazing disinterestedly at the various products displayed on metal shelves. Air freshener ornaments and motorcycle helmets. Chamois cloths, key chains, tail cases, and leather storage compartments. In the corner of his eye, he saw the man pick up the phone and mumble furtively into it.

Three minutes later, the door opened and a tall man squeezed through the doorway. He was as solidly built as a brick wall, with bristly gray hair. A quick dip of the chin was the only confirmation.

Hades picked up his backpack and rose to his feet. He followed Sebastian into the other room.

"Here on business again?" Sebastian asked.

"Yes. What do you have in stock?"

"Depends. What are you looking for?"

"Ideally, a bike," Hades said. He had acquired his previous motorcycle from the dealership. Not only was it cheaper than buying a car, but he also preferred the open atmosphere that a bike provided him. Besides, if he was forced to engage in a chase, a motorcycle would allow for greater maneuverability in urban settings.

"Price range?"

"Ten thousand or less. I need something functional, in excellent condition. Fast."

"Mmm, I think you might be in luck."

An hour later, with his backpack eight-thousand dollars

lighter and his dark hair hidden underneath a module helmet, Hades drove back onto the interstate.

Unlike with Randy, he wasn't concerned about Sebastian ratting on him. Acting on Dimitri's orders, he had done business with Sebastian before and knew that the man was reliable. Most of the vehicles the man sold were legitimate, while others, like the motorcycle Hades now rode, had been acquired and altered through less than ethical means.

Even so, the license plate and VIN numbers wouldn't attract attention. The motorcycle itself, while outdated, wasn't too flashy or dingy to draw notice. Not like it really mattered. If he was pulled over, he figured that he wouldn't remain under the radar long enough for a cop to run the plates.

Hours passed as he lost himself in the monotonous rhythm of the road. Long sessions in the sensory deprivation tank had taught him how to detach himself from time and circumstance—and indeed, even from his own body—and focus on single-minded tasks of concentration. He lapsed into a depersonalized state, stepping away from the groan of stiff muscles and the hot throbbing in his gut.

Reality turned into a blurred fever dream, and the places he passed through became nothing more than smoky figments of his own imagination. Small towns fell away behind him, sinking from existence the moment he lost sight of them past the horizon. As for the gas station clerks and drive-through employees who greeted him and the motorists on the road behind him, they ceased to be people at all. They were ghosts playing flesh.

Neon lights, the darkening sky. Rumbling thunder and

the tang of ozone. Sowed fields, forests, the splintered moon rising.

His periods of dissociation were always accompanied by a sense of profound, overwhelming isolation, and this time was no exception. As Hades trekked across the Midwest, he felt as if he were a restless spirit wandering the world of the living. The thought should have soothed him, but instead it left him discontented. Anger ate away at him like acid.

This is happening to someone else, he told himself over and over, fading in and out of clarity. He forced his murderous rage deep down, into a place away from himself. *Someone else. Someone else.*

He wanted to be someone else.

Hades drove seventeen hours in the first day. He stopped only for quick meals and toilet breaks, to refill his tank, and for a brief nap in an Indianan culvert along a rural backroad. From a convenience store, he had purchased basic toiletries; in lieu of a shower, he cleaned himself with baby wipes, dry shampoo, and deodorant spray. His wound ached, and constipation left him feeling like he had a bellyful of stones, but a couple hydrocodone pills took the edge off his discomfort and allowed him to fall asleep slumped against the cold cement.

When dreams came to him, he found himself entangled in Subject Nine of Subset A's arms. He was fifteen again, not Hades but Subject Two of Subset A, and Nine was still alive, warm and radiant. They didn't have names or families, but that didn't matter, because they had each other. And then she was gone.

In early morning, he awoke to moldy breath on his face and hands trying to tug his backpack out from beneath him. A pocked moon face loomed down at him past a wiry beard. He shoved the vagrant away and reached for his revolver, but by the time he pulled the gun from its holster, the rat man was already fleeing down the tunnel.

Though he stood, he did not pursue. Even shifting his weight from foot to foot aggravated his stiff muscles. The backpack was still with him, unopened, and considering that he had no wallet and his motorcycle keys were hidden in an inside jacket pocket, there was nothing of value the man could have taken from his pockets besides loose change.

The drifter meant nothing to him. Shooting him in the back would bring him no closer to the Academy.

Spitting out the sour, gritty taste of sleep, Hades sat down again and opened the pack. He curbed his pain with aspirin, saving the opiates he'd stolen from the senator's medicine cabinet for the night hours. To dull his hunger, he ate a couple of protein bars and drank a meal replacement shake that he had purchased at a gas station the day before. The chocolate-flavored beverage tasted even chalkier than the pills and left a sandy residue on his tongue.

Every time a car passed overhead, the structure rumbled. As he massaged his legs and performed simple stretches, he assessed the damages. An area on his neck, which neither his helmet nor jacket collar had protected, was sunburnt. His kneading fingers did little to loosen the knots in his muscle fibers, and his jeans had chafed the hell out of his ass. Even with the aid of the aspirin, his stomach hurt. He would need to redress the wound at the next rest stop.

He wheeled his motorcycle into the intense sunlight. Somewhere else, it rained, but here there was not a cloud in sight, the sun irritatingly bright. He stopped and stared upward, feeling a touch delirious, as if at the edge of a dream. Had the sky always been this blue or had he simply never noticed?

Another thousand miles lay ahead of him, and he wasted no time in returning to the highway. He picked his way through scrub grass and chunks of rusty metal and wheeled the motorcycle up the road's shallow, packed-dirt slope. Passing motorists honked at him, and as the cars sped past, sheets of hot air slammed down on him in their wake. Exhaust fumes stung his nose, and acrid dust coated the inside of his mouth before he had a chance to put his helmet on.

A shiny new convertible roared by. Hades caught a brief glimpse of the young couple inside. Their laughter sliced into him like razor blades, and as he saw their grinning faces, he felt a sudden, toxic loathing for the pair. How the hell could they be so happy? What did they possess that made them smile and laugh like that, and why didn't he have it?

Maybe he would find that out when he met his mother. Maybe once he finally came face-to-face with the woman who had brought him into this poisonous world, he would finally realize what made him so different from everyone else.

He waited for a break in the traffic before accelerating back onto the highway. Once more, he sunk into the dream.

Cold asphalt. Rolling farmland, green meadows, small towns, autumn leaves. Illinois to Iowa. The scents of gasoline, alfalfa, burning fires. A hamburger at a drive-through, gas station coffee, water, protein bars, energy drinks, and wrapped sandwiches. Sore muscles, dirty bandages, filled drainage jar—murky with blood. Welcome to Nebraska. The sun arched overhead like a flipping coin in slow motion, turning bloody as it descended lower, lower.

CASE NOTES 15:

ARTEMIS

Two states away, Shannon watched the sunset without appreciating it. She had spent the night before on a futon mattress in the living room, only to fall into a restless sleep sometime after midnight. She had awoken now and then to find Dr. Miller taking Tyler's vitals or examining his wounds. Once in the night, in an exhaustion-induced haze, she had believed that Miller was preparing him for burial.

A breakthrough had occurred just two hours after the treatment, when Tyler woke briefly, in a state of panic. He had been confused and in pain, and after blabbering about killing someone, had drifted off again in her arms. He woke several more times in the day that followed, and though he was well enough to speak, drink, and eat, he confessed to being too tired to maintain a conversation. All he wanted to do was sleep.

Now, Dr. Miller kept a closer eye on him, hanging over the sofa like a vulture. Her presence made Shannon uneasy, and suggested that even though Tyler had regained consciousness, his condition had somehow worsened. At last, Shannon worked up the confidence to confront the doctor about it.

"Oh, it's not that at all," Dr. Miller said, rising from the armchair. "In fact, it's just the opposite. He's doing extraordinarily well, all things considered. The worst is already past. He has a long recovery ahead, but let's take this day by day."

"I thought you were going to dump us to the curb as soon as you could," Shannon said drily.

"Yesterday, I stayed up all night, thinking about you two," Dr. Miller said. "I can't just abandon you. It wouldn't be right. When I became a doctor, I took an oath to do no harm."

That worked well.

"What about Charles Warren?" Shannon asked.

"I'm hardly the only researcher affiliated with Project Pandora who lives in this state. He hasn't contacted me yet, and even if he does, he has no reason to suspect that you two came here."

Shannon maintained a placid expression, concealing her growing suspicion. Dr. Miller had all day to contact Warren, but she hadn't—or had she? If Miller had spoken to Warren, was it possible that he had told her to keep them there? And if so, why?

No, that was just too far of a stretch. She was overthinking things again. She needed to put a rein on this ridiculous paranoia before it drove her nuts.

"There's something I've been wondering about," Dr. Miller said. "There's some unusual scarring here on his body. Did he mention having any previous surgeries?"

"No."

"Any problems with his kidneys that would require a biopsy?"

"Biopsy?"

"Where a tissue sample is removed to make sure there are no irregularities," she explained.

"No, he's never said anything like that."

"And nothing about needing a skin graft? When a piece of skin is removed for a graft, it leaves a distinctive scar. But normally grafts are taken from other less-noticeable regions, like the thigh. Never the neck."

Shannon blinked. She hadn't even noticed a scar on his neck. "We never discussed stuff like that."

"Shannon," a weak voice said from the sofa, stealing her attention.

Shannon hurried to Tyler's side and dropped to her knees in front of him. She grabbed his hand and was relieved by the warmth and pressure of his grip.

"How are you feeling?" she murmured.

"Could be better," he said, with a faint, distracted smile. "I need to go."

"Where?"

"Pee."

"Oh." She laughed, feeling a surge of relief. "I'll help you."

Dr. Miller cleared her throat. "I think it would be better if I assisted him, Shannon."

"I think I can walk on my own," Tyler said, sitting up with some difficulty.

"No," Dr. Miller said firmly. "Now's not the time to overexert yourself. Besides, I want to check if there's blood in your urine."

As Dr. Miller eased Tyler into the wheelchair, Shannon waited close by, wishing that there was more she could do

"Is there anything I can get you?" Shannon asked him.

"A drink, please."

"Okay," she said, but didn't move as Dr. Miller wheeled

him off. She watched him until he entered the bathroom, then went into the kitchen.

A few scant drops of orange juice remained in the bottom of the bottle. Shannon brought him water instead. She set the glass on the coffee table and picked up the blanket, searching for a bloodstain against the red wool. Nothing.

"Thanks," Tyler said, once he sat down again. He leaned against the sofa cushion as he drank, watching her from over the rim of his glass. He waited until Dr. Miller left the room before speaking. "So, she's the one from the files?"

"Yeah," she said. "Dr. Miller."

"How'd you get her to help?"

"At gunpoint," she admitted.

"You can't trust her," he murmured.

"I don't."

"I'm so tired."

"That's normal, I think," she said. "Are you in any pain?"

"Just a little."

"I think she's getting you some painkillers."

"I know of a better way," Tyler said and set the glass down. He reached for her with his good arm, touching her cheek. She eased to her knees before him, and as he leaned forward, she turned her head up, moving into his kiss.

He seemed to relish her warmth and the softness of her skin. His fingers traced her cheekbones gently, almost reverently.

"You saved me," he murmured.

"Oh, Tyler, I was so afraid," she said, choking on her words. "I thought you were going to die."

He chuckled mirthlessly. "So did I."

Before they could continue their discussion, Dr. Miller returned with a second water glass and a small bowl containing an assortment of pills. "Take them one at a time," she said. "We don't want you to choke."

"What are they?" he asked.

"Antibiotics and painkillers," Dr. Miller said.

Tyler glanced at Shannon. She didn't like the thought of him taking mysterious pills, but infection seemed like a greater possibility than poisoning.

"There is nothing to be afraid of. You can trust me."

"I know," Tyler said, though his eyes told just the opposite.

CASE NOTES 16:

HADES

Daylight dimmed, and soon enough, twilight swept over Hades. The stars appeared in the deepening sky, and bats swooped over the road, feeding on insects.

He passed trailers and farmhouses, his motorcycle's headlight gleaming off the eyes of cattle huddled behind barbed-wire fences.

As the moon appeared in the bruised sky, the bike heaved beneath him, and its motor began to rattle. The metallic clatter tore him from his foggy reverie, returning him to his own body. For the first time since his last rest stop break, he became aware of the aching.

Sensing that the motorcycle was about to die out, he moved to the right. He didn't need to apply the brakes. Even as he eased his grip on the throttle, the motorcycle slowed on its own and trundled to a stop along the dirt shoulder. He climbed off and wheeled it further away from the pavement. Each step he took jarred him all the way up his spine, traveling through stiff muscles.

The handlebar jabbed him in the side, and a sharp pain radiated from the sutured wound. As the wheels reached fertile field soil, he felt moisture trickle down his stomach. Probably just sweat or discharge spilled from the drainage tube, but if he wasn't careful and ended up tearing open the stitches, it could end up being a whole lot worse than that. The last thing he needed right now was a nasty infection.

He engaged the kickstand and took off his helmet, resting it on the ground. When he unzipped his jacket and peeled his shirt up, he was unsurprised to find that the bandages were discolored with blood and pus. The wound would need to be cleaned soon and the bandages changed, but that could wait until later. First things first.

Hades zipped his jacket back up and knelt beside the motorcycle.

After five minutes of examining the motorcycle, he realized that he had absolutely no idea how to repair it.

Marksmanship and combat had been his specialties. Vehicles were of lesser importance, as it had been assumed that wherever he ended up, he would have the supplies he needed to complete the objective. The only skill of his that came anywhere close to repair work was hotwiring. Not like that would do him much good out here in the middle of nowhere.

Stepping away from the bike, Hades looked around him. The landscape consisted of flat, rolling farmland. No sign of houses or oncoming motorists. He recalled seeing some rundown structures, but that had been at least two miles back. He wouldn't be able to drag the motorcycle that far, not in his condition. Not to mention that the bike might need some tender loving care from a mechanic to even get it to work again. It would be better to just dump it.

In that case, there were really only two options. He could wait along the road for a car to drive by, though evening was edging into night and he had passed few motorists since coming down this stretch of highway. Or he could continue on foot and search for a home.

Chances were, either possibility would end in bloodshed. He did not want to harm bystanders. It would only make his true mission more difficult to complete. But sometimes violence was necessary.

Just as he began walking, the rumble of an engine startled the bats from overhead and sent them fleeing into deeper darkness. Headlights washed over the low rise of a hill, and a truck hauling a small flatbed trailer came trundling down the slope.

Hades yanked down his jacket and rested his hand over the bulge formed by the handle of the revolver. He raised his other hand, waving down the trucker.

The window rolled down, and a man poked his head out. Hades could see nothing of the man's body, but his face was that of a laborer, all dust and tanned leather.

"Looks like you're having some trouble. She broke down?"

At first, he wasn't entirely sure what the man meant when he referred to "she," but then realized that he was talking about the motorcycle.

"Yes," Hades said, "but I don't know what's wrong. Phone's dead, too, so I haven't been able to call a mechanic."

"Wouldn't do you much good out here anyway, I'm afraid. Service is off and on, picky as a green mule." The man parked along the road and climbed down from his cab. As he circled around to the other side of the vehicle, Hades reached under his jacket, touching smooth steel.

"Let's see here," the man said, looking at the motorcycle. He might have had the face of a farmer, but his body was burdened under fifty extra pounds of padding. His biceps were all flab. He would be easy to take care of if need be. "I got one like this back home. Not such a beauty, though. Well, I can't tell you what's wrong with it just from a glance, but I live a short drive down the road. We can take a look at it back at my place and see if we can fix it, and if not, I can call you a mechanic."

There had to be something the man wanted in return.

"What's the catch?"

"Catch?" The man let loose a good-natured chuckle. "There's no catch, son. We get a lot of stranded motorists out here. Something to do with the roads, I figure. It's part of our responsibility, living in this beautiful county."

As he considered the man's offer, his gaze swept from the man's waist, down his legs, then up again toward the small of the back when he bent over the bike. No visible holsters or sheathes. No telltale bulges that would suggest a concealed weapon. But there might be a knife nestled in one of his cowboy boots, or a small piece in an ankle holster.

"All right," Hades said. "Thank you, sir."

"Ah, a polite teen," the man said. "We don't see a lot of those around here."

The man pulled down a ramp from the flatbed. With their combined effort, they wheeled the motorcycle up the shallow slope. Once the bike was all the way in and the steering column locked, the man secured it with ties retrieved from the steel lockbox at the back of the flatbed. After checking to make sure that the motorcycle wouldn't tip over, he turned and gave a thumbs-up.

"We're good to go."

Hades got into the cab. He didn't buckle his seatbelt, and throughout the entire drive, kept his hand at his side, resting on the revolver handle. He watched the man in the corner of his eye, wary of any sudden movements.

The man introduced himself as Ben Pinkerton. He began the ride by talking about motorcycles but turned to more personal questions after Hades responded only in monosyllables.

"So, what's your name, son?"

"Eli."

"Eli, huh? Is that short for Elijah, or Elias maybe?"

Short for Elizabeth, Hades thought, and smiled.

"Elijah," he said.

"You from around here, Eli?"

"Nearby," he said, without elaborating. "I'm travelling. I'm off on fall break."

"Oh, congratulations. Going on a little road trip then, huh?"

"Yeah."

"What do your folks think about this?"

"They're fine with it."

"Mmm. When I was your age, I hitchhiked from coast to coast all summer long. You really get to know people that way. Folks these days are too distrusting and bitter. It was different back then. Some of the people I met on the road became lifelong friends."

That was the last of the bothersome questions, as Pinkerton spent the remainder of the drive talking about his childhood adventures. It was a rather short trip, which was a good thing. After the five-minute mark, Hades found himself fantasizing about pistol-whipping the man into silence. He distracted himself by massaging the sore muscles in his legs, working loose the knots and kinks.

Soon enough, they turned off the road and onto a dirt driveway. A small, white terrier ran up to the truck as it passed through the gate and followed them barking to the door. They rolled the motorcycle down to solid ground.

This time, the pain that shot through Hades's body was sharp enough to rip a groan from between his gritted teeth.

"You all right, Eli?" Pinkerton asked.

"I'm fine," he said, gently touching the gauze through his jacket. He couldn't tell if the area over the wound was damp, not through the layers of cloth. He had a feeling that if he removed his clothes and peeled away the gauze, his skin would be slick with blood.

"How long were you standing out there for, anyway? You look a little under the weather."

"Just a few minutes."

"You're lucky you didn't break down during the night. The weatherman says it's going to be a cold one. Cold enough as it is today."

"I see." The cold didn't concern him. Come midnight, he would have already arrived at his destination.

"Maybe you should get a drink first," Mr. Pinkerton said. "Here, come inside."

As Mr. Pinkerton led him down the dirt driveway, Hades followed warily, muscles tensed in preparation for violence. The man's demeanor hardly came across as threatening, but his hospitality alone was reason for suspicion. Every favor was expected to be reciprocated. Every debt must be repaid in some way.

Mr. Pinkerton turned out to be neither a sex fiend nor an axe murderer. There were no decapitated heads in the refrigerator—only fresh meat and produce, an icebox cake, and a pitcher of lemonade.

With the family portraits on the walls and the scent of freshly baked bread lingering in the air, the home seemed well lived in. Hades wouldn't go so far as to call it cozy, but it was...something.

"Do you want to call your parents and let them know

you're okay?" Mr. Pinkerton asked as he poured Hades a glass. "They're probably worried about you."

Hades accepted the lemonade but didn't drink it. "Actually, do you have a computer I can use? My dad's out of the country right now, so he wanted me to email him."

"Be my guest. It's in the living room. Here, I'll show you."

Mr. Pinkerton led him to an ancient, lumbering PC that seemed ready to collapse the desk it rested upon. Hades sat down and turned the computer on, and while he waited for the machine to load, he thought about where he would go from here.

What would he do once he found his mother?

The computer lagged like hell. It took eight minutes just to access Dimitri's email alone, and another five to search his emails for the woman's name. He didn't expect to find much, if anything, for most of Dr. Kosta's data had been saved to external hard drives or to his work computer, not on the web.

As he waited for the results to load, he reached under his shirt, touching the bandages. They were damp in places, but he had sweated while out on the road, so maybe he had nothing to worry about.

He pulled out his fingers and looked down at them. His skin was splotched with translucent reddish liquid. Great. He wiped the discharge off on his jeans and turned his attention back to the screen.

His mother's name showed up in over fifty emails. The most recent message was from four weeks ago, while the oldest dated all the way back to his earliest days with Dimitri. There could have been more that were marked as spam or stored in other archives. He didn't have time to look through them all, so he added "mailing" into the search bar to narrow down the results.

No messages showed up.

Next, he tried "address." This time, there was a hit. The email in question was two years old, but because there were no additional results with those same keywords, he suspected that the address his mother had provided was up to date. If not, by going to her old address, he might be able to find some clue of her current whereabouts.

He wrote the address on a scratch piece of paper on the desk and searched for directions online. These, too, he jotted down. Once he was done, he deleted the search history and cleared the web cache. He almost wiped off the keyboard and mouse out of habit, and then remembered that he wasn't on a job. Fingerprints and DNA evidence weren't a concern here.

By the time he was finished, Mr. Pinkerton had already moved the motorcycle into the barn.

Inside the dusty, sawdust-strewn space, a vintage car rested on cinderblocks. Tools and automobile parts were scattered about. Cans of solvents and chemicals sat on homemade shelves. Another motorcycle leaned against the back wall.

"Did you get through to your parents?" Mr. Pinkerton asked, bending down in front of Hades's motorcycle.

"Yeah. I emailed them. Thank you for letting me use your computer."

"Of course." As he worked, he spoke merrily. "You see, Eli, repairing things is sort of a passion of mine. Got it from my father. Every day after school, he and I would work on the old car he had out back. We fixed her up as good as new. Ah, those were the days. I tried to get my daughter, Sarah, hooked on cars at a young age, but now that she's gotten older, she'd prefer to sit around in her room, talking on her phone all day instead of giving her old man a hand."

As Pinkerton recounted his childhood experiences, Hades pretended to listen, interjecting now and then with a nod or brief response. When Pinkerton asked for a tool, Hades handed it to him. At all other times, he stood afar, looking through the barn doors at the dimming fields until the setting sun burned afterimages into the backs of his eyes.

Although Pinkerton seemed about as dangerous as the grazing cows he kept, Hades refused to let his guard down. While Pinkerton worked, Hades listened for any noises to suggest the man was coming up behind him.

His skull clamped down on his brain in the birth of a nasty headache, so he downed a couple aspirin with a lukewarm energy drink purchased hours ago at a service station. He could have taken something stronger, but he knew it would only be a matter of time before he turned back on the highway. He'd dealt with worse pains before, without the aid of drugs. Just had to suck it up and distance himself from it.

Time passed, and his patience thinned.

"We might have to call a mechanic," Pinkerton admitted.

Hades's smile tightened. "Can you recommend one?"

"Wait. I think I have it. Give me a minute."

More like twenty.

"There we go," Pinkerton said and smiled at the purr of the engine. He patted the seat cushion. "Good as new."

"Thank you," he said drily. "How much do I owe you?"

"Keep your money. We're good Christians here. The way I look at it, anyone who doesn't help a stranger in need is the worst."

He didn't share the man's religion, let alone his philosophy, but he smiled and nodded like he did. As far as he was concerned, faith was shared by the weak. He didn't need God, and the fear of heavenly retribution did not frighten him. He knew what Hell was like. He had spent the last two years of his life walking its lavish, wainscoted corridors.

"Why don't you give her a test drive?" Pinkerton asked. "Let's put my handiwork up to the test."

He just wanted to leave, not drive around a stranger's farm at last light, but before he could refuse, a teenaged girl appeared in the doorway.

"Dad, dinner's almost done!" she said, then froze at the sight of him. Her eyes widened, and a blush reddened her cheeks. For a moment, she just stared at him gape-mouthed, until she found her voice again. "Hey, who's this?"

"Sarah, this is Eli," Mr. Pinkerton said. "His bike broke down along the road, and I've been helping him fix it."

"Daaaad, what did Mom tell you about this?" Sarah chastised, then turned back to Hades. "He does this all the time. The last hitchhiker Dad picked up stole my iPod. No offense. Not that you look like a thief or anything."

As Sarah spoke with her father, Hades found himself staring at her. The girl's platinum hair had a brassy tint that betrayed its color as artificial, but in the right light, it looked soft and flaxen. It reminded him of Nine's.

"I don't need your mother's permission to do a good deed," Mr. Pinkerton said. "You're home early. How did the dance recital go?"

"Fine," Sarah said in a tone that suggested otherwise, then turned back to Hades. She scanned him up and down and smiled. Probably liked what she saw. "Hey, why doesn't Eli stay over for dinner? You know Mom makes enough to feed an army."

He decided to make the decision easy on the man and said, "I need to get back on the road, anyway. I have a few more hours to go before I stop for the night."

"Then that decides it," Mr. Pinkerton said. "We wouldn't want you driving on an empty stomach. To be entirely honest, son, you look like you're about to collapse from exhaustion."

What was wrong with these people? Did they have such a thing as common sense? What kind of idiots invited a stranger over for dinner, unless they planned to pull a *Texas Chainsaw Massacre* on him?

"I'm fine," he assured the father and daughter.

"Besides, it's been a while since we've had a visitor stay for dinner," Pinkerton continued, as if never having heard him.

He felt as though he'd stepped into an alternate reality. It was the first time in his life that a person had invited him to break bread with them. Against his better judgement, he found himself agreeing.

The Pinkerton family's hospitality belonged to another era, as if the cornfields that surrounded their home had trapped them in a bubble, isolating them from the rest of the modern world. While he waited for dinner to finish cooking, he sat with Mr. Pinkerton and Sarah out on the front porch, drinking soda as they pestered him about his home life.

Both father and daughter took an interest in him, or at least pretended to, and when he realized that he couldn't get away with silent gestures and one-word answers, he began to lie. He told them that he was the eldest of five siblings, that his father was a military man and his mother was a doctor. The more Hades spoke, the more elaborate his lies became, and the more he began enjoying himself, until he found himself describing trips he had never taken and celebrations he could only dream of. He spoke of fair rides and school dances. He spoke of sailing with his father on a lake—the boat was called "THE UNDINE" like the boat he had seen in one of the photographs on the senator's walls.

He knew the effect that he had on people, and occasionally flirted with them just to feel a brief connection and reassure himself that he was still alive. But this was different. He didn't want Sarah's admiration or attraction, just a sense of family. A feeling of being.

"That's incredible," Sarah said when he got to the part about saving a little sister who had fallen overboard. "That's like something a hero would do."

Although the experience had only happened in his imagination and he'd never stepped foot on a boat in his life, he felt a brief, unexpected pride. But as soon as he recognized the emotion as such, it soured into anger and disdain.

How stupid could these people be? Couldn't they tell that he was lying through his teeth?

These two idiots were content with his lies, but he didn't need any of that. He didn't need a boat, or friends, or a family like the one he described. Revenge was the only real thing in the world, so why was he sitting here with these backwater hicks when he should just get up and leave?

By the time dinner was served, the sun had dropped from sight and the sky was murky with stars. The kitchen was uncomfortably warm, even with the air-conditioner rumbling away.

"Would you like me to hang your coat up for you?" Mrs. Pinkerton asked, using her napkin to mop the sweat from her brow. Her face was red from the heat of standing over the stove.

"No, thank you, ma'am," he said. "I'm fine."

"My god, you must have ice water for blood. It's practically broiling in here. I swear, the oven warms up the whole house." She turned to Mr. Pinkerton. "Honey, we really need to start working on getting a new A/C. Someday I'm going to have a stroke, and it's all because of that useless air conditioning."

Hades forced himself to smile, already regretting his decision to join the family for dinner. He felt out of place, distanced from the cheerful chatter. Indeed, it began to frustrate him after a while, as he tried to make sense of what the hell they were even talking about.

Mrs. Pinkerton was almost as nosy as her husband. When he told her that he was going on a road trip, she sighed. "Aren't you a little too young to be travelling the country on your own?"

"I'm eighteen," he lied. He wouldn't be eighteen until two months from now, in January, if he even lived that long.

"That's still awfully young."

Sarah rolled her eyes and smiled at him. "You're so old-fashioned, Mom. People do it all the time. Danielle's going to France next summer, and all by herself!"

Hades glanced up, hearing the whirr of a helicopter pass overhead. He was used to helicopters, but he didn't expect to hear one out here.

"Wildfires," Mr. Pinkerton said.

"What?" he asked, turning his attention back to the dinner table.

"They fly along the powerlines every now and then, searching for wildfires. Or at least that's what I've heard."

"Oh." To dissuade further small talk, Hades shoveled a

heaping spoonful of mashed potatoes into his mouth. The food was pretty good, all things considered. Maybe not as delicious as the stuff he used to eat at the Georgetown safe house, where there had been one kitchen for catering and another for personal use, but still decent.

"Eli, it looks to me like it's been a long time since you've sat down for a good meal," Mrs. Pinkerton said.

He lowered his spoon and finished swallowing the food in his mouth before responding. "What makes you say that?"

She leaned forward, her eyes narrowing behind her horn-rimmed glasses. "Are your parents treating you well?"

He didn't know how to respond. Why would she ask him something like that? Had there been some sign of it in his face or the way he ate?

Sometimes, he thought that people could see all the things he had done if they just looked into his eyes for long enough. Was it true?

"Mom," Sarah whined, her cheeks turning red. "Do you really have to get into this right now?"

Mrs. Pinkerton ignored her. "I don't mean to pry, dear, but I couldn't help but notice those bruises."

His hand went to his neck as he realized what she was talking about. His throat was still slightly sore from being choked out, but compared to his other pains, the bruises had faded into an afterthought.

"They're nothing," Hades said, pulling up his collar to hide the oval marks.

He felt strange, knowing that this woman was worried about his welfare. He was used to being treated like a machine, where the only reason his physical health was important was because it meant he could operate at his full potential. Scrapes and bruises were inconsequential.

However, if he had been crippled in an accident or damaged beyond repair, Dimitri surely would have seen it fit to euthanize him. But not before wrecking what remained of his sanity with electroshocks and drugs, not to mention lengthy sessions in the sensory deprivation tank. In the end, he had been nothing more than a guinea pig to the doctor.

He was glad that Dimitri was dead. He just wished that he had been the one to off the bastard. If he'd had his way, the doctor's death wouldn't have been as merciful as a gunshot wound.

Dimitri would have suffered.

"They certainly don't look like nothing," Mrs. Pinkerton said, fingering the gold chain around her own petite throat. "They look an awful lot like fingermarks to me."

Mr. Pinkerton cleared his throat. "Honey, I think that's enough. You're making the poor boy uncomfortable."

"It's fine," Hades said, then turned to Mrs. Pinkerton. "I appreciate your concern, ma'am, but I'm fine. They're hickeys."

"Hickeys," Mrs. Pinkerton repeated, looking unconvinced.

"My girlfriend has a biting habit."

A blush colored Mrs. Pinkerton's cheeks. Across from her, Sarah's awkward smile dissolved into helpless laughter.

By the time dessert was served, his headache had intensified into a hot, throbbing pain, and his stomach hurt, too. He felt detached from this entire situation, like he had stepped foot on a movie set without knowing it. He couldn't tell sincerity from falseness, and the longer he sat here, the more aware he became of the staggering gap that separated him from the Pinkertons.

They might have been sitting only inches apart, close

enough to touch, but there was definitely a divide between the Pinkertons and him. One that could never be conquered.

"May I please use the bathroom?" Hades asked. As friendly as the family was, he didn't want to stay here any longer, and decided that it would be better to get himself cleaned up now instead of waiting for the next opportunity to do so. He still had a long journey ahead of him. The sooner he returned to the road, the better.

"Of course," Mr. Pinkerton said. "It's on the second floor. Sarah, can you show Eli where it is?"

"Okay." She stood. "Follow me."

Hades got to his feet. He retrieved his backpack from the floor and slung it over his shoulder.

As soon as he stepped into the hall, Mrs. Pinkerton said, "Ben, you could've told me we were having a *guest* over." From the way she said it, Hades had a feeling that she disapproved of her husband's philanthropy. Luckily for her, he had no intention of delaying himself further.

Sarah led him upstairs, past framed needlepoints and a vase of dusty silk sunflowers.

"It's a little dirty," she said as she stopped in front of the third door. "I hope you don't mind."

"I'm sure I've seen far worse."

The bathroom was, as it turned out, far cleaner than he expected, though slightly antiquated. The yellow linoleum floor curled up in places, and there was a faint ring of mildew around the inside of the toilet bowl, but the room was otherwise in good condition. A lemon-scented air freshener hid any unpleasant odors.

Sarah hesitated in the hallway.

"Do you have a Facebook?" she asked.

"Sorry, I don't know what that is," he said, shutting the door in her face.

CASE NOTES 17:

THE PINKERTONS

Mr. and Mrs. Pinkerton began talking the moment the kid was out of earshot.

"I can't believe you would bring a stranger home without my approval," Mrs. Pinkerton whispered, leaning so far over the table that her necklace fell into the bowl of mashed potatoes. "And with Sarah in the house, no less! You should've just called a mechanic for him."

"Believe me, honey, I wouldn't have done it unless I had a good reason to."

She sighed as if she had heard that excuse a hundred times before. "And what would that be?"

"I think you're right about those bruises," Mr. Pinkerton said. "Them being fingermarks. When we loaded the bike onto the truck, his jacket rode up a bit. Got a good look at him. He's got some nasty scars. His back's covered in them, least from what I could tell. Never seen anything like it. Looks like someone beat the living shit out of that kid. Maybe more than once. Bad enough to put him in the hospital." He shuddered at the memory. "Not to mention he practically inhaled his dinner, like he thought we were going to take it away from him."

Mrs. Pinkerton's frown deepened.

"He says he's from nearby, but he's driving a bike with West Virginia plates," Mr. Pinkerton said. "Says he's on fall break, but Sarah's break ended almost a month ago. Now, I don't know about those high schools back east, but I'll bet you a dollar to a donut they don't let out in early November."

"Did he tell you where he came from?"

"When we returned home, I asked him if he would like to call anybody, but instead, he just wanted to check his email. Probably met one of those predator types online who said they'd help him. I tried talking to him out in the barn, asking him where he's from, how's his life at home. At first he just avoided the questions, then once Sarah showed, well, he began telling stories. Probably feels more comfortable talking to another teen. Still, the way he talked about his family…I think he was lying, or at least embellishing. Telling us what he thought we wanted to hear." Mr. Pinkerton chuckled drily. "Truth is, I've been trying to delay him for as long as possible, raking my brain, trying to figure out what to do. I'd feel horrible if I just let him go on his way and something bad happened to him."

"Maybe we should call the police," Mrs. Pinkerton said.

"That's what I thought, too, but I'm worried it'll just freak him out and he'll run away again. You should've seen the way Eli acted when I brought him out to the barn. At first, I thought he was nervous, being alone in there with me, but after a while he began looking out at the road, like he expected someone to show up there any moment. Poor kid's probably terrified of being dragged back home. This might not be the first time he's run away."

"Call Tom," Mrs. Pinkerton suggested. "He'll know what to do, and you know how good he is with kids."

Thomas Ransom was a retired policeman and a good friend of the Pinkertons. He lived a couple miles down the road. These days, he spent his free time welding metal sculptures, which he sold at the town's annual art shows. On weekends, he coached soccer.

"Think I will," Mr. Pinkerton said, climbing to his feet. He went to the telephone on the wall and thumbed in Tom's number.

"Hello?" Tom answered on the first ring.

"Hey, there, Tom. It's me, Ben. Are you busy?"

"No, just trying to get this damn TV to work. It's been acting funny all evening. Maybe you'll know how to fix it."

"I would, but I've got a little issue of my own, Tom. Think you can drop by in the next couple minutes? There's this kid here, Sarah's age. He broke down along the road. I think he's a runaway. He's got some nasty bruising on his neck and wrists, like someone's been abusing him. Seems scared out of his wits."

Tom listened to what Mr. Pinkerton had to say. When he spoke next, his voice was hardened: "I'll be right over."

Less than five minutes later, the doorbell rang.

"Sometimes, I wonder if he can teleport," Mr. Pinkerton said, rising to answer the door. As he stepped into the front hall, the bell rang a second time. "Hey, hold your horses, old fellow. I'm coming."

As Mr. Pinkerton opened the door, his smile faded. "Who are you?"

CASE NOTES 18:

HADES

As Mr. Pinkerton spoke with Tom Ransom over the telephone, Hades relieved himself in the upstairs bathroom. After washing his hands, he took off his jacket and threw it over the closed toilet seat.

A dime-sized maroon spot stained his shirt, and when he pulled it off, he found the dressing underneath discolored. He carefully peeled off the tape affixing the bandage to his skin, then tried to remove the bandage itself, grimacing when the damp gauze adhered.

Clotted blood obscured the wound, and trails of pus had dried on his skin.

He removed the first aid kit from his backpack, set it on the sink counter, and opened it. He cleaned himself up using a pad of gauze dampened with hydrogen peroxide. The peroxide fizzed and bubbled and ran down his flat stomach, pink with fresh blood.

At the sight of the wound, he gritted his teeth. The edges of the incision swelled against the sutures, and faint red lines crept across his skin. When he smelled the soiled bandage, he detected a subtle malodor.

The collection jar at the end of the drainage tube was

filled halfway with ruddy liquid the color of beef broth. He emptied it into the toilet. He had half a mind to remove the drainage tube, but now wasn't the time to play doctor. For the time being, it was an inconvenience he would have to put up with.

After he cleaned the wound, he dressed it in clean gauze. He waited to see if pinpricks of blood would appear through the bandage, and when they didn't, he pulled his shirt back on.

Parting his hair, he found the stapled incision and gently traced a finger over the scabs and steel. Compared to his other wounds, the pain was minimal. No swelling or pus. The drainage tube wasn't the only bit of medical equipment he had to worry about removing; soon, the staples would need to come out, too.

He searched his first aid kit for antibiotics, but all he found was aspirin, aloe vera gel, and over-the-counter topical ointment. He opened up the medicine cabinet next to the sink and riffled through its contents, reading the labels on the prescription bottles.

One of the Pinkertons must have suffered from chronic pain, because there were two bottles of prescription painkillers with recent fill dates. Another bottle contained the pharmaceutical equivalent of speed. These people were so naive, they kept their medicine where visitors could steal it, but they didn't have any antibiotics to spare?

As he returned the first aid kit to his backpack, he heard a shrill scream from downstairs.

To a person who was a stranger to violence, the cry might have been mistaken for one of surprise, but Hades recognized the terror embodied in that sound. It was the cry of someone staring death in the face.

In an instant, he forgot about the ache in his stomach

and the threat of gangrene. The shriek awoke a rabid awareness in him, an animal instinct, throwing him back into his old habits.

He left his backpack on the floor and took the revolver from its holster. As he cocked the hammer, he listened for any sound of movement in the hallway outside. Adrenaline spurred his heartbeat to a feverish gait, and his muscles tensed at the thrill of the hunt and the kill.

The Project knew he was here.

Another scream. The echo of frantic footsteps. Voices, but he couldn't make out what they were saying over the blood rushing through his ears.

This couldn't just be a domestic dispute or a home invasion. That was too much of a coincidence. Dimitri's email account must have been rigged to alert the organization if anyone accessed it.

From somewhere nearby, a door opened, then slammed shut, and Hades eased open the window. The bathroom faced the front porch, and as he crawled onto the roof, the doorknob rattled as someone tried to open it. The hinges were flimsy metal, and the door was cheap wood laminate. The lock wouldn't hold for long.

"We know you're in there, A-02," a boy called from outside the bathroom door. "There's no use hiding. If you surrender now, we won't harm you. You're more valuable to us alive than dead. We have orders to take you back to the Academy."

We know you're in there. That meant there was more than one. But how many more?

The tarpaper scratched his skin. It would have been easier to crawl with both hands free, but he didn't trust the revolver to stay in its holster. Besides, he felt more secure when he had a gun in his hand.

Hades went to the next window and tried opening it. At first it wouldn't move, but as he tugged at the frame, the pane creaked up by an inch. He wrenched it up the rest of the way, and slipped through, entering a bedroom.

As he eased himself onto the carpeted floor, something moved in the corner of the room. He levelled the gun, only to make out a waifish figure cowering against the bed, her face pressed against the comforter to muffle her gasping breaths. The dimness robbed her blond hair of its brassy undertone and made it appear almost platinum.

Nine, I thought you were dead, he thought bizarrely, but the moment she turned to him, the illusion broke like a reflection on restless waters.

Sarah saw the gun in his hand and moaned. She didn't speak, and rather than flee from him, just crumbled against the bed. Her eyes were dull and resigned. They didn't even seem like human eyes anymore.

He lowered the revolver. She wasn't a threat to his safety, so he saw no point in drawing attention to himself by shooting her.

He raised a finger to his lips, then stepped closer. Sarah flinched as he reached her side, cowering over herself.

"How many are there?" he whispered.

"Don't know." Sarah choked on a sob. "They…oh, God."

"Get under the bed and don't make a sound," he said and crept over to the door. As he reached for the knob, a crash echoed from down the hall. The bathroom must have been breached.

He opened the bedroom door, and after making sure that he was alone, stepped into the hall, silent as a cat. He edged closer to the bathroom, whose door hung broken on its hinges.

"Fine, be that way," the assassin said from inside the

bathroom. "We'll break a few limbs if we have to." He was careless. He had probably never killed before. There would be others, but for now, he was Hades's main concern.

With his body pressed against the wall, Hades glanced into the bathroom, looking into the mirror. He couldn't see the boy's entire body, but from the reflection alone, realized that he must be leaning out the window.

Hades didn't wait. He moved. As he lunged into the bathroom, the boy turned to him. He raised the revolver and slammed it down on the boy's head so hard that the impact jarred his wrist.

The boy dropped his gun and went down like a sack of bricks. Blood oozed down his shaved head, where the heavy weapon had made a sizable dent.

Facing toward the door, Hades squatted beside him. The boy wore a black quilted jacket, but underneath that, he found a vest held in place with Velcro straps. Kevlar. The assassin had come prepared.

With one eye turned to the hall, Hades set his gun on the floor. He undid the vest's straps and slid the boy's arms through the openings. The boy's limbs were limp and unresisting, and it took Hades mere seconds to separate the vest from its owner.

Weeks ago, the vest wouldn't have fit, but his brief hospitalization had eaten away at him, and dehydration further shrunk his powerful frame. When he pulled the vest over his shirt, it fit snugly against his back. With some tugging, the straps closed. It was like wearing a corset, and the Kevlar pads pressed uncomfortably against his bandaged wound, but it was better than nothing.

Pressing a finger against the boy's throat, he detected a faint and irregular pulse. He doubted that the boy would be getting up anytime soon, if at all. In all likelihood, even if the boy did regain consciousness, he would be in no condition to fight. A vegetable. Brain dead.

He took no chances. Even in his weakened state, he was able to snap the boy's neck with relative ease. In the silence that followed the crack of breaking bone, he felt himself enter a state of calm detachment. This meant nothing at all. This was not a person; this was the enemy.

He must search and destroy.

The dead boy had a small contraption clipped to his ear, visible against his blond stubble. Hades pulled the device off and held it to his own ear.

The speaker crackled and hissed.

"No sign of him in the backyard," a girl said. "Found a bike in the barn. It has West Virginia plates. I think it might be his. Any luck on your part, E-08?"

"Not yet," another boy said.

All right, so there had to be at least two of them. During mock missions, teams had been divided into groups of three or four. This was probably a case of the former.

After clipping on the headset, he picked up the handgun that the boy had dropped. A suppressor was screwed onto the end, and the extended magazine protruded. It must have held at least twenty rounds. Judging by its heft, there would be more than enough bullets left to take care of the others.

He returned his revolver to its holster, seeing no point in using it now. The dead boy's handgun would be better for a silent approach, and he wouldn't have to cock the hammer every time he wanted to fire.

If he was lucky, he would get five to ten shots out of the pistol's suppressor before it deteriorated completely. He doubted that he would be able to maintain his cover long enough for that to matter.

"Check the hayloft," E-08 said, ignorant of his comrade's demise.

Soon they would notice the silence. He needed to move quickly before they realized that their team was one less.

After putting his backpack on, he went back into the hall, hurrying at a swift but quiet pace. He paused at the top of the stairs, listening for movement below. After a short hesitation, he walked down the stairs, holding the pistol out in front of him.

The washing machine grumbled from its alcove like a hungry, discontent beast. In the foyer, he found Mr. Pinkerton sprawled on the floor, face-down. Gore darkened the carpet beneath him.

Hades was seized by a sudden profound shame, the emotion so strong that it took his breath away. He couldn't even have a simple meal without bringing death to everyone around him. Every attempt at formulating a human connection just ended with blood. No matter what he did, no matter where he went, he would always be alone.

Why is this happening to me? He clenched his jaw, burying his shame beneath mounting rage. *What the hell did I do to deserve this?*

This bloodshed, this destruction of a family—it felt *personal.* He had let his guard down for a moment, relaxed, enjoyed a meal, and now this. He had given up on the idea of having a peaceful or fruitful future a long time ago, but still, he was so tired of this constant velocity and constant violence. It was eating away at him like the throbbing pain in his gut.

Don't think about it. The weight of his gun grounded him as he continued deeper into the house. *Don't feel it. The only thing that matters is the kill.*

In the kitchen, blood congealed on the linoleum tiles, coating broken china. Soap suds dyed pink as water from the kitchen sink streamed down the cabinets and ran across the floor. He walked around the puddle instead of splashing through it.

Mrs. Pinkerton lay slumped in the corner.

He did not stop to check if the woman was dead. If she was still alive, he would not help her. She was collateral damage.

As he entered the family room, the lamp on a nearby side-table shattered. Porcelain shrapnel stung his forearm. He barely had time to duck back through the doorway before another bullet whizzed past, taking a chunk out of the door's decorative trim.

Without the aid of the table lamp, shadows gathered in the room beyond. The only other light source was that which came in from the hall. If he moved, he would be backlit like a shadow puppet. He might as well paint a target on his chest.

"I've found him!" E-08 said into the receiver. "He's in the house. I've got him corner—"

Hades leaned out from behind cover and raised the gun, firing off five rapid shots at the figure crouched behind the couch. The bullets punctured the cloth upholstery and went through to the other side. He couldn't tell if he hit his mark, but he must have, because E-08 groaned. A leg slid into view.

Even so, he ducked back against the wall and remained where he was, aware that it could be a trap. Yet, when he glanced out again and saw the same leg, unmoving, and a line of blood inching across the hardwood floor, he realized that the sound had been no feint after all.

He stepped into the living room, his gun pointed at

the inert figure. He pulled the trigger once more, and the leg shuddered as a dark hole appeared in its thigh. The silencer softened the gunshot to a dull rap only marginally quieter than actual gunfire. Other than that, there was no response. Not so much as a dying moan.

He stepped around the couch and found E-08 sprawled out on the other side. He didn't check to make sure the boy was dead. Blood streamed down E-08's face, or rather, what was left of it.

He traded E-08's gun for his own and took the spare magazine he found protruding from the boy's pocket, but otherwise made no attempt to scavenge the body. Time was of the essence.

"E-08, are you there?" The girl's voice crackled in his ear. "Can you hear me?"

"I'm afraid he's not here anymore," Hades said, focusing on the sounds he heard through the headset as he slipped through the house. Was that the crunch of hay beneath her feet? Was that the wind?

The girl didn't respond. Her hoarse breaths pushed through the speakers, the only indicator that she was still listening.

"There's still a chance for you to leave," he said, knowing that she never would. "You're going to die, you know."

"Shut up."

"Have you ever killed before? I mean, aside from unarmed hicks. The others in your squad sure didn't act like it. They were like lambs to slaughter."

Silence as deep as the grave.

"Oh, I see," he said. "You were the unlucky ones. You're just a distraction until they can send in better soldiers."

"We were only sent to retrieve you."

"That didn't go very well for you now, did it?"

"We were given orders not to harm you unless we had to."

"Why?"

"The Leader wants to see you. He'll forgive your transgressions if you come quietly."

"Yeah, right," Hades said. "Then he'll beat me to death."

"It's me, A-07. We were friends. Do you remember?"

Hades said nothing.

"I don't want to have to hurt you. If you surrender now…"

"Sorry, Seven. If what you say is true, you're going to have to take me by force."

That *was* the wind. He imagined she was circling the house now, or perhaps standing in the shadow of the barn, reluctant to step beyond the threshold.

With his advantage of surprise gone, the suppressor had become unnecessary. He unscrewed the metal cylinder from the end of the barrel and stuck it in his pocket. If he continued using the suppressor, the gunfire would eventually render it useless. He would rather save it, in case it came in use later.

He left the earpiece in the laundry room, next to the washing machine. He doubted she would be fooled by the rumbling, but he thought she might suspect he was still inside the house somewhere, holed away and wary.

He slipped outside through the front door, past the dead man, and instantly dropped into a crouch. As he hurried from under the porchlight to the cover of the plowed field, he surveyed the barren landscape. The barn was just a distant shadow. No sign of her.

Broken corn stalks bristled from the earth, devastated by the harvester and too short to conceal him. But the darkness was plentiful here, thick as wool. He settled down in an irrigation rut, flat on his stomach in four inches of muck. He smeared his face with the black mud that puddled in the algae-encrusted trench as he waited for his eyes to adjust. It occurred to him that A-07 might have night-vision or infrared goggles, but he would take his chances. The camouflage was better than nothing, and the coolness of the earth would help lower his body temperature.

Holding his gun out in front of him, he watched the home and the barn beyond it, searching for any sign of movement. If she was smart, she wouldn't rely on a flashlight. Surely her eyes had already acclimated to the night.

As he considered heading toward the barn, a shadow freed itself from the outer darkness. A-07 wore all black, but it was her face and untamed hair that gave her away, and the whiteness of the arms she held in front of her. She swung her arms to and fro, hunched over with her shoulders rolled as if anticipating a punch.

He couldn't tell if she was wearing a bulletproof vest, but even if she was, the force of the bullet would still stagger her. In fact, if she came close enough, it might even crack her ribs or knock her unconscious. Then it would only be a matter of finishing her off.

As she approached the house, he opened fire. She stumbled, cried out, but kept moving nonetheless, and disappeared behind the corner.

Keeping to the darkness, crouched down and gun held at the ready, Hades followed the curve of the irrigation trench. He knew that he had hurt her. He had seen the trail of black blood she left in the moonlit soil, but he couldn't tell if it had been a disabling wound.

If he made a single misstep, everything would end. He wasn't prepared to die without dragging Project Pandora down to Hell with him.

Before he could leave the cover of the culvert, an engine rumbled from the front of the property. Headlights washed over him as he pressed his body against the cement wall, panting in exhilaration.

A rusty pickup truck trundled to a stop in front of the house, and a man got out.

From where he crouched, he didn't have a good view of the stranger. Considering the vehicle's condition, he doubted the man had anything to do with Project Pandora.

The man took a couple steps toward the front door, then paused. He cocked his head toward the barn and headed in that direction.

"Sarah, is that you?" the man called, disappearing around the corner of the house. "You sound—"

A soft thud, then silence.

As Hades edged away from the barn, he considered how much time had passed from the time the man had turned the corner to the time he had fallen silent. Five seconds, maybe less. And the man had been close enough to hear her breathing or groans of pain, so that meant she hadn't picked him off from afar. She had to be near the house. Perhaps in the shadow of the eaves, waiting.

Circling around the house, he discerned a faint choked sobbing over the whistling breeze. He saw her gun before he saw her. The weapon lay in the dirt, in a growing pool of blood.

He found A-07 leaning against the door of the root cellar, bleeding from her arm and neck. She pressed her left hand against her throat, for her right one was useless. As she noticed him, she reached for her gun with her left hand, but it slipped from her blood-drenched fingers. Dark liquid guttered from the hole in her throat. He kicked the weapon aside before she could reach for it again.

"You could have run," he said, seized by a sudden, irrational anger at the sight of her familiar face. "You should have. I would've let you go."

It was much too late for that now. The bullet might have missed her jugular vein and carotid arteries, but it had devastated her trachea. As for her arm, the amount of blood pumping from the wound was enough to confirm that he'd struck her brachial artery. It was only a matter of time before she bled out.

Putting her out of her misery was the least he could do. He owed her that much, as a former comrade—no, *friend*.

A-07 looked up at him through dimming eyes and tried to speak. Sounds gurgled from her mouth, black with blood. "You...aren't Two."

"No. Two died a long time ago."

"What...what are you?"

Hades pointed his gun at her head.

"I am the end."

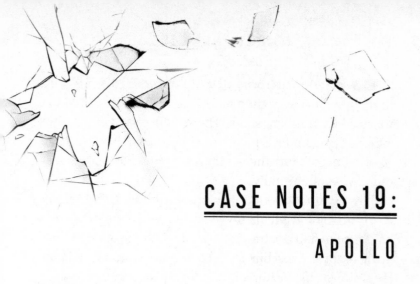

CASE NOTES 19:

APOLLO

Once Tyler proved well enough to walk, Dr. Miller decided to move him to the upstairs guest bedroom. The room was right across from hers, which meant that she could check on him in the night without disturbing the rest of the household. More importantly, the bed was large enough to prevent accidental falls if he rolled over in his sleep, and a lock on the door kept Caroline from disturbing him.

"I really don't mind her," he said as he sat down on the king-sized bed. "I wish I had a little sister."

It occurred to him that he very well might. Was there a way to find out who his real parents were? He wasn't sure he wanted to.

"I appreciate your amiability, but you need all the rest you can get," Dr. Miller said, retrieving two extra pillows from the closet. "You shouldn't exert yourself more than necessary. In fact, it's impressive that you were even able to walk up those stairs."

"Not without help."

"There's something I've been wondering," she said. "Have you broken any bones before?"

"I don't know," he admitted. "I got punched pretty hard in the nose, like, almost a week ago, and it sure felt like it was broken, but I guess not. The swelling went down after a day or two, and it doesn't hurt anymore."

Her bright-blue eyes regarded him intensely. "How did that happen?"

"Some lunatic," Tyler said, then sighed. It felt wrong to dismiss Hades as simply a lunatic, when the other boy had been just like them. Brainwashed and deadened. "No, uh, actually, he was like us. Like Shannon and me, I mean. He was sent by Dr. Kosta to kill me."

Dr. Miller's brow creased. "This boy, is he still after you?"

"He's dead. He got shot right in front of me."

"Oh. I see. You two have been through so much."

"I'm kind of used to it by now," he admitted. "At first, it felt like a dream, but now...I don't know. I feel numb to it. It's like my life has always been this way."

Dr. Miller nodded, then responded with another question. "Have you had any other surgical procedures? Such as an exploratory laparotomy? Or organ biopsies?"

"Not that I'm aware of," he said, taken aback. "I don't even know what those are. Why?"

"You have some interesting scars over your major organs."

"It's probably from the white ward." He frowned, puzzled at the words that had left his mouth. A sense of déjà vu overcame him, and he felt so close to remembering something. Something that was like a dream but wasn't.

The creases in her forehead deepened. "The white ward?"

"I meant the hospital," he said. "Back with Dr. Finch—I mean, Dr. Kosta. Dr. Kosta. That's what I meant."

For some reason, Tyler thought about the dream he

had the night after he was shot. He could only remember bits and pieces, and the moment he tried to recall more, he was struck with a sudden debilitating anxiety.

"This kind of scarring isn't consistent with Dr. Kosta's method," Dr. Miller said. "He didn't perform surgeries."

Tyler wished she'd just shut up. Why was she asking him about this? It didn't matter. They were just scars. Who cared about where he got them?

"I guess I got them before. I don't know. I don't remember. I'm sorry. I don't know." He felt at the brink of terror, as if those three words—*the white ward*—had unlocked the doorway to an unbearable memory. His childhood memories were almost entirely absent, with only the vaguest recollections that were more like *sensations* than actual visions. Like the scent of antiseptic, or the coldness, the touch of firm vinyl and crinkle of paper, or the blinding glow of white fluorescents.

Don't think about it, a frantic voice whispered in his head. *Just don't think about it, and don't you dare open that door.*

If he opened the door to his past, it would destroy him. He knew it would.

Dr. Miller must have sensed his growing unease, because she laid a hand on his arm.

"You must be tired," she said, though it was only early evening and he had slept through half the day. "You should rest. How is the pain?"

He was still feeling the effects of the previous dose of medication, but he liked the way it made him feel. The drugs numbed the worry along with the pain, leaving him warm and hollow. Right now, that was what he needed most of all, to be empty.

"Pretty bad," Tyler lied.

She sighed. "I'll get you another pill."

He felt slightly pathetic, as if by asking for another dose, he was giving into weakness.

Miller left. A couple of minutes later, Shannon entered, carrying a glass and a small saucer.

"Dr. Miller wanted me to bring you these," she said, holding out the saucer. "It's time to take your antibiotics, too."

"Thanks." He took the three pills with a swallow of water.

"How are you doing?"

"I'll live." He smiled.

"You have a nice setup here," she said, looking around. "It's like the Hilton. I guess I get the couch tonight, huh?"

"Actually, it's a pretty big bed. I think there's enough room here for the two of us."

She laughed. "I don't think Dr. Miller would approve."

"Probably not."

"Besides, I have a feeling you're not supposed to overexert yourself."

"You say that like I'm an old man."

"I say it like you've just been shot. Twice." Shannon took the empty water glass from him and headed toward the door. "I'll check on you later."

"Shannon?"

She turned back. "Yeah?"

"Do you remember a place called the 'white ward?'"

Her smile faded. "The white ward?"

"Like a hospital ward," he said.

"No, I don't."

"I mean, from before Dr. Kosta. From the Academy."

She shook her head. "Do you mean the sickbay? That's where they used to take us when we got injured, remember? And there was that doctor with the witch's wart on her nose. Do you remember her?"

"I don't," he admitted. "Never mind. It's nothing."

"Actually, now that I think about it, you mentioned something like that back in the car, after you'd been shot."

"Really?"

"There were thirty," she said.

He shivered, suddenly chilled. A strong sense of disquiet engulfed him.

"You said that, too," she told him. "Do you remember what you meant?"

Tyler shook his head. "I'm sure it's nothing. I was just out of it."

"You had a pretty bad dream, too, after it happened."

"Just forget it," he said, regretting that he brought it up in the first place.

"Is there anything you want to talk about?"

"No. I'm tired. I don't feel good. I just want to go back to sleep."

"Oh. Okay." A worried crease appeared between Shannon's eyebrows. "But you know I'm here for you, right? We survived that place together. So, if you ever want to talk, I'm here."

He smiled until the door closed behind her.

CASE NOTES 20:

HADES

Deeper into Colorado, a dry storm. Each time there was a burst of lightning, the pine trees popped out like teeth against the sky. The wind clawed at the motorcycle's wheels, and underneath his jacket and unstrapped Kevlar vest, his shirt was drenched in sweat. The fabric chafed his skin, and though he had applied antibiotic ointment to the sunburn on the back of his neck, it ached as if scalded.

The pain tethered Hades to his body, and yet, at the same time, he felt as though he were floating above himself. Riding on a high of sleep deprivation, fever, and caffeine overload, he felt at the edge of a holy experience. A great epiphany.

Though he was using a clear visor, his vision acquired an eerie depth as the lightning faded. In the glow of the motorcycle headlight, the entire world appeared to be drowned in an oily black-green ichor, as if he were nestled inside a vast amniotic sac. The air was wet and heavy, thick with the vinegary scent of ozone.

His gunshot wound throbbed, and it felt as though a hand had reached into him and grabbed him, held him, tugged at something deep inside him. He could almost believe that the hole was an umbilical cord connecting him to her. The pain was his labor. Birth spasms. He was getting closer. So close.

"Mom," he murmured, and took his hand off the handlebar long enough to slip it under his shirt and touch the slick, muddy bandages, the surgical tape detached from his skin. The collection jar had fallen off somewhere back at the farmhouse, and bloodied discharge oozed down the waistband of his jeans.

With a long, breathless sigh, he traced the groove of his abdominal muscles and followed it down to the damp denim, around to smooth leather, the steel butt of the revolver. The other gun waited in the tail bag, disassembled, silencer unscrewed, but ready to be put to use. Maybe soon. Soon he would find out. Were her eyes like his own? Did she have his face? Share his mind?

What would it be like to have her embrace him and call him her son? Would she weep and ask for his forgiveness?

Something was going to happen to him. Once he reached her, he would know his purpose in life. He would know what he had to do next.

An idea suddenly occurred to him, and he knew at once that it was true: what if she had been forced to relinquish him? Yes, that must be it. They must have forced her to do it, and when she finally met him, her only child, her son, her very flesh and blood, she would dissolve into tears. He could even imagine the words she would say as she hugged him: *I'm sorry, I'm so sorry. I should have protected you from them. I had no choice. You're my only child, the most important thing to me in the world, and I love you, and I'll never let them touch you again.*

"Home." His voice was just a whisper now as he guided his hand upward again and fingered the raw end of the drainage tube. Flexible, moist and weeping, yes, like an umbilical cord. Gummy clots of blood stuck to his skin, and as he touched the swollen lips of the incision, he moaned in pain and yearning.

His eyes fluttered shut and he came very close to falling off his bike, but the crash of thunder slammed him back into reality.

"I'm coming home."

His body was so warm, and though it was already night, the sky grew darker still. Veins of lightning throbbed through the clouds, and the world was like a womb, swaddling him. He felt as though he were in the process of being born, that the purr of the motorcycle beneath him was the strain of muscles enclosing him, and each feverish mile forward was another step toward the distant light.

The gun pressed against his flank, hot as a second heart.

Soon.

CASE NOTES 21:

APOLLO

Tyler slept through the evening, and at eleven o'clock, woke to a knock on his door. The sound was so soft that he thought he had imagined it, until he heard it a second time.

"Come in." He sat up and reached for the bedside lamp, turning it on once he found it.

The door opened, just a crack. A little radiance came in from the hallway, but neither light source was strong enough to expose the silhouetted figure who stood just beyond the threshold, hidden behind the door. The shadow was too short to be a human, and in his doped-up state, he first thought that it must be a dog like the one barking outside. Then reason caught up to him, and he laughed.

"Hey, there's no need to be shy," he said. "I don't bite. You're Caroline, right?"

"Yeah. Mom says I shouldn't come in here." Caroline stepped into the room and shut the door behind her. She crossed her arms and shyly met his eyes. "Are you sick?"

"Something like that."

"Like the flu? Mom makes me stay in bed when I get the flu, too. She says it's, um, caw...cun..."

"Contagious," Tyler guessed. "And, uh, no. I just hurt my arm and chest is all, and I'm supposed to rest until I get better." He glanced at the alarm clock on the nightstand. Fifteen minutes until midnight. "Isn't it way past your bedtime?"

"No. I'm always awake now."

He grinned at her flimsy lie. "If you say so."

"Do you want to play checkers?" she asked.

Tyler opened his mouth to tell her that he was too tired right now, but he would play with her tomorrow. Then, seeing the eagerness in her face, he relented. Maybe playing a game would take his mind off of the discomfort that survived through his pleasant opiate haze.

"Okay, but just one game."

With a delighted laugh, Caroline went to the closet. This room must have been used as a storage place when it wasn't occupied, because the closet was stacked floor-to-ceiling with board games, appliances, and moving boxes. She stood on her tiptoes to reach the lowest shelf. As she sorted through the cardboard cartons, he found himself vacantly reminiscing about his past.

He still hadn't regained his childhood memories in entirety, but he recalled enough to cut through the warm, cottony effect of the painkillers. The rows of white beds. Harsh lights. The chill of an air conditioner, so cold, even in the heat of summer. Fragile things.

The past didn't matter. Didn't mean a thing. It would be better if he never remembered.

"I want to be red," Caroline said, clambering onto the foot of his bed. "Red goes first."

"Be my guest," he said. If only he had such simple desires.

"Huh? What's that mean?"

"You can be red."

Six-year-olds made poor opponents, and after the first few moves, he began to play to lose. He pretended not to notice when Caroline moved her game piece an extra space, and he placed his own checkers right in the line of fire. He wished that he could predict Pandora's movements with the same ease. Maybe then they'd have an actual chance of survival.

"I was asleep," she admitted, "but Andy woke me up."

"Who?"

"Miss Lily's dog. He's really nice, and Miss Lily lets me pet him all the time, but Mom doesn't like him that much. Mom says dogs are filthy."

That dog still hadn't stopped barking. Maybe Andy's owner should have invested in a shock collar.

"Sometimes Mom says she wants to give him arsenic," Caroline said matter-of-factly.

"Wait, did you just say 'arsenic?'"

She nodded. "Yeah. I think it's a goodie like a Scooby Snack."

Tyler decided not to destroy her innocence by informing her that arsenic was a deadly poison. Instead, he just moved his checkers piece down a square.

"I win!" she announced when she claimed his final piece. "You're really bad at checkers. You're worse than Mom."

"I know. I bet Shannon's a better player. Maybe you can play against her tomorrow." He wondered if they would be here tomorrow. He didn't trust Dr. Miller, and he didn't want to rely on her charity for much longer, but what choice did they have? If they left now, he would just drag Shannon down.

"One more game?" Caroline asked. "Please? Just one

more. You can be red this time."

The dog stopped mid-bark. Its owner must have brought it inside.

"No, I'm sorry," he said, brushing the pieces back into their box. "It might not be past your bedtime, but it's past mine. We'll play again, okay? I promise."

"Oh, okay." As she stood to return the box to its shelf, the bedroom window exploded.

Tyler was on his feet before the first shards of glass struck the carpet. "Get down!" he shouted and tackled her to the ground. He landed on his knees and elbows, and even with the painkillers to soften the blow, his body screamed in such intense pain that he almost blacked out. Broken glass struck his back, but those mild lacerations were nothing compared to the burning inside of himself. It felt like a fire had been ignited in his bloodstream.

Another bullet tore a groove through the bedpost, and his instincts took over, blanking out the excruciating pain. He covered Caroline with his body and held onto her wrists so that she could not break free and bolt into the line of fire.

That didn't stop her from shrieking for her mother and kicking out at him. Her mother had trained her well—most of her blows landed uncomfortably close to his crotch. She wore soft-toed slippers, but a single hard kick was all that it would take to reduce his limbs to water. His only consolation was that her aim was worse than her skill at checkers. For now.

"Stop moving!" he shouted. "Just stop moving! I'm not going to hurt you."

"Caroline, what's wrong?!" Dr. Miller yelled from down below, and he heard her footsteps pound up the stairs.

Caroline twisted in his grasp, writhing like a snake.

"Mommy! He's hurting me!"

"Don't come in here, doctor!" His back hurt so much. He could barely speak straight, and the words came out hoarse and trembling. "Don't you fucking open that door! There's someone shooting at us through the window! If you open that door, you're dead!"

"Tyler, where are they firing from?" Shannon called from over Caroline's frantic sobs.

"I don't know. I think it's from the house next door. They've got us cornered here, Shannon."

"Caroline, do what Tyler says," Dr. Miller said. "Don't move, okay? Don't move. Everything will be all right, just do what he says. We're going to help you, I promise. Just do what he says."

Her mother's reassurances were enough to still Caroline's thrashing limbs, but it didn't keep her from shrieking out when the bedside lamp exploded, engulfing the room in darkness.

CASE NOTES 22:

ARTEMIS

Standing in the second-floor hallway, Shannon listened to the child's sobs and felt a black anger roll over her. Wherever they went, they were never safe. This would go on forever.

As she drew her pistol from its waist holster, she turned to Miller. "Do you have a gun?"

Her face was as pale as parchment paper, and deep in the hollows of her sockets, her eyes blazed with a feverish light. "Yes. It's in my bedroom, in the gun safe."

Shannon winced. All this time? Why hadn't she thought to confiscate it earlier?

"Get it," she said. "Be careful. There may be another gunman. Do you know what house he's talking about?"

Miller nodded. "It's the Rosenbergs'. The brick colonial. They don't live in it anymore."

Shannon remembered passing that house on her way here. There had been "For Sale" signs on the front lawn.

"I'm calling the police," Dr. Miller said. "I can't take any chances. Not with Caroline."

"I know," she said and turned from the woman. Her anger wasn't meant for Dr. Miller, but as she hurried down the stairs again, she seethed at the injustice of it all. It wasn't fair. The doctor didn't deserve to have faith in the justice system when she was a part of the reason they couldn't seek out the cops in the first place.

As she crossed the living room, she listened for footsteps, the snap of breaking glass, or the creak of a door being opened.

There had to be more than one shooter. If she had to make a logical guess, there were at least two others. Yet, considering their proximity to the facility, there could very well be a whole platoon of them waiting on Dr. Miller's doorstep.

Stay calm, she told herself as she edged toward the backdoor. *Just take things one at a time.*

Pep talk or not, she felt strangely detached, as if she were drifting above her body, connected only by the thinnest line. Maybe she had just grown accustomed to constant terror. Maybe it was the end and a part of her knew it.

She hesitated once she reached the door and waited. No one entered, and the windows around her did not disintegrate in a hailstorm of bullets. Through the glass, she saw no flashlight beams or searchlights, only the flash of faraway heat lightning. Ducking down, she turned the knob and eased the door open.

If there was a moon, the clouds obscured it. The entire yard was bathed in darkness. Fragrances of gardenias and roses turned sour in her nose, and the squelch of mud and earthworms beneath her shoes made her stomach twist with nervous tension.

She breathed through her mouth, then, fearing it too noisy, breathed through her nose instead. Each time she took in a breath, she expected it to be her last.

CASE NOTES 23:

APOLLO

"I t's okay, it's okay," Tyler repeated over and over. "It's just the dark. It's nothing to be afraid of."

If that calmed Caroline, he couldn't tell. She just kept wailing. Could the neighbors hear her?

"I'm scared." Her voice warbled through her sobs. "I don't like it! Make it stop! I want my mommy."

Just his luck. Stuck in a room with a six-year-old who was afraid of the dark, and with a shooter outside who could kill them in an instant if they moved out from behind cover.

"Shh. It's okay. Close your eyes."

Her sobs softened into quiet weeping. "I'm scared."

"I won't let anyone hurt you. You're safe, I promise. Nobody's going to hurt you."

"It's too dark."

"I'm here for you."

"I don't want to go there."

"Go where?" he asked, hoping that by starting a conversation, he would be able to distract her.

"Back there."

"What do you mean?"

"I don't want to go back in there."

"Don't worry. We're not going to go there. Just close your eyes." For all he knew, her eyes were already squeezed shut. "Pretend we're at the movie theater, right? We're at the movies with your mommy, and we're watching *Frozen* or some shi…or something."

"Don't want to go into the dark place," she repeated, and went silent for good.

"Caroline?"

She wouldn't answer. His eyes had adjusted enough now that he could see her face, the subdued trembling of her limbs, her parted lips and blank stare. Her eyes were just wet gleams.

"Caroline, I'm going to try to get my gun, okay? Just stay here. Don't move."

Silence.

Tyler let go of one wrist, then the other. He pressed a hand against her cheek, briefly. Her skin felt cool and clammy. Was she going into shock?

"Can you hear me?" he asked.

Nothing.

When he was certain she wouldn't move, he crawled off of her and inched toward the nightstand. He kept his body low to the ground, with one shoulder pressed against the wall. Each time he put pressure on his left arm, he clenched his teeth to keep from crying out.

As he reached for the drawer's knob, a bullet cut through the air, missing him by inches. Splinters stippled his skin, and he threw himself back, landing on his ass. He rolled onto his stomach, winced at the radiating pain, and returned to Caroline's side, shocked that the gunman had missed him.

No. That wasn't right. The shooter would have waited

for him to move his entire body into the crosshairs before firing to kill. This was a warning: *I can see you, and I can shoot you whenever I want to.*

But inside that message, there was another.

They wanted him alive.

CASE NOTES 24:

ARTEMIS

As Shannon crept over to the low stone wall dividing the Miller property from the Rosenbergs', she heard the snap of breaking glass from the front of Dr. Miller's house. She turned in that direction but forced herself not to approach it. Taking out the gunman in the neighbors' house was of the utmost importance. As long as the sniper was still active, she wouldn't be able to move anywhere on the property without the danger of entering his crosshairs. Even passing windows could mean death.

She climbed over the wall and sunk into a crouch the moment her feet touched the ground. Shrubbery scratched at her face and tangled in her hair. She parted the foliage with her left arm while keeping her right one directed forward, finger on the trigger.

She intended to circle the house to find a quiet entry point, but as she approached it from the front, she saw that the door had been left ajar. She narrowed her eyes and studied the opening. It reeked like a trap to her, but there was just something too off about it. Why would they leave the door open in clear view of the neighboring houses? Why leave it like that when forcing her to manually open it would create enough noise to alert the gunmen to her position?

Instead of slipping through the open door, she followed the curved colonnade to the other side of the house. Mud squelched under her shoes as she tested windows. She found one that was unlocked, opened it, and crawled inside.

The kitchen she entered was even darker than the night outside, and she hadn't gone more than ten steps in before she jarred her arm on the marble countertop. By sheer luck alone, she avoided pulling off a shot in reflex.

Elbow throbbing, she searched the entire bottom floor before returning to the entry hall and the grand staircase. She took the stairs one at a time, moving with the utmost caution. Her senses were in overdrive, and each sound, even that of the creaking wood beneath her, seemed amplified. She could almost imagine that the air waves created by her subtlest movements had a sound of their own, and that the sniper upstairs possessed the extrasensory perceptions capable of detecting them.

As if to confirm her suspicions, the floorboards groaned deeper in the darkness.

CASE NOTES 25:

APOLLO

"**Y**ou're going to be okay, Caroline," Tyler said, pressing his fingers against her inner wrist. Her pulse felt slow but regular. He didn't know whether to be relieved or worried.

The door opened.

"I told you not to come in…" His stomach dropped.

The person's broad shoulders filled the doorway, and he was much too tall to be Dr. Miller. He turned on the lights, revealing a square face with piggish eyes and a mop of red hair hanging over a low forehead. He had a gun tucked under one arm, and he gestured at Tyler with its barrel.

"Stay right where you are and keep your hands where I can see them," he said. "If you try anything, I'll shoot you. Or I'll shoot the brat. Do you have a preference?"

"Relax," he said, lifting his hands. His shoulder screamed with pain at the motion. "I'll behave. I promise."

"I'm going to toss you a pair of handcuffs. Put the first cuff around your right wrist and the other around your left ankle." The young man pulled the handcuffs from his pants pocket and threw them at Tyler. They skittered across the floor and stopped six inches shy of him.

Warily, he extended his hand. He feared that any sudden movements would end with a bullet in his face. The last thing he needed right now was another hole in him.

"What's your name?" Tyler asked, picking up the handcuffs. The metal was as cold as ice against his skin.

"So, it's true then," the redhead said. "You're defective."

"What do you mean?"

"We don't have names. You know that as well as I do."

"Then what name do you go by? My name's Tyler." He wanted to humanize himself in the boy's eyes, but also to waste time. The moment he put on the handcuffs, he would be helpless. Left unable to defend anyone, least of all himself.

The redhead didn't take the bait, just looked at him with green eyes the color of pond scum and a sneer twisting his ruddy lips. His gums were receded, making his teeth seem longer than they truly were.

"Listen, you don't have to do this. We both grew up in that place. We're the same, you and I. We're not just pawns to be controlled and discarded. We're people."

"Now, put them on."

Tyler slipped the cuff around his wrist.

"Tighten it."

He took no chances. While he didn't think that the boy would shoot him, not now, at least, he feared that Caroline didn't possess that same immunity. She wasn't a part of this.

"What's up with the girl?" the redhead asked, scowling.

"I think she's in shock. She's harmless. She's only six. Just leave her alone."

"Your ankle now."

By chaining his wrist to his ankle, he would be practically hogtied. No way to free himself, let alone rise to his feet. In other words, about as useful as a turtle on its back.

Left with no choice in the matter, he closed the second cuff around his ankle and tightened it as well. The position put pressure on his wounds and left him bowed over himself, his knees shoved up painfully against his chest. He felt like a trussed turkey.

"The killing has to stop," Tyler said. "Please, just listen to me. You can join us."

"That's ironic, coming from you."

"What?"

"I've heard all about you," the redhead said. "You killed three others just hours ago, and now you say the killing has to stop. Do you think I'm stupid?"

Tyler stared at him blankly. "What are you talking about?"

"Where's the doctor?"

Tyler wondered just the same.

"She escaped," he lied. "She's already left."

"We'll find her," the redhead said, stepping into the room. "It's only a matter of time. Now, where's your gun?"

"It's in the drawer."

The redhead walked up to Tyler and kicked him in the ribs, knocking the air out of his lungs and hurling him onto his back. His entire world flashed red. He landed hard and found that, also like an overturned turtle, he could only roll around helplessly, coughing and gagging, until he righted himself.

The boy stepped past him, glanced only briefly at the stunned girl, and went to the dresser. He opened the drawers one at the time, and when that revealed nothing, turned to the nightstand.

"You mean in here?" the redhead asked, looking over his shoulder.

Between gasps, Tyler said, "Right."

The redhead removed the gun from the top drawer and took his hands off his own weapon long enough to examine it. "The safety's on. That's a surprise."

"I didn't want to shoot anyone by mistake."

The redhead smiled, but before he could say another word, he collapsed against the bed. More window glass tinkled to the floorboards, and blood oozed down the bed linen.

The boy did not get up.

CASE NOTES 26:

ARTEMIS

Shannon hesitated, unsure if the creaking noise had been a product of her anxious mind or whether it was truly there. She waited for a recurrence, then continued forward. Even if there was an assassin lurking through the house, staying on the stairs would only put her at a disadvantage. He could fire at her through the railings in the bannister or from down below, and she would have little cover of her own.

At the top of the stairs, she ducked against the wall. There was no furniture to conceal her. The movers had cleared everything out. Only dust and shadows remained.

By the time she entered the third room, her eyes had adjusted to the extent that she could make out a figure sitting beside the window, his back against the wall. A rifle lay across his legs. The stench of gunpowder and carpet cleaner thickened the air.

She swung the pistol up before the blond-haired boy could react.

"Drop your gun and put your hands in the air." As she pointed her gun at his head, she was aware of how easy it would be to just pull the trigger. "If you try anything,

I'll shoot you!"

He didn't move.

"I said I'll shoot!" She doubted that the crack of the gunshot would make it past the home's thick brick walls, except she couldn't bring herself to outright execute him. He was still human. Maybe she could bring him back from his trance like Tyler had done to her.

The sniper did not respond. His silence was eerie. He showed no sign of having heard her at all and sat as still as a statue. It didn't look like he was wearing earmuffs. Was he wearing earplugs or just ignoring her?

"I'm not joking around! Put your hands in the air!"

She was suddenly struck by the oddness of his posture. He wasn't just sitting against the wall, but slumped against it, his head bowed unnaturally to the side. His hands lay in his lap, fingers unfurled. The rifle rested on his ankle, not his lap, as if it had been dropped there without much thought.

Then, as she stepped forward, she also noticed the dark splotches of liquid on the white carpet under the window.

Before she could convince herself to reach out and touch him, he slid sideways along the wall and landed atop the rifle with one arm bent beneath him.

Blood darkened his hair. He had been shot once in the head.

Hearing footsteps, Shannon swiveled around and raised the pistol, but no one lurked behind her. Her finger twitched against the trigger. Worried that she might fire by mistake, revealing her location to everyone nearby in the process, she rested her finger against the guard.

Shannon ran into the hall and found herself alone. She pivoted on her heel, turning to the stairs.

No one. Dead silence.

Maybe the noise had just been her imagination, or the wind, or the tapping of the pipes.

As she returned to the bedroom, her mind swam with questions.

What could it mean? Who would kill their own comrade? It just didn't make any sense.

Shannon grabbed the sniper's shoulder, grimacing at the sweaty warmth of his skin and the tackiness of blood on her fingers. She avoided looking at the bullet hole in his skull, and when he fell onto his back, the sight of his murky eyes made her squeeze her own eyes shut, just for a moment.

A memory from her adolescence returned to her: sitting in a darkened room with a dozen other teens, watching a film play on a large projector. Scenes of death and carnage. She remembered a man telling them that the violence was necessary. Needed. Good.

Not for the first time, she wondered who the real Shannon was—the girl who had calmly executed multiple people on Dr. Kosta's orders, or the one she saw when she looked in the mirror. Who was she really, Shannon Evans or Artemis?

Just don't think about it, she told herself as she pushed the corpse aside and reached for the rifle. The scope was a high-tech piece of equipment, clearly electronic, probably used specifically for low-light situations. Her fingers touched the steel barrel, still warm from recent use. The wooden stock felt cold in comparison, even with the blood streaked across it. More blood on the trigger, sticky. In the dimness, she could almost pretend it was ink.

She didn't like the thought of leaving a loaded rifle here for anyone to use, but as she searched for the bolt release, she discovered that the bolt had already been removed. Without it, the rifle couldn't fire.

Shannon set down the rifle, hands trembling ever so slightly. She took another brief look at the boy's face and forced herself not to turn away when she encountered the devastation of his wound. Bitter saliva flooded her mouth, and she had the sudden urge to retch.

He was her enemy, but if circumstances had been different, she could have died in his place.

Her legs felt watery. Her bowels, too, as if her bladder was filled to capacity and ready to burst. She took one step back, then another. Unused cartridges and empty shells rolled under her shoes.

Bearing the pistol in front of her, she returned to the grand staircase. Once again, she sensed that another person occupied the house, and had taken these stairs only minutes before her. Her suspicions were verified when she found a second trail of muddy footprints exiting the home and the front door closed. A bloody handprint rested on the post beside the door, as if the killer had stopped there, briefly, to collect himself.

Caution fled her as she rushed out into the murky night. The image of the dead boy remained seared in her brain. One shot to the back of the head. Close range, maybe point-blank. Execution style.

Just who the hell was capable of that? If they weren't her enemy, then who were they?

As she stepped out from under the shade of the colonnade, the wind blew against her face, cold and piercing. In her absence, the clouds had parted, revealing a sliver of moon like a half-closed eye.

As she hurried back to the wall, she listened for screams or footsteps. If there were any, she couldn't hear them over the rattling of leaves.

She made it over the wall without incident. As she rose from a crouch, two gunshots cracked out. She instantly ducked down again, though she knew the bushes would provide her no protection.

Just as she hid herself, it occurred to her that the hunters would be using silencers. Unless enough shots had been fired to render the suppressors useless, Tyler or Dr. Miller had been the one to open fire.

The killers were inside the house.

She dashed out from behind cover and raced across the lawn. Her shoes slipped in the wet grass, and mud slapped across her pantlegs. The back door was closed, and just as she reached it, hands seized her from behind and slammed her into the unforgiving wood. She didn't even have time to cry out before her arm was twisted behind her back and the gun knocked from her fingers.

"Who the hell are you?" a boy asked, his breath fanning against the nape of Shannon's neck.

"My name's Shannon." Shannon took a deep breath as water blurred her eyes. Her head throbbed from hitting the wood, and her arm ached.

"What are you? Some runaway he picked up?"

His questions confounded her. They made no sense at all. Hadn't the killers come here looking for Tyler and her?

"We only need your boyfriend, the doctor, and the brat."

Cold metal pressed against her back. She refused to tremble or cry. As she heard the cock of the hammer, her life did not flash before her eyes. All she saw was the white door.

Then blood as it splattered across the painted wood.

Gasping, she pressed her hands against her stomach. Dry cloth, no wound. The boy no longer held her arm, and when she turned around, he lay unmoving at her feet.

Blood oozed from his temple.

"Are you real?" a voice murmured, and she swiveled in the direction it had come from.

A figure stood to her right, in the shadow of the tree. He held a handgun whose barrel was elongated by a silencer, and as he stepped forward, he lowered the weapon.

A cruel, handsome face stared back at her, one that she recognized all too well. Unkempt black hair and deep-set eyes. Sensuous lips pressed into a flat smile, hardly a smile at all. His cheeks were smeared with blood, and more of the same stiffened his hair in tufts, as if he had absently pushed the strands out from over his eyes.

"Hades! You were dead! How could you be here? We left you. I thought…"

Try as she might, she just couldn't wrap her brain around the fact that Hades was really here, when she and Tyler had left him for dead, bleeding out in a basement stairwell.

Then, before she even had a chance to recover from the first shock, another realization struck her like a hammer blow, and Dr. Miller's face filled her mind. Those eyes. That hair. Even the face was so similar.

It couldn't be.

"So, you're really here," he said, his voice flat and hoarse. As he stepped under the porch lamp, the yellow glow painted him in a sickly light, eroding his beauty. The skin around his eyes was smudged with bruised shadows. The hand that held the gun trembled ever so slightly. Sweat dewed on his brow, and through his tangled, blood-stiffened hair, his gas-flame blue eyes smoldered with madness or fever.

"Who are you again?" he asked.

"Shannon Evans," she said.

"Oh. Yeah. Artemis. D-05. I remember you."

"You don't look so good," she said.

"You feel that?" Hades closed his eyes and tilted his head up. A faint smile twitched across his lips as he lifted a hand to his face and stroked his own cheek, leaving a trail of blood. "My evolution. It's going to happen soon."

She realized that there was something seriously wrong with him. He wasn't just speaking cryptically, he was talking like he was out of his freaking mind.

"Tyler's still upstairs," she said. "We need to help him."

"Who's that?" he asked, opening his eyes.

"Apollo," she said, using Tyler's old codename. "The boy you were sent to…"

She trailed off. This wasn't the time to remind him that he had once tried to kill Tyler.

"Oh. Yeah. I saw him."

"What?"

"Through the tank hatch," Hades said. "Or, no, the scope. That's right. It was a scope, but it was like the hatch. The deprivation tank."

"You were the one to shoot the sniper." She could hardly suppress a tremor at that realization. Whether Hades was high, delirious from injury or sickness, or just plain bat shit crazy, he had enough sense left in him to perform a cold-blooded execution. Killing was so engrained in him that it had become second nature.

As he reached her side, she almost gagged. He was close enough now that she could smell him—sweat, blood, gunpowder, infection. He smelled like he hadn't showered in days, and judging by the mud stains on his clothes, that estimation wasn't too far off.

"I've been seeing things," he said, "but I think the one upstairs was real, too."

"Oh, God. You didn't shoot Tyler, did you?"

"No. Just the enemy."

"I need to help him." She picked up her gun. She avoided looking at the corpse and didn't dare think about the drops of warm liquid sinking through the back of her shirt. "You should wait here."

If he was hallucinating, she didn't want him covering her.

As she entered the house, she heard the floorboards creak behind her. Deciding that the last thing she needed was another assailant, she had no choice but to let him follow her.

They passed through the kitchen and entered the hall, looking into archways. The living room was deserted. Shannon saw no overturned furniture or broken glass to suggest a struggle. There was no blood, either.

Passing the stairs, she resisted the impulse to rush up them and assist Tyler. Before she helped him, she needed to make sure no gunmen waited downstairs. Losing her cool in this situation would only get her killed. She must stay calm, take deep breaths, and not think about the blood dripping down her back. Rely on instinct, not emotion.

Bathroom. Linen closet. Office. All clear.

"Just wait down here," she told Hades as they returned to the stairs. "Cover me, okay? Make sure no one gets past."

His burning eyes drew to her. Though he kept his hands steady, with his hips and spine aligned in the perfect shooter's stance, it was clear that he was suffering from something other than just poor hygiene. His breaths left his mouth in raw, ragged gasps. Even as she spoke, his gaze wandered and focused on objects he had no reason to look at, like a picture on the wall or the floorboards at her feet. Odd expressions cycled across his lips—a faint smile, then a frown, and then a lost distant look.

Did he understand what she was saying? Could he even *hear* her?

"Just stay here," she repeated quietly.

This time he grinned. "No."

CASE NOTES 27:

APOLLO

Tyler scooted over to the corpse like a crippled crab. With only the use of his left hand and right leg, he could move just inches at a time. Each muscle torsion brought tears of pain to his eyes and aggravated the wounds under the bandages. A particularly vicious contortion left him temporarily paralyzed and gasping for breath. It took him the better part of a minute to reach the body, and even longer to search all the pockets.

Where the hell was Dr. Miller? Had she fled, leaving her daughter behind?

One minute had passed since the gunshots rang out from inside Dr. Miller's house, and he dreaded to think what they meant. He wanted to believe that the doctor had been able to defend herself against the redhead's companions, but he feared the worst.

He found the key, unlocked the handcuffs, and threw them aside. Pins and needles crawled up his legs as he climbed to his feet. He considered taking the boy's weapon, then decided he wouldn't be able to handle the submachine gun's vicious kick in his current condition. He rolled the corpse onto its side, pushed the boy's gun under the bed where it couldn't be retrieved, and picked up his own pistol. The magazine held ten bullets. He hoped that would be enough.

"Come on, sweetheart," Tyler said, helping Caroline to her feet. She didn't collapse like he feared she would, but remained standing, swaying ever so slightly. Her face was blank, her brown eyes glassy. She was a china doll petrified in shock and horror.

He held Caroline's hand and led her to the door, taking care to shield her face from the corpse. Shannon must have secured the sniper's position, but that didn't mean there weren't others still in the house, where her scope wouldn't reach. He couldn't leave Caroline here with the corpse and the gun, not to mention the threat of armed killers. He would find a hiding place for her, then continue his search, and if he encountered anyone along the way, he would do anything in his power to protect her.

As soon as Tyler entered the hall, he eased Caroline behind him. The position extended his arm awkwardly, and he felt the muscle tension as an ache that radiated from his shoulder all the way to the tips of his fingers.

He turned the corner in the hall and narrowly avoided a full-on collision with Dr. Miller. She gasped when she saw him and raised her revolver, but thankfully recovered from the shock before she pulled the trigger.

"Oh, Caroline," she said, scooping the little girl against her.

"I think she's in shock. She just stopped crying and moving."

Hugging her daughter, Dr. Miller glanced up at him. "I got one of the bastards. He tried to attack me. I...I can't believe it, but I got him. I shot him."

There was a raw sort of satisfaction in her voice that

sent a chill down his spine.

"Tyler," Shannon called from down below. "Tyler, Dr. Miller, are you two still up there?"

"Shannon, we're here."

"There's no one left downstairs," she said. "You clear?"

"We're clear," Dr. Miller answered.

"Okay, we're coming up," Shannon said.

Dr. Miller looked at him, a question in her eyes. "We?"

Before he could answer, let alone ask Shannon who she meant, she stepped into the hall. A dark-haired boy followed close behind her, a gun lowered at his side.

"Holy shit," Tyler said, getting a good look at the boy's face.

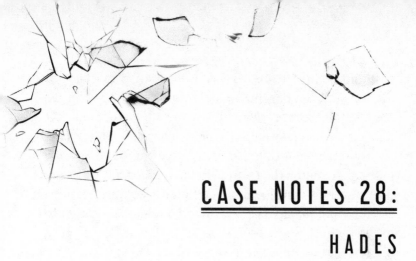

CASE NOTES 28:

HADES

The amniotic darkness ebbed, submerged Hades, and then receded once more. His stomach throbbed with a steady burning, but goose bumps rose on his shoulders as he was racked by a terrible chill. Standing there, drenched in sweat and trembling, he felt torn between two opposite forces—extreme heat and extreme cold, the unbearable need to be *somebody* and the numb indifference that usually governed his life.

His mother had hair as dark as his, and eyes like his, too, just like he knew she would. But as he stared at her, her features distorted, rippling like a watery reflection. At first he saw a face like his, then she became an absolute stranger. One moment, he was certain he had seen her before. The next, he knew with absolute conviction that he had never met her.

He had come here to kill her. He had come here to be loved by her. Which one was it? Why had he travelled so far? Why was he even still alive, or was he dead and he just didn't know it yet? And the blood on his hands, soaking through his gloves—what had he just done?

Frantic questions filled his head, adding to the

pounding ache. He felt like his skull would split open any second, and the darkness would enter again, pouring in and blotting out every thought, every little part of him, just like it did when he went into the sensory deprivation tank.

Hades didn't want to go back into the tank. He hated it in there. He hated the IV infusion pump that administered drugs into his veins, and the catheter used during longer sessions, and the dry skin and bladder infections. But most of all, he hated how he felt when he left it, like a bit of himself had dissolved into the water, gone forever.

If they made him go back in the tank, he would make everyone suffer. He would kill them all.

No, that wasn't right. Dimitri Kosta was dead. No tank. Just his mother standing before him, trembling herself. Trembling with joy. She must be so happy to see him.

But why wasn't she smiling?

"I'm home," Hades said softly. Though he couldn't remember ever stepping foot in this house, he felt certain that he must have. She must have raised him here at some point, nursed and rocked him, cared for him until cruel circumstance forced her to relinquish him to the Project.

There was no other alternative.

"No," his mom said and shook her head like she couldn't believe it. "Not you. This can't be happening."

"Mom," Hades said, testing the word. He liked the sound of it. It felt *right*.

"How are you here?" she asked.

Was he here?

He wasn't sure.

His gaze swept to the child briefly. A spark of an idea occurred to him—*can't be, it's not possible, she wouldn't dare*—then fizzled out in an instant. And the little girl dissolved from his thoughts like so much smoke.

"Is this where it happens?" he asked. "Am I evolving?"

A strong sense of déjà vu overpowered him. Yes, he had been here before. He had been in this very moment. Something would happen to him soon.

"Drop the gun," his mother ordered, and in her expression, he saw none of the warmth he expected. Just an emotion he didn't have a name for. And then, as he halved the distance between them, she lifted her revolver and pointed it at his chest.

His fingers tightened around the handle of his own gun, driven by the instinct to destroy. Then his grip loosened, and his finger slipped from the trigger. She was not the enemy. She couldn't be the enemy, or everything he had envisioned would mean nothing.

"I am ordering you to drop it!"

"So how does this happen?" he asked. "What should I do?"

"Wait." The blond boy—what was his name again?—reached for Mom's hand, but she jerked away.

"Dr. Miller, calm down," the brown-haired girl said. "I don't think he's going to hurt you."

Who was Dr. Miller? Oh. Right. That was his mom's name. Dr. Francine Miller. Why did people have to have names? It only complicated things, and he could never seem to remember them.

"Drop the gun, now!"

"This isn't how I imagined it," Hades said, disturbed by how harsh her voice was. "You're doing it all wrong."

"I said drop it!"

"Is this a test?" he asked. That was the only explanation. It had to be a test, like the tests that Dimitri had often put him through. Respond this way and you get rewarded. Respond that way and you need another session in the tank, or another change in your medication, or a few more jolts of electricity. *And it hurt.*

But the rules were never explained to him. Sometimes, he did the things Dimitri wanted and was punished anyway. And sometimes there was nothing he could do to get a positive response. Like when he watched those special videos, electrodes plastered all over his skin, and there was a reaction Dimitri didn't want, but Hades couldn't help it because it was his body betraying him. Was this like that time?

"I think he's sick," the brunette girl said. "I think he's delirious."

Who was she speaking about?

"Drop it or I'll shoot!" his mom said.

Hades spread his arms and allowed the handgun to drop from his slack fingers. As it fell, he felt his internal organs plummet with it. A sickening hollow formed in the pit of his stomach. This was wrong. Why wasn't his mother crying or smiling? He'd killed them for her. Shouldn't she be happy to see him?

Did she want him to hurt someone else?

"Now, kick it over."

"This is a test, isn't it?" He was almost certain of it now. There was a way she wanted him to respond, a way that would open the doorway to her heart and allow the situation to proceed exactly as he had foreseen it.

"Now!"

"How am I supposed to respond?" he asked

"Kick it over."

A light kick sent the weapon sliding down the hall.

"Now get on your knees."

"He saved my life," the girl said.

Hades took a step forward, then another.

"I told you not to come any closer," his mom said. "Get down on the ground!"

As he reached her, her revolver's barrel poked him in the chest. He vaguely recalled having tightened the straps of the Kevlar vest when he had arrived, but now they felt constricting, choking him. His midsection was damp.

A faint stirring of trepidation cut through the haze that swaddled his mind. This wasn't right. This went against everything he had been taught, all of his training. Why had he dropped his gun?

The thoughts emptied from his head as he tried to hug his mom, and she pushed him away, shoved him hard enough that he stumbled back. He tried to hug her again, and this time she rammed the revolver's barrel into his chest hard enough to bruise him, and he slipped and landed on his butt.

"Why are you doing this?" he asked, and his voice wasn't his own anymore. It was the trembling, wounded cry of the boy he once was, A-02 who had died so that Hades could live. It wasn't right, and it *hurt*.

It hurt so much. The throbbing heat he felt inside were not birth pangs after all, but a kind of death. A part of him was withering away.

She hated him. She hated him, and he was going to die because of it. No one. He had no one now. No one to turn to.

It's happening. I'm alone again.

"We need to get out of here," the blond boy said. "There may be more on their way."

Hades looked down at his hands. There was blood on the gloves, and more on his wrists. He couldn't quite remember how it had gotten there. Was it his own?

So tired. He closed his eyes and opened them again

when a hand touched his shoulder.

"Am I dead?" he asked.

"Are you hurt?" the brunette girl asked.

"Who are you again?" he asked.

"Shannon. I asked if you were hurt."

"I think I'm dead." Sometimes, Hades felt like he was dead. Sometimes, he hurt himself, just to see if he would bleed and to reassure himself that he was still alive. Sometimes, he needed to hurt other people. But it had never felt like this before, and he couldn't be sure.

"Are you injured?"

"It was never supposed to feel this way," he said in wonder. "That bitch. She was supposed to cry and say she was sorry, say she didn't abandon me. So why didn't she stick to the script?"

"Come on, you need to get up," she said, reaching for his hand.

"I'm tired," Hades said.

"You can't sleep here."

"I don't want to go in the tank," he said as he took her hand.

"You'll never have to anymore."

As she helped him to his feet, he leaned against her, enjoying the warmth of her body. She was so warm.

"Hey, Nine?"

"I'm not…" She sighed. "What is it?"

"It's funny. I thought you died."

"I'm still alive."

"I'm glad. Thank you for saving me. I love you, you know. I'll destroy them for you."

In the time it took to blink, he found himself sitting down in an unfamiliar place. Shafts of light passed over him, and as he rolled his head to the side, he discovered their source. Street lamps. He was in a moving car. He could not recall having entered the vehicle, but he didn't feel particularly surprised. Everything after the farmhouse massacre felt like a dream, with strange transitions and blackouts.

He closed his eyes again and waded back into the dark.

CASE NOTES 29:

APOLLO

F ew words were exchanged during the several hours it took to reach Dr. Miller's cabin near the Wyoming border. Tyler thought he'd never fall asleep after what had happened, but he drifted off repeatedly, lulled into a false sense of security by the gentle jostling of the SUV.

Once during the drive, he awoke to panic and confusion. He lurched up, breathing rapidly. His hand went to his side, but he wasn't wearing the shoulder rig. Then he remembered where he was, and that the pistol was in the glove compartment, there if he needed it, and he calmed.

"You okay?" Shannon whispered from behind him. She shared the backseat with Caroline and Hades, and when Tyler looked back, he could only see the faintest outline of her features.

"Yeah," he whispered and reached back. It was uncomfortable to extend his left arm, and he knew that he was putting unnecessary strain on his shoulder, but he needed to touch her. He needed to feel something other than the gnawing, lingering terror and the chill of the air conditioner.

Warm fingers enclosed his own. Even though the muscle extension sent sharp needles of pain travelling down his arm, he savored her touch. It was funny, in a sad way. He had never imagined that holding someone's hand could bring so much comfort. Just this brief contact brought the same warmth as kissing or hugging, and yet was so understated.

The moment was ruined when Hades groaned in his sleep, drawing Tyler's attention away from her silhouetted figure. Shannon had told him what Hades had done, and although Tyler knew that he should be grateful, all he felt was anger. Mostly toward himself.

Shannon's fingers slipped away. As soon as she let go of him, he felt the despair take hold again. He turned his attention back to the road ahead, staring at the thick forest that pressed down on either side of them. They were deep in the mountains now, and each mile took them further away from civilization.

As the lights of a small town faded behind them, he felt like a shipwrecked sailor adrift, clinging to the shattered pieces of the world he had once known. There was only restless night now. This was his life.

By the time they arrived at the cabin, the sky was a predawn indigo, the sun just a red glower past the rising peaks. He welcomed the dawn. It meant that he had survived another day.

At the start of their drive, Dr. Miller had spoken briefly about the property and had explained that it was purchased under a different name that could not possibly be traced to her. Another safeguard against the possibility of total anarchy—or, more likely, prosecution by the justice system. However, her description wasn't enough to prepare him for the sight of it: a one-story cement building with narrow windows and a flat roof. An architect might have called the design Modernist, but to him, it just looked like a prison or bunker. Hardly the cozy log cabin he had imagined.

As soon as the car slowed to a stop, Tyler got out. As Dr. Miller unbuckled Caroline's seatbelt, he stretched his legs and enjoyed the crisp breeze. The mountain air was cool and refreshing and carried none of the ugly odors he had grown so used to.

Dr. Miller looked at her home and sighed. For the first time, it occurred to him that something traumatic must have happened to her long ago, perhaps before she had even become a doctor. Past her curt professionalism and her adoration for her daughter, there was another side of her that was only glimpsed through her possessions: the hoarded medical supplies, this bunker-like home, and the gun she carried close even as she led Caroline inside.

He felt bad for the little girl. Caroline appeared normal now, and even mumbled his name when she passed him, but he couldn't get her screams or catatonic stare out of his head. What damage had been done tonight to her fragile mind? How many lives would be destroyed before this all could end?

Shannon joined him, rubbing her back. She looked around, and took a deep, appreciative breath. "It smells great out here. I thought I was going to suffocate back there."

"I kept thinking, if only the car had a trunk we could stuff him into," he said, then felt a pang of regret. It felt obscene to make jokes right now.

But that didn't keep him from coming closer and putting his arms around her. Her shoulder blades pressed against his hands, rigid. She leaned into him, but even then, she was so tense.

"I'm sorry," Tyler murmured as she rested her head on his shoulder. He stroked his hand through her hair. "I should have been able to protect you."

"It wasn't your fault," she murmured, running her fingers down his chest. "You did everything you could do."

As he pressed his lips against the crown of her head, the door to the backseat swung open.

As Hades approached, Tyler glanced inside the car, estimating the number of seconds it would take to open the glove box, take out his gun, switch off the safety, and pull the trigger. They had relieved Hades of his bag the moment he had fallen asleep—including the loaded revolver, the box of ammunition, and bundles of cash stored inside it—but it wouldn't surprise Tyler if the other boy had another weapon hidden on his person.

"Where am I?" Hades asked, stopping at a wary distance. His right hand went to his side, to the empty holster, while his left one flexed, tensed, and tightened into a fist. There was dried blood and dirt on his face, and he didn't even seem aware of it.

Although Hades's coordination was slightly off balance and his eyes were clouded and at half-mast, Tyler sensed that if the other boy felt threatened, he'd attack with the viciousness of a rabid wolf, going straight for the throat. Even in sickness, he possessed a restless, animalistic presence.

"Relax, we're in a safe place," Tyler said, deciding to leave it to Dr. Miller to explain.

The other boy licked his lips and looked about, then turned his gaze toward the sky. "What day is it?"

"Wednesday, I think," Tyler said. "But it's, like, four in the morning. You've been sleeping for hours."

Gone was the trembling, bloodied boy who had pleaded to his mother. Hades was clearly still sick, but he seemed to have regained at least a little of his awareness. Looking at them again, his eyes narrowed. "I slept?"

"You were pretty much out cold," Shannon said.

"I thought...I feel drugged." Pressing a hand against his stomach, Hades turned to the house. His jaw worked silently, teeth grinding, and the fingers on the other hand, his right one now, continued to twitch. Opened, closed, opened, closed.

If Tyler didn't know any better, he would have thought that Hades was a recovering smoker. But he had a feeling those grasping fingers craved to curl around something a little more dangerous than a cigarette—like a knife handle or the trigger of a gun.

Shannon must have had a similar suspicion, because she slipped her hand into her pocket.

Before the tension could spill over into violence, Dr. Miller returned. "Tyler, Shannon, go inside. I'd like to have a minute in private with—"

"Subject Two of Subset A," Hades said coldly.

The home's decor was as drab and sterile as its exterior, designed not to be aesthetically pleasing but to serve a purpose. No paintings hung on the walls. The furniture in the living room was steel and black leather, covered in opaque plastic sheeting. In the kitchen, dust skimmed the black marble counter. Though the fridge and freezer were barren and unplugged, the walk-in pantry yielded an ungodly amount of canned and jarred goods.

To pass the time, Tyler browsed the shelves. Dr. Miller was meticulous with her organizing and had not only labelled every single product with its name and expiration date, but had also arranged them according to their use.

Airtight silver bags contained powdered eggs and milk, while plastic barrels held flour, rice, and sugar.

Only a single shelf was devoted to normal staples, like cereal, macaroni, and baking mix. Apparently, Dr. Miller intended to sit out the apocalypse snorting dehydrated dairy products.

Tyler sat down at the kitchen table and gently rubbed his upper arm, where a grinding ache had developed. Shannon remained standing but rested against the table edge. Though they didn't speak, it made him feel good just being next to her. A little more at peace.

"I guess now she can't betray us," Shannon said, echoing what was on his mind.

The front door opened and closed, and Hades followed Dr. Miller into the kitchen. As he passed the stove, he lost his balance and stumbled against the counter. Dr. Miller reached out to stabilize him.

"Don't touch me," he growled, shrugging her hand away. "I'm fine. I just slipped."

"If you say so," Dr. Miller said calmly and led him through another archway.

Two pairs of footsteps receded deeper into the house. Tyler waited until he heard the sound of another closing door before he responded.

"Are you still worried about that?" he asked. "Her betraying us, I mean."

"Aren't you? Don't you think it's just a little suspicious how those people knew where we were?"

"I don't think they came to the house looking for us. I think they were looking for him."

She bit her lip and looked at the floor. "Do you feel like you owe her something?"

"No," he lied.

"You don't owe her your trust or anything. She doesn't deserve it."

He sighed. "I'm just sick of being so paranoid of everyone around me, Shannon. I want to believe that she has some good in her, okay? People can't be all bad."

Before they could continue their discussion, the doctor entered the kitchen, her hands sheathed in stained latex gloves.

"I think it's time we all went to bed," she said, dropping a bundle of soiled gauze and plastic tubing into the empty trash bin. She stripped off her gloves and tossed those as well.

"Is Hades okay?" Shannon asked.

"The boy will live." At the sink, Miller washed her hands under hot water until her skin reddened from the heat. Even after all the soap suds swirled down the drain, she kept on scrubbing. "He's got a slight infection and has the classic symptoms of sleep deprivation and dehydration. I've given him some antibiotics and medicine to reduce his fever. He should be fine after a good night's rest." After wiping her hands dry on a dishtowel, she retrieved an empty jug from the cupboard and filled it with tap water. "I need to bring him a drink and check on Caroline. I'll be right back."

Once she had left the room, Tyler turned to Shannon. "She needs to know how dangerous he is."

"What? So she can shoot him?" She sighed. "I've been reading his files. I know what was done to him."

"It was done to all of us."

"No, it wasn't. Not like that. Dr. Kosta didn't just try to brainwash him, Tyler. It *began* with him, and for as long as Dr. Kosta was with him, it didn't stop."

"Just because something bad happened to him doesn't

mean he's not responsible for his actions. You remember how he acted, back when we first met? The only reason he hasn't tried killing us yet is because he's so out of it, he probably doesn't even recognize us."

"He sided with us."

"Doesn't mean the truce is still in effect."

Shannon looked at the ground. "It bothers me. The way she just called him 'the boy' and 'the kid.' I mean, he's clearly her son."

"He didn't give her much of an alternative," Tyler said, but realized then that it bothered him, too. Ever since learning the truth about his conception, he had played with the idea of finding his own birth parents, if indeed they were still alive. Until now, his main concern had been that his search would lead him to a pair of graves, but what if his reunion was just as depressing? What if his parents were alive, satisfied with their other children, and wanted nothing to do with him?

"I don't trust her," she muttered. "I can't trust anyone who sells their own son, no matter how he turned out."

"She saved me."

"At gunpoint."

"But afterwards, she had a hundred opportunities to rat us out."

"Maybe she did."

He sighed. This conversation was going nowhere. They could argue about Dr. Miller all they wanted, but he knew that in the end, Shannon was right. The doctor couldn't be trusted. His gut feeling told him that much. Everything that the woman did after this would be an act of self-preservation.

As for Hades, Tyler couldn't stand to think that the other boy had rescued Shannon while he had been helpless to do anything but writhe around in handcuffs. It sickened him.

"Tyler, what's really bothering you?"

"Nothing."

"You sure?"

He brushed her hair out of her face and kissed her. "I promise."

"Stop that, please," Dr. Miller said, putting an end to their romantic moment. When he turned, he found her glowering at them from the doorway, arms crossed.

"The last thing I need to worry about right now is hormonal teenagers." She beckoned with one hand. "Come. I'll show you two to your rooms."

Dr. Miller stopped at the first door they came to. It led into a room with white wicker furniture and the first splash of color he had seen so far—a pink rug on the floor. Plastic storage containers were stacked along one wall.

"The previous owners left this house furnished," Dr. Miller said, looking distastefully at the rug. "I never had a chance to redecorate it all the way. This is your room, Shannon. Please don't touch the boxes. They are filled with supplies and sealed to preserve freshness. The bathroom is over there. There should be extra toiletries under the sink and clean linen in the closet. I'll bring you a change of my clothes in a bit."

"Thank you," Shannon said.

"Night," Tyler said, once Shannon stepped inside.

"Good night," she said, then shut the door.

Dr. Miller led him to another door, but instead of opening it, stopped just outside of it.

"You'll be sleeping here," she said. "I'm sorry, but I don't have any clothes for you. I'll see about acquiring some tomorrow."

"It's fine. I'm kind of used to this."

"I want to thank you. You sheltered Caroline, and you didn't have to."

"Will she be okay?"

Dr. Miller nodded. "Children are resilient. Traumatic memories can be forgotten. She reacted exactly as I expected her to, considering the circumstance. There will be no lasting psychological impact, I can promise you that."

"Well, good night." Tyler entered the room—and froze.

There were two beds. The one furthest from the door was occupied.

No way, he thought, *there's no way I'm having him as my roommate.*

He turned to Dr. Miller to ask if he could sleep on the couch, but found the hallway deserted. No wonder she hadn't wanted to come inside.

He sighed and shut the door, then eyed the still form under the sheet warily. "Are you awake?"

The lump beneath the thin coverlet didn't stir. Of Hades, all Tyler could see was a tangle of dark hair and one pale shoulder.

As Tyler took a step into the room, the shape rolled over.

Hades hoisted himself into a sitting position. The sheet slipped down to his bare waist, revealing a square of bandages taped against his side. Bruises girdled his throat, shockingly dark against the surrounding skin. It appeared as though he had been throttled.

"I'm trying to sleep," Hades said, picking up an ice pack from the mattress and pressing it against his neck.

"I guess we're sharing a room." Tyler glanced down at the pile of filthy clothes sitting next to the half-filled water jug. "Are you naked under there?"

"Doctor's orders."

"That's great," he said, walking around to the other bed. He stripped off the plastic sheet covering the comforter and dropped it on the floor. No pillow. He turned to Hades. "Give me one of your pillows."

"Get your own."

He decided to take matters into his own hands and took a step toward the other bed.

"Back off," Hades said, his voice chilling over.

The lamp had been left on in the attached bathroom. Although the light wasn't bright enough to prevent shadows from colonizing half the room, the honeyed glow reached the bed and flitted across the knife that edged out from under the pillow. The message was clear: *Come any closer, and I'll bite.*

Tyler couldn't help but be slightly impressed. Hades must have taken the blade from the knife block when he had passed through the kitchen, using his stumble as a diversion.

"You shouldn't sleep with knives," he said as Hades dropped the ice pack and hurled a pillow at him. "That's just asking for a second puncture wound."

"Then give me my gun back."

"It's out in the car, with the rest of your stuff. You can get it tomorrow. Are you really that afraid of being killed in your sleep?"

"As if you wouldn't love to smother me." He slid the knife out all the way and rested it on his knee. The blade was five inches long, slender, tapering to a lethal point. One single flick, and it could rip you open.

By the way Hades held the knife, Tyler suspected that the other boy was no stranger to close combat. Or disemboweling people.

"If I wanted to kill you, I could just shoot you," Tyler said.

Hades looked him over. "You're not carrying a gun, and you wouldn't want to make it look intentional."

"Are you faking it? Being sick?"

Hades didn't respond.

"You shot that boy."

"Which one?"

Tyler tried not to think about the connotations behind that answer. "The red-haired one, the one who was in my bedroom."

"Oh."

"If your fever's that bad, how could you still handle a gun?"

"Not that sick," Hades said. "Just overheated and tired. I feel a little better now."

"That still doesn't explain it."

"Autopilot. Hours and hours of practice in the forest. Sometimes, I practiced for so long, I couldn't move my hand afterwards. The M40 is my favorite. Can dismantle it, reassemble it with my eyes closed, if I have to." His voice turned caustic, and a cold, mocking smile cut across his lips. "That all you wanted to ask, or do you want to suck me off now, too?"

Tyler sighed. That was a bit more like the Hades he remembered. "No, uh, I wanted to thank you."

No reaction. The smile hardened, but Tyler knew better than to assume the expression was a response to actual emotion. Whatever Hades might be feeling, he hid it well.

"I mean it," Tyler said. "And I'm sorry about what happened with your mother."

"I don't need that." He slipped the knife back under his pillow and settled down again. After drawing up the sheet, he turned his back to Tyler, revealing a raised, jagged briar of old scars. "It doesn't mean anything. It's just a lie."

Tyler sighed again. Just a lie. Just like everything else in their world. Day by day, it seemed like the life he once knew slipped further and further away. For Hades, it must have been the same.

"Just get some sleep," Tyler said, turning off the bathroom lamp. "We can talk more in the morning, if you want to."

There was enough light coming in through the window now that he was able to find his way through the room without falling. He reclined on his side and closed his eyes, but remained hyperaware of every rustling sound coming from the other side of the room.

Tyler wished he had brought the pistol in from the car, just to have it at his side. Maybe he should start sleeping with a gun under his pillow. If anyone was going to get smothered in their sleep tonight, it would be him.

"Revenge," Hades murmured as Tyler began to drift off. "That's all I want now. It's the only thing that's real."

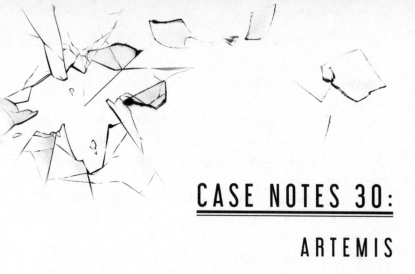

CASE NOTES 30:

ARTEMIS

Shannon couldn't fall asleep that night. The bed was comfier than any car seat, but every time she began drifting off, she remembered the way the handgun barrel had felt when it jammed into her back. As the room lightened, she removed all the books from the tall bookcase and dragged it over to the window. It made for lousy cover, and an armor-piercing round could easily penetrate the soft wicker backing, but it was better than nothing.

Once she was standing, she felt too restless to lie down again. Her stomach rumbled in discontent. Maybe a snack would help her fall asleep.

As she went into the hall, she noticed a light coming from the kitchen. She approached the doorway but lingered just beyond it. Cigarette smoke stung her nostrils.

"Who's there?" Dr. Miller demanded. "I'm armed."

"It's just me," Shannon said and stepped into the room.

Dr. Miller sat at the kitchen table, a coffee mug in one hand and a cigarette in the other. Her revolver rested within hand's reach, and loose papers covered the tabletop. The entire room was veiled in a cloud of smoke, and judging by the number of cigarette butts crammed in the ashtray beside her, she had already gone through at least one pack.

"Can I have a cigarette?" Shannon asked, sitting down. She had smoked every now and then with her best friend, Victoria, and her other friends, but had never actually developed a habit.

"No, you may not." Miller pushed the mug toward her. "Have some coffee instead."

"Where did you get cigarettes, anyway?"

"In the event of a structural collapse, they would make good currency. Usually I have enough self-control not to dip into my stockpile. They're a year old, but they do the trick."

"I can't sleep," she said, taking a sip of the brew. Bitter. Miller drank it black.

"Yeah? You're not the only one."

"I know how you feel."

Dr. Miller scoffed.

"I mean it," she said, passing the mug back. "I know what it feels like to kill someone, or at least how it feels afterward, knowing you did it."

"That's not what I am referring to, but I appreciate your sentiment," Dr. Miller said drily.

"Did you give Hades a name before you gave him to the Project? That's what you did, isn't it? Abandoned him?"

"Good god, just shut up," Dr. Miller said and extinguished her cigarette in the half-inch of lukewarm coffee at the bottom of the mug. She carried the ashtray and cup to the kitchen counter. "I can't deal with this right now."

"Why did you do it?"

"I don't want to talk about him," Dr. Miller said, dropping the glassware into the sink.

"I don't mean him," Shannon said. "I want to know

why you helped start the Project in the first place. You invented the artificial womb, right? You could've gotten millions from it, I'm sure, so why not patent it? Why use it for the Project?"

Sighing, Dr. Miller gripped the edge of the counter and stared into the basin, her back to the kitchen table. "To save our country," she said quietly.

"By killing people? By brainwashing kids, treating them like chess pieces?"

"There are people out there who believe that the Civil War was fought between America and Great Britain," Dr. Miller said, just when Shannon thought she wouldn't answer. "And there are people who don't know the slightest thing about politics, but who vote for a candidate because he has a nice catchphrase. The majority of Americans are blathering idiots. Do you really want those kinds of people determining our country's future?"

"I'd rather have them vote than a bunch of bigots," she said.

Miller turned. "Excuse me?"

"As far as I'm concerned, you're just Neo-Nazis without the swastikas."

Miller took a deep breath and brushed a hand through her hair. "Yes, I'll admit, race did play a part in determining cell donors. Whites make up the vast majority of our political and military leaders. That's just the way it is in America. We also chose cell donors whose heights were above average, who were healthy, and who had high IQs and good facial symmetry. It was based on a carefully-designed profile. It's all based on statistics."

"It's crap."

"You know, most children are conceived by mistake," she said. "Almost half of newborns are born out of wedlock.

You're special. Every part of your birth was intentional and planned with the utmost care, from conception onward."

"And what about Hades? Was his intentional?"

"I don't appreciate being chastised by a teenage girl," she said tersely. "With A-02, it was complicated, and I don't feel the need to justify my decision to you. Believe me, I wouldn't have done it if I didn't have a good reason to."

"I just don't get it. I don't buy your whole 'for the good of the nation' bullshit. There's been so much killing. I just don't get it. Why are you people doing all of this?"

"As I've told you and Tyler repeatedly, I am no longer affiliated with the Project. And when I was affiliated, the plan was never to use you kids to kill other people. You were meant to be raised as politicians and military leaders, ambassadors and diplomats."

"Fine, you're not involved, but the other Project over-seers still are. Why? What do these people want? Why go to this much trouble?"

"Are you aware of how much money private donors contribute to presidential campaigns, and even lesser governmental posts?"

Shannon didn't know.

"Hundreds of millions of dollars each year," Miller answered, returning to the table.

"But that doesn't mean that they'll win."

"No, you're right, there's no guarantee, but there are ways of improving the odds," Dr. Miller said. "And if we have a candidate in each party, well, that of course would also affect the chances of winning such an election."

"But what if it still didn't work? Then everything would go to waste."

"You're looking at this the wrong way, Shannon. You see it as a one-time deal, but it takes years to cultivate a political career. Even if you don't go on to become President, you can still find yourself in the Senate or Supreme Court. The Executive Branch is only one of three." She tapped her cigarette on the chair arm. "As far as expenditures go, the majority of costs are accumulated in the first eighteen years. In total, about $200,000 per child. After that, the child becomes largely self-dependent. The cost decreases to several thousand dollars a year, if anything. By the time the child begins his political career, other donors unrelated to the Project will pick up the slack and back him."

Miller paused.

"Cost is hardly a factor, however. Even in the beginning, when the Project was in the first stages of its conception, we had donors who were interested in contributing to the cause. I am talking about men and women you have never heard of, and whose net worth would make the Rockefellers look like bourgeoisie. People who have so much money, they wouldn't be able to spend it all in a hundred lifetimes. When you are rich beyond imagination, money loses its meaning. Then you begin to crave power and control."

"But why not just buy out a politician?"

"Because politicians, even corrupt ones, still have free will," she said stiffly. "They may have political views that contradict our own, and even if they accept a bribe, that doesn't mean they won't allow their consciences to get in the way. What we needed were individuals whose moral compasses could be molded like clay, individuals who had been raised since birth to obey their leaders' commands."

"You mean slaves."

"Forget it," Miller said and picked up one of the stapled leaflets.

Shannon stood to leave.

"Wait," Dr. Miller said. "I have a question."

Shannon turned.

"Has Tyler ever mentioned the name 'Prometheus' to you?"

"Prometheus? No. Why?"

"Remember when I told you that I thought Tyler would live?" Dr. Miller took a deep breath. "I lied. He should have died."

Shannon eased back into her seat.

"There was another project being conducted at the same time as Project Pandora," Dr. Miller said. "It was called Project Prometheus."

"What's with these names?"

"In Greek mythology, Prometheus created humans," Dr. Miller explained. "He was the one who created Pandora, the first woman."

"Oh, so a god."

"A titan," she corrected, "but essentially the same thing. Now, Project Prometheus was the pet project of one of our wealthiest donors. It involved altering the genetic codes of zygotes, with the purpose of causing beneficial mutations."

"You mean like X-Men?"

Dr. Miller laughed. "Nothing nearly as grand, I'm afraid. I'm talking about increased bone density, adaptability to hostile weather conditions, perhaps a slightly accelerated healing rate."

"Oh," she said, slightly disappointed.

"Unfortunately, the entire project was a failure. Of the fifty children, forty percent were stillborn or perished shortly after birth. The thirty who survived had an average life expectancy of seven years, with many of them suffering from serious birth defects. Only eight lived past the age of fourteen, and it was around that same time that the man responsible for funding the project died. Our resources are not infinite, and no one wanted to contribute to a project deemed a failure. The matter was put to a vote, and it was decided that the experiment would be terminated."

"Terminated." Shannon didn't like that word one bit.

"All remaining test subjects were euthanized."

"You can't be serious!"

"Statistically speaking, it was unlikely that any of them would have survived to adulthood," Dr. Miller said. "Of the eight remaining, three of them had serious health issues. The others were bound to die as well. They had spent the majority of their developmental years in an environment that made them unsuitable to be transplanted into Project Pandora."

"You mean they weren't bred to be killers," Shannon hissed.

"There was no other alternative."

"You could have dumped them at a hospital some-where!"

"And risk exposing the project?" Dr. Miller sighed. "That just wasn't an option. And, please, stop with the 'you' thing. I only assisted during the earliest stages of Project Prometheus. By the time they decided to terminate Prometheus, I was no longer a part of it. The only reason I know all of this is because I have remained in contact over the years with some of the key scientists related to the Project."

It almost seemed like Dr. Miller was relieved to speak of her own culpability, as if she took a slight pleasure from revealing her role in the Project.

What do you see me as? Shannon wondered. *Am I one of your successes or your failures? Am I even* human *to you, Doctor?*

"Why are you even telling me this?" Shannon asked.

"Tyler should be dead," Dr. Miller said. "Considering his injuries, it would have been a miracle for him to have survived long enough to reach a hospital. But this…this is just unbelievable. There have been rare cases where humans have survived massive trauma, but for someone to recover so quickly from the brink, it's extremely unlikely. I would love to have a look at his genome."

"Over my dead body."

"Relax, it's a little too late for that." She brushed her hair out of her face. "In any case, after I treated Tyler, I began thinking about Prometheus. Then I remembered the scar on his neck. At first I thought it was from a graft, but, you see, it wouldn't be uncommon for the subjects to be tattooed or branded in some way. The project wasn't like Pandora, where a transition to outside life was an end goal. The subjects would live and die in captivity."

Shannon's stomach twisted, and her hatred for this woman and the entire organization was bitter as bile, eating away at her tongue as she held back the words she wanted so much to say.

"If there was a physical mark, it's possible that someone removed it. Then it would only be a matter of hiding him in plain sight, perhaps by exchanging him with a subject of Project Pandora set for transit. But what I can't understand is why one of the scientists would go to such lengths to hide a subject and not attempt to retrieve it."

"Seriously? Did you seriously just call Tyler an 'it?'"

Dr. Miller winced. "Sorry, this is all in speculation. It was a slip of the tongue."

Shannon clenched her hands in her lap. Punching Miller wouldn't be worth it. It might make her feel good, but that was about it. "Maybe they weren't able to reach him."

"That's possible." Dr. Miller considered it. "But they may have considered him a failure, nonetheless. Genes themselves cannot be changed, but gene markers can be switched on and off. It's possible that as a result of the severe trauma, something changed in his epigenome."

"Ever since I met him, I've felt like Tyler's…different. Not in a bad way. He's just so kind, and I feel like he doesn't really care that much about his own life. After he got shot, he told me to leave him behind."

"Survivor's guilt isn't uncommon. Even if he doesn't remember, subconsciously he might still be aware that he is the sole survivor of that doomed experiment." Miller paused. "And unlike you, he wasn't conditioned for violence."

"I want you to stay away from him," Shannon growled.

"I'm not going to harm him."

"I don't want you telling him what you just told me, you hear me? He can't know about this."

"If it's true, deep down, he might already know."

"I don't care."

"What are you afraid of?"

"He has enough to worry about," she said. "He doesn't need this right now, especially if it's not true."

"I won't tell him," Dr. Miller said. "You have my word."

"Good. I just have one more question. Let's say he does have something wrong with one of his genes. Can it still hurt him, like it did with the others?"

"It's possible," Dr. Miller said. "He might be more susceptible to cancers or certain diseases. An atypically large percentage of the children suffered from leukemia."

Shannon sighed. Poor Tyler. If he didn't die of violence, he could die of cancer instead. This world could be such a crapshoot.

CASE NOTES 31:

ARTEMIS

When Shannon woke, she wasn't sure what time of day it was. With the window blocked by the bookcase, the room was thrown into a perpetual dusk. She crawled out from under the covers and trudged down the hall.

In the kitchen, a feast greeted her: cereal, pancakes, and canned fruit. Her stomach grumbled at the aroma of cooking food, only for her appetite to sour at the sight of the raven-haired boy lounging at the table.

Even in repose, Hades exuded a primal, almost animalistic vitality. She felt like she had stumbled across a sunbathing panther, where any unexpected action on her part might lead to a sudden mauling.

Ally or not, he was dangerous.

"Morning," she said civilly, retrieving a bowl and spoon from the stack on the counter.

"Good morning," Hades said, watching her. He wore the spare change of clothes she'd seen in his backpack. His shoes were on and tied tightly, as if he expected to make a run for it at any moment. She didn't even have to glance at his waist to know that he was armed.

"Where's Dr. Miller?" she asked, pouring herself some cereal. "And Tyler?"

"She's trying to feed the girl, and your boyfriend's still asleep."

"Caroline," Shannon said. "That's her name, not 'the girl.'"

"Who needs names? They don't define a person. They're just there for the convenience of others, or a way to show you own someone." As he spoke, he used his fingers to roll up a pancake. Before each bite, he dipped it in maple syrup. "These are pretty good. Even if they're just mix and water."

"Ever heard of table manners?" Shannon asked, sitting across from him. "Like a fork?"

"This is faster."

She glanced at his laced shoes. "You in a hurry to go somewhere?"

"Not really."

"Can you stop looking at me like that?" she asked, growing uncomfortable at his persistent, unwavering eye contact. He had striking eyes—intensely blue, framed by long, sooty lashes—but they were dangerous eyes, too. Looking into them was like looking into a dark sea. It was impossible to see to the bottom, let alone what lurked just beneath the surface.

"I'm just thinking about you," Hades said, licking the syrup from his lips. "It's interesting. I never thought I'd see you two again after what happened in Georgetown, but here we are. It's almost like fate. The doctor filled me in on your current situation, but I'd like to know, what are you doing here?"

"I could ask you the same."

"Ladies first," he said pleasantly.

She sighed and began telling him her story. When she reached the part about wanting to take the records to the police, Hades laughed.

"Do you really think that will do anything?" he asked.

"They can't just cover it up."

"Of course they can," Hades said. "And in case you forgot, you killed people."

"While brainwashed!"

"Just saying." He shrugged. "Just because you didn't knowingly commit a crime doesn't mean they won't charge you for it. The only thing you've got going for you is that you're a girl, but Tyler? Life sentence."

"Then what—you think we should just hide, and wait, and do nothing?"

"That's not what I'm suggesting. Running away won't solve anything." He paused to chew and swallow. "If you have no future, then there's only one thing left for you to do. Make sure the people who hurt you can't continue with what they're doing. Destroy them completely."

As he reached for another pancake, Shannon noticed a series of straight black lines on his inner arm. At first she thought that he had doodled on himself, then she realized they were tattoos.

"So, what are those supposed to be?" she asked and gestured to the tally marks. "On your left arm."

"Oh?" He looked down. "These? They're notches."

"Notches?"

"Like what you would make on a gun," he explained. "For kills."

She lost her appetite.

"That's sick." Then, worried that he would mistake her bluntness for praise, she clarified: "Sick as in disgusting."

He shrugged. "It helps me keep track."

"Why would you want to keep track of something like that?"

"I have a bad short-term memory sometimes," Hades said. "Most of the time, it's just like a dream."

"Killing, you mean." That made a little more sense. When she thought back to last night, the memories were blurred like wax figurines left on a hot windowsill, starting to ooze. If she wanted to hard enough, she suspected she would be able to convince herself that it was all a dream. Not real. No consequences.

"No, I mean life in general." He rubbed the black lines. "If I wake up a few days later and see one of these, I know that what I remember actually happened. And then that means the other memories are usually true, too."

"Is that how you tell time?" Shannon asked sourly. "By how many lives you've taken?"

"By the sound of water in the dark," he said and picked up the pancake he had his eyes on. "And the pauses between recordings."

"You're doing it again. Being unnecessarily cryptic."

"It's nothing," he said, dredging the pancake in syrup. "Sometimes I just expect people to understand what I'm thinking."

Her gaze was drawn back to the lines. Silently, she counted them. Eighteen. He had killed eighteen people.

Did he even see them as people?

"Are you going to add the three from last night to your list of conquests?" Shannon asked drily.

"No, I'm not. I don't need to do that anymore." After inhaling another pancake, he added, "Memories mean shit."

She sighed and rubbed her face. She wished Tyler was awake so that she would have someone sane to talk to. "You know what? I just want my life to go back to being normal. I'd kill to be in school right now. Even trig."

He stared at her.

"Trigonometry," she clarified, and seeing the confusion in his eyes, sighed. "Math. It's one of my least favorite subjects."

"Oh."

"And I don't mean that I'd literally kill to go back. I just miss it."

"I knew what you meant. I'm not stupid."

"I never said you were," she said. "It's just…"

"You don't trust me," he said. "I get it."

It was true, but she didn't want to admit it. "It's not that, it's just that you shouldn't be alive."

"That seems to be a popular opinion around these parts." He took a bite of his pancake. "Is that disappointment I hear in your voice?"

"Very funny," she said. "How did you escape from the hospital? Or did you?"

"Oh, so that's what it is. You're worried that I'm a spy. You're wrong. If the organization wants me brought in alive, it's only so they can waterboard me, not because they value my life. Anyway, if I wanted to kill you, don't you think I would have done it back there? You still haven't thanked me for saving you."

"You didn't do it for me."

"Are you always this distrusting?"

"Last time I checked, you wanted to kill us."

"It was Tyler I was after," he said, "and I was only following orders. Anyway, it's not like you two are free of blame. In case you forgot, you hit me on the head pretty hard. I had to get stitches. And besides, we were allies, remember?"

"I thought you didn't follow orders."

"I know what you're trying to do," Hades said. "You're trying to make me trip up, and that's not going to work.

I hate to disappoint you, but as far as the organization's concerned, we're the exact same thing. Dissidents and failures. But I also lived with Dimitri and spent a lot of time with other members of the Project, so I know more about the organization than either of you, and that makes me more dangerous. Not to mention that I'm not afraid to get my hands dirty."

"You mean kill people."

"They're the enemy."

"They're just kids like us," Shannon said.

"That kind of thinking will get yourself killed."

She gave up. Arguing with him would get her nowhere. The last thing she and Tyler needed right now was another threat on their hands. She decided to take a softer approach. "I read about you, you know. In Dr. Kosta's records."

The change was instantaneous. His whole body tensed, and his eyes narrowed. His jaw clenched, but his lips drew up ever so slightly in a smile that was not a smile.

"Why exactly are you telling me this?" he asked.

"What he did to you was unforgivable, Hades. The drugs, the electroshocks, the tank. He treated you like an object for so long. I can't imagine how lonely it must've been. You must feel so violated."

"Is this your attempt at humiliating me?"

"I understand it now, why you're —"

"Don't act like you understand a damn thing," he said, "and don't act like you're sorry. What happened to me means nothing to you. You read it in the files, who gives a shit? It's nothing more than data."

"Why you are the way you are," she finished. "That would turn anyone into a killer."

"A killer." He paused only long enough to drop his mangled pancake, crushed into crumbs and dripping syrup, back onto the plate. He stared her down with those intense, glacier-blue eyes of his, and then he smiled. "Would you like to know something interesting, Shannon? A secret I've told only two other people?"

She did not respond. The hairs prickled on the nape of her neck as he leaned in, and she suddenly became aware of a subtle scent that clung to him. Hot and spicy, like scorched firewood. For as long as she lived, she would never be able to attend another fall festival without thinking of the words he told her next.

"I committed my first kill before I came into Dimitri's care, back at the Academy," he murmured sensuously. Still smiling, he lifted his shirt to show her a vicious scar on his hard, chiseled midriff, inches from the bandages. Obviously a defensive wound instead of self-inflicted.

"My first notch."

Before Shannon could respond, a noise from the front of the room caught her attention. She turned in her seat to find Tyler stepping through the doorway.

"What time is it?" Tyler asked.

Shannon glanced at the microwave clock. "Almost 12:30."

"You should have woken me up," he said, frowning.

"Shannon and I were just about to discuss our next course of action," Hades said, wiping his hands on a napkin. In the blink of an eye, his entire demeanor had changed. His smile remained, but his voice held only amusement now, and he reclined instead of leaning forward.

"Our?" Tyler glanced at her. "You seriously want him helping us?"

"I never said that," she said.

"It's time we take the offensive," Hades said. "We need to hit them where it hurts, and we need to do it as soon as possible. If we want to destroy Project Pandora, we need to target the facility itself."

"What exactly do you mean when you say 'target' it?" Tyler asked, unsmiling.

"Oh, I'm not saying we should bomb the place. Just infiltrate it. You two can liberate the others or whatever you're planning on doing, and well, I'll do what I need to do."

"Easier said than done," Shannon said.

"It's actually not as difficult as you might think," Hades said. "The fact is, the fence is there to keep people in. So are the guards."

"But they already know we're in Colorado," Tyler said. "They've probably upped their security."

"Yeah, but who's stupid enough to walk back into a place like that?"

Shannon chuckled. "Some people, obviously."

"I'm going to get straight to the point," Hades said. "I know of a way to get inside."

"Are you serious?" Tyler asked.

"I'm serious," Hades said, and nothing in his demeanor or expression suggested otherwise. "I wouldn't be telling you this if I wasn't."

"Well, of course not," Tyler said sarcastically.

"You know, we're all here for the same reason," Hades said. "Because one way or another, we failed their expectations. We weren't leadership material, so they used us as cannon fodder. I don't know what you two did to get blacklisted, but me? I conspired to escape."

"Clearly, that didn't go well," Tyler said.

"Actually, I never had a chance to try. The only reason I failed is because I was naive enough to tell someone about my plan and believe that she wouldn't betray me.

The plan itself was practically flawless."

"Well, go on," Tyler said. "What is it?"

"Before I tell you, I want to make one thing absolutely clear," Hades said. "I'm going to kill our beloved leader, Charles Warren."

"No," Tyler said, glaring at him. "We're not killing anyone unless we have to."

"Tyler's right," Shannon said. "Violence is a final resort."

"Actually, I think there's been a slight misunderstanding. That wasn't a request, and this isn't up for discussion. You two need my help, and the only way our little alliance is going to work is if you understand that I have no intention of letting that man live. He's the reason all of this is happening."

"If you kill him, you'll become just like him," Tyler said. "You can't just go around murdering people."

Hades smirked. "Isn't that what we were born to do?"

"No, it wasn't!"

"Listen, you can pretend to be a good person all you want. Just see how well that goes for you when you have to make a split-second decision between killing and being killed. If you go into this thinking no one will die, you're not just naive—you're so stupid, there's no hope for you."

"Don't put words in my mouth. All I'm saying is that there's a better way to get rid of someone like that," Tyler said. "All we need to do is expose these people to the press, and the law will take care of them for us."

"Oh, yeah, the justice system." He rolled his eyes. "By the way, how are your bullets treating you? Do you really think you're in any condition to take part in this? You're just dead weight."

"I can still help somehow."

"You can be a decoy," Hades suggested, "and get yourself killed in the process."

"You're an asshole."

"I'm being realistic."

"See, I told you," Tyler said, turning to Shannon. "He'll shoot us in the back if it suits him."

"I really don't like it when people talk about me right in front of me," Hades said.

"He isn't our friend."

"I said I don't like it."

"Don't even try to deny it," Tyler said. "You know it's true."

Having been silent this whole time, listening to them bicker, Shannon decided to interject: "If you two keep arguing like this, we're going to get nowhere. We all have our differences, but that doesn't mean we can't work together."

"You're pretty hostile to me, Tyler," Hades said, "when I'm just trying to be honest."

"I'm hostile now? In case you've forgotten, you tried to shoot me once."

"You would have done the same. Oh, wait, no. I forgot. You're the Second Coming. You can do no wrong."

She sighed, annoyed that they were ignoring her. Boys could be so immature. Some things never changed.

"Not to mention that you sounded like you were about to cream your pants when you pulled the trigger," Tyler added in disgust.

Hades opened his mouth to respond, but before he could get a single word out, Shannon slammed her fist into the table, rattling china.

"Enough!" she said. "Hades, just tell us your plan. If it's so great, then prove it."

"Warren—"

"You can crucify him for all I care," she said.

Tyler scowled, but held his tongue.

"There's a water treatment building near the back of the facility," Hades said. "I think it's a brick building, or maybe cement. It's by the shed where they store the training gear."

"Oh, now that you mention it, I remember that," Shannon said. "It was brick, and it didn't have any windows. Everyone in my group thought it was a prison."

Hades smirked. "Where they tortured the bad kids who forgot to return equipment?"

"Yeah, that sounds about right."

Tyler frowned and said nothing. Glancing at him, Shannon wondered if he even knew what they were talking about. Just how much did he remember? Could Dr. Miller be right about Project Prometheus?

"It was the summer before my sixteenth birthday when I found out what it really was," Hades said. "The sewage main's there, and there's a drainage pipe large enough to crawl through. It leads right under the fence. There's a locked grate on the other side, but it's just padlocked. Easy to break with the right tools. I planned to shoot it off."

"How do you know all this?" Tyler asked warily.

"I have my methods."

Tyler snorted. "Yeah, like bullshitting."

"Just trust me."

"I want to know how you found it."

"I don't want to talk about it," Hades said.

"Why?"

Hades swallowed, and his gaze swept from Tyler to Shannon to the window across the room. He licked his lips. "I think the pipe leads out into a river, or, no, a water-filled ravine," he said. "His bones are probably still there, underwater."

Tyler's cynical smirk began to fade.

"I think I bashed his head in with a rock."

"You think?" Shannon asked.

"Some memories are hazy. Give me a moment." Hades rested his face in his hand and closed his eyes. A thin smile crept across his lips as he reached down and under his shirt, surely touching the scar, that first notch. "No, it was a brick. He brought me there. It was damp and cold inside. I knew what he wanted. I didn't know what I intended to do. I'd seen the way he looked at her. The little treats he put aside for her. Nine was so beautiful, and I knew that soon he would go for her. He liked them more. The girls, I mean. Young, but not too young. I'd heard the rumors. I'd never let him have her. I thought I could break his neck and stage it as a suicide, but then I found myself, my hands, covered in blood. I did it all for her."

Opening his eyes, Hades looked at Shannon, but his gaze remained distant. Though he stared into her eyes, he didn't really seem to see her. Maybe he was thinking about that other girl, the one he spoke of.

"I searched for a place to hide the body, and I came across the sewage main. The manhole was locked with a sliding bolt, easy to open from the inside. I followed the pipe down, and then I saw it for myself. The outside world."

CASE NOTES 32:

HADES

Hades had waited one month after his discovery of the sewage pipe before desperation drove him to attempt escape, but it took them only two hours to plan for the infiltration.

Dr. Miller sat with them, interjecting here and there with little tidbits of information that allowed them to hone their plan further. Hades felt no attachment to her now, nothing but aggravation and aching betrayal. He considered his previous night's behavior to be the result of stress and fever, not a true need for love or acceptance. And why would it be? He had spent his whole life without a family. Blood ties meant nothing.

Even though it hurt, he forced himself to sit still and listen as she recited everything she knew about the Academy and its overseer, Charles Warren.

"Charles has a very rigid schedule that he rarely deviates from," Miller said, after checking on her whiny little spawn for the fifth time. "On the third Thursday of every month, he visits the Academy and stays over the weekend. Usually, he leaves early Monday morning or late Sunday night. If there is a serious incident, he will also go out there."

The third Thursday. Fifteen days away. If Charles Warren arrived on Thursday evening, they would have a three-day window to act. Better to play it safe and arrive Friday evening. That gave them sixteen days to plan. Sixteen days for his wound to heal. Good enough. Hades doubted he'd get a second chance.

"It sounds like we're done here," he said, pushing out of his seat. "I'm going back to sleep, so don't bother me."

Instead of going to his room, he stopped in front of the master bedroom. Squeaky cartoon voices leaked through the closed door. He reached for the knob and turned it.

As he entered the room, the little girl sprawled on the bed looked up at him. Her eyes were large and dark like drops of oil. Like the eyes of a rodent.

A rodent. At the thought, a vague memory returned to him. One winter, some boys in his subset had found an abandoned nest of rats living behind the barracks' radiator. The baby rats became Subset A's secret pets, and although the majority of them died within the first several weeks, one lived well into Hades's ninth year. Until the night a boy from Subset B found the boys playing with it.

"What's that?" B-05 had appeared out of nowhere. He didn't belong in the Subset A barracks, but it wasn't uncommon for kids to sneak around between floors.

"Nothing," said A-06, a chubby boy with curly brown hair and a face like a toothless puppy. A-06 reached for Ratty, but before he could pick it up, B-05 grabbed the rodent by its tail.

"Gross, it's a rat!" B-05 declared and gave a little yelp as Ratty tried to right itself by crawling up his hand. He flung his arm around in a panic, and the rodent lost its grip and sailed across the room.

Ratty struck the wall with a sound like the crack of a frozen twig and fell twitching to the floor.

At the time, Hades had been sitting on his cot, reading a book on military maneuvers and thinking about how he might apply them to the paintball wargames. But when he saw the dying rodent, something snapped in him. As the creature squealed pitifully and blood beaded on its whiskers, Hades's vision faded.

Now that Hades thought about it, that was the first time he had a rage-induced blackout. He couldn't remember dropping the book, or getting up, or punching B-05 in the face. But he remembered waking up to find himself straddling B-05, slamming his fists down again and again into the boy's head and stomach, and blood damp on his hands.

Hades also remembered weeping for the little animal, but he had trouble believing that part of the memory was real. It was just too bizarre and irrational. Why cry for a pest?

Now, he stared into Caroline's eyes, and thought about how he could end it like B-05 had. In a single moment, he could end it. He could show his mother the monster that she had created.

"...my brother?" Caroline's was saying.

"What?" he asked, feeling disoriented all of a sudden.

"Are you my brother?"

Her question took him off guard.

"What makes you think that?" he asked.

"Well, you look a lot like Mommy," she said, sitting up. "You have big, pretty blue eyes like she does, and all my friends' brothers kind of look like them."

"You guessed correctly," Hades said. "I'm your brother."

She looked at him in wonder. "Really? Cool! Mommy

never said I had a big brother."

He shut the door and took a step into the room. "Before your cell donor made you, she made me. And she threw me away."

Caroline's smile faded. "My what? Cell donor? What's that?"

"She tossed me out like trash," Hades said, hearing a razor's edge of anger in his voice.

It would be easy to lose himself in that black, roiling rage. Give in, let it consume him, and destroy everything.

He had done it before.

If he did it again, he might be able to find peace in the solitude of being the only one alive around him. Then this terrible yearning and jealousy worrying at him like a pair of starved wolves would just let go, go away, and leave the emptiness he *needed*.

"So, what makes you so special?" he asked, approaching the bed. "Why did she keep you? Is it because you're a girl, or is it something else?"

"Um…"

"If you had never been born, maybe she would have come for me instead," he said softly, looking down at her. "Then none of this would have happened, and Nine wouldn't be dead. Because of you, I have *nothing*."

Caroline nibbled on her lip, then brightened. She crawled over the bed and fished a raggedy teddy bear from under the covers.

"Here," she said, holding the stuffed animal out to him. "This is Sunny. Mommy gave him to me the first time I got sick. Now, you can have him."

Hades took the teddy bear from her. If its color had been its namesake, only a few patches of sunshine-yellow hair remained. The rest of the stuffed animal's coat was a dirty pus color, and it smelled nasty. Turning it over in his hands, he came across several crusty patches of dried food.

"Why are you giving me this?"

"He makes me feel better when I'm sad, so maybe he'll help you, too," Caroline said. "He's my favorite, so take good care of him, okay?"

As the little girl smiled up at him, Hades was hit by an unexpected emotion. Not envy, anger, or loathing, but a deep profound exhaustion. Everyone around him either died or went away, and he was so sick of it. He didn't want to live this way anymore, in a world not meant for him. He was just so sick of everything.

This is all just a trick of hers so that I feel sorry for her. If not for her, I wouldn't be this way. Those bad things wouldn't have been done to me. It's all her fault I have no future, and someone needs to pay for it.

He couldn't bring himself to believe it. The more he tried to see Caroline as a conduit for his rage, the more his anger slipped away from him, until he felt lost and confused.

Why was he feeling this way? These emerging emotions, they had been dead for so long, so why were they coming back when he didn't need them? Emotions just got in the way of everything. It would be so much easier if he felt absolutely nothing.

"Are you okay?" she asked, stirring him from his daze.

"Why do you ask?"

"You look sad."

"I'm not sad."

"And you're squeezing Sunny like you're trying to kill him!"

"Oh." He chuckled mirthlessly and held the teddy bear out to her. "Here. Take it."

"Keep him, he's yours. Hey, do you want to play checkers?"

Hades had no idea what checkers was or were, but before he could respond, he heard the door creak open.

"What are you doing in here?" Dr. Miller asked, her voice as cold as ice. She was finally showing her true colors.

"Sibling bonding," Hades said, turning to her. "Caroline and I were just about to play checkers."

"I see," she said dully. "May I have a word with you in private?"

He followed her into the adjoined bathroom.

"I told you that I don't want you with her unsupervised," Miller said, crossing her arms. Now that she was alone with him, her mask had crumbled to reveal a frigid core. Just like he knew it would. She was no different than he was.

"You don't have the right to tell me what to do," he said. "I'm done following orders."

"What did you tell her?"

"Just the truth. I'm curious, what did I do to make you hate me so much that you gave me to the Project?"

Miller narrowed her eyes. "I don't hate you. I never did. I just… At the time, I saw it as an opportunity for progress. It was an experiment."

It was an experiment. Those four words shook Hades to the core in a way he never imagined words could, bringing the anger back in an instant, leaving him trembling in rage and wrenching anguish.

He felt violated, as if by bringing him into this world, she had committed the ultimate transgression against him. Even the sensory deprivation tank sessions at the Georgetown safehouse couldn't compare to this…this feeling of dehumanization, of being *nothing*.

She had given him life, but to her, the act had been

no more personal than DNA in a petri dish, than the indifferent mechanisms of the artificial womb.

So what was he?

Did she even see him as human? As alive?

"My life isn't an experiment," he said in a tight, strangled voice he didn't immediately recognize as his own. "It isn't an experiment. Everything I've endured so far, *it isn't a fucking experiment.*"

Darkness bled across the edges of his vision. A low metallic ringing filled his ears. The shaking intensified. Aware that he was moments away from losing himself, he took a deep breath.

This is happening to someone else, he told himself, and exhaled slowly. *The person she is speaking about is dead. This is happening to someone else. A-02 is dead. He died back in the deprivation tank, and I am all that he became. This is happening to someone else.*

The overwhelming emotions faded with the trembling. His grip around the teddy bear's head loosened, and a familiar, soothing calmness washed through his veins like a dose of sedatives.

As Hades looked around at the bathroom's decor, he had the impression it was different than how it was a second ago. Changed. Not real.

That's right, nothing's real. It's all just a lie anyway.

"Are you even listening to what I'm saying?" Dr. Miller asked, and he realized that she was still talking. He wasn't sure how long she had been talking for, or how long he had been standing there for. Not that it really mattered.

"I'm listening, I just don't care," he said, dropping the teddy bear. He felt numb and washed out. Except for the soft, persistent ringing in his ears, it was a good thing. "Now, I need to go patrol the perimeter."

"Excuse me?"

"I'm going for a walk outside." Some fresh air might help make his lingering tinnitus go away. At the very least, he would be able to acquire a good picture of the land's layout, allowing him to prepare for an attack. In the event that the Project found this place, he wanted to be aware of every rock formation, cluster of trees, and surrounding building that could offer a tactical advantage during a firefight.

"Wait. Don't walk away from me. Tell me what I can do to—"

With his emotions smothered, Hades returned to a state of cold, indifferent practicality. "What can you do? The way I look at it, you really only have two options. You can either betray me or you can help me. You and I both know that Project Pandora is cleaning house. And you were once the one who authorized it. See, I don't remember much, but I remember that little poker game. The one where you poisoned a man."

Miller didn't answer.

"Now, if I have to make an educated guess," Hades said flatly, "I would say that something's changed since then. Changed in a big way. You're not very high up in the organization anymore, or else you would have already turned those two in. The risk of selling them out must have been greater than the risk of harboring them. Am I correct?"

Silence.

"In any case, with what happened last night, I think it's fair to say if you crawl back to Charles Warren, you're dead. Knowing him, he'll kill your daughter as well. And we both know him so well, don't we?" He paused to gather his thoughts. "I'm going to give you a way out. I need weapons, I need the right tools, and I need information. But that's as far as your involvement in this mission will go. Aside from that, I want nothing to do with you. And once this is over, I'm done. Gone. I don't want to be a part of your family."

"I understand," Miller said. "I'll do whatever I can to help you."

He smiled at her. "I'm glad we've reached an understanding."

Enjoy this truce while it lasts, you life-ruining bitch, because someday you're going to wish I died in the machine you created.

He left the bedroom and walked down the hall. When he entered the kitchen, Tyler and Shannon stopped talking and looked at him. Ignoring them, he went to the backdoor and stepped outside.

As he reached the edge of the tree line, the back door slammed behind him. He stopped and turned. "What is it?"

"We need to talk," Tyler said.

"Not now." Hades felt suddenly vulnerable, exposed, like his conversation with Dr. Miller had torn apart his armor. Although he felt something like kinship toward Tyler and Shannon, who had also endured Kosta's brainwashing and experiments, he didn't want to show them this side of him. The moment he showed other people his weaknesses, he would be opening himself up to betrayal.

"I know why you came here."

"I didn't come," Hades said. "I was brought."

"I'm not going to let you hurt her."

"Do you mean Dr. Miller?"

"Your mother," Tyler said tersely.

"Right now, my cell donor's the last thing on my mind," Hades said and thought that would be the end of it. But apparently Tyler was intent on launching a personal attack against him, because as Hades turned to head deeper into the woods, the other boy just kept on blathering.

"Just admit it," Tyler said. "The only thing you care about is getting revenge, and as long as you get your way in the end, you don't care how many lives you destroy in the process. You're dead inside, and you want everyone else to suffer just as much as you have."

He stopped. "Does this mean you disapprove of my plan?"

"I disapprove of the fact that you want to murder innocent people just to get to the man you hate."

"What exactly are you fighting for, Tyler?" he asked, turning back. "Why are you doing all this, if not to get revenge?"

"Justice. These people need to be brought to justice, but that doesn't mean you should act as their goddamned executioner!"

Hades paused, giving it some thought. Then he chuckled. "You say it like there's a difference between the two. Justice and revenge, they're just different sides of the same coin. One's just a lie used to justify the other."

"That's not true," Tyler snapped, narrowing his eyes.

"Oh, it's true, all right, and you know it," Hades said. "Deep down, we're more similar than you'd think."

"We're nothing alike."

"Do you ever wonder if the world truly exists?"

"No."

"You never feel invisible when you're walking through a crowded street? Or look up at the night sky on a starless night and wonder if it's really there."

"Never."

"I used to travel a lot for Dr. Kosta," Hades said, taking a step closer to Tyler. "Going into towns I'd never seen before, just passing through. And I used to play a game with myself to pass the time, imagining the earth falling away behind me, the same way it did whenever I entered the tank. The funny thing is if I ever passed through those towns again, I actually felt a little surprised, seeing that they were still there. I think a part of me really, truly believed that those places ceased to exist the moment I left them. I got the same feeling whenever I returned to Georgetown. The streets were so familiar, but at the same time, they were different too, like the neighborhood was just a movie set made to look the same."

"Do you get some sort of amusement out of telling other people how screwed up you are?" Tyler asked mirthlessly. "Or do you just think everyone thinks the same way as you?"

No. Hades knew that he was an outsider, but that didn't mean he wanted to remain one.

"Isn't it important to confide in others?" Hades asked. "Isn't that a part of making friends?"

"You want to be my friend," Tyler said, unconvinced.

"What would you prefer me to be? Your enemy?" He smiled. "We're after the same thing, Tyler. We might as well get to know each other. We can bond over our past experiences."

"Oh joy, like how much I enjoyed shooting someone, without even realizing it."

"Did you?" Hades asked.

"Are you kidding?"

"Actually, I enjoy talking to you. I find it curious the way you behave."

Tyler didn't answer. As Hades strode closer, he took one step backwards. His amber eyes darkened with confusion—and something else. Was that fear? Anger? Despair?

"You know, I remember that Dimitri had me reteach you how to use a gun," Hades said. "I find that interesting. He thought it was just short-term memory loss related to the programming, but really, it was like you'd never fired a gun before. You weren't bad at it once you got the hang of it, but you were more of a novice than I expected, all things considered."

"Why does that matter?"

"It fascinates me, really." He leaned forward. "How could you forget how to fire a gun when we were taught how to shoot the moment we could hold a pistol? How could you be born there and end up like this?"

"It's called a conscience. Normal people have it, and it's something you're obviously missing."

"We weren't raised to have consciences."

"Speak for yourself."

"How exactly did you break free from your programming?" Hades asked.

"I don't know. It just happened. Why are we even discussing this?"

"You're different from any of us, Tyler, and I want to know why. What makes you merciful? Why are you willing to sacrifice yourself for others, or try so hard to expose what you can destroy instead? Don't you want the people who hurt you to suffer? Don't they deserve to feel pain?"

"They deserve justice."

"You're not from the Academy, are you?" Hades asked, staring him down.

"Excuse me?"

"Who are you?"

"You're on crack."

"Now you're just avoiding the question," Hades said pleasantly.

"Because it's stupid!"

"Is this a test? Another experiment?"

"The hell's that supposed to mean?"

"I'm looking forward to it," Hades said, "to finding out who you are beneath your programming."

CASE NOTES 33:

ARTEMIS

Club 451 had all the trappings of an upscale establishment: valet parking, bouncers in three-piece suits, and an army of gorgeous hostesses that made Shannon feel both ugly and underdressed the moment she stepped through the glass double-doors.

"So, are we supposed to just wait here for him?" Shannon asked, looking around. She wished she had put on a little makeup before leaving the cabin, but she didn't own makeup anymore. Oh well. Looking pretty was the least of her concerns right now. Their planned infiltration was only five days away. Time was running out.

"At least there's a nice view," Hades said, pausing to track the swish of a hostess's miniskirt.

Shannon cleared her throat. "Really?"

He looked back at her and smiled. "What?"

"I'd hate to see what's going through your head right now," she said, rolling her eyes. "It would probably scar me for life."

"Actually, I think you'd enjoy it."

"Yeah, no. I'm not a sadist."

"Neither am I," Hades said, then glanced down at her

hips with a smirk on his face. "I was just thinking how good you'd look in a skirt like that."

Cheeks searing in embarrassment, Shannon turned to greet the man who approached them.

Unlike the other employees at Club 451, the man's greatest attribute was size, not beauty. He was nearly seven feet tall, with a shaved head the size of a bowling ball, no eyebrows, and a nose like a gnarled mushroom. He looked like he could shatter boulders using his pit-bull jaw alone, and judging from the state of his teeth, that estimate wasn't too far off.

"Boss is ready to see you now," the man said, ushering them forward.

At this early hour, the club was crowded, but not filled to capacity. Some people lounged on the tufted leather couches, chatting and sipping martinis. Others hung around the bar. Only a few looked up as Shannon and Hades passed. If the clientele wondered how two teenagers had gotten into such a high-end establishment, dressed as grungy as they were, they kept their curiosity to themselves.

The bald man led them past the horseshoe bar and through an unmarked metal door that he opened with a keycard. He held the door for them and closed it as soon as they stepped into the storage room on the other side.

Crates and shelves crowded the room. Extra chairs were piled against one wall, dismantled stage lights against the other.

A dark-haired man waited for them inside. He was as wiry as the first guy was huge, and carried a pistol on his hip, in full sight. He took Hades's backpack, dumped its contents out on an empty table, and sorted through the pile. He inventoried the belongings in an emotionless drawl:

"Cash. Pistol, loaded. Suppressor, detached. Holster."

"Hands against the wall and legs spread," the bald giant said gruffly. "You first, *pretty boy.*"

Upon hearing his new nickname, Hades looked like he wanted to kick the guy's teeth in, but he did as he was told, pressing his hands against the smooth plaster. As the man patted him down for concealed weapons, Hades stared at the wall. He kept his expression placid and his body still, but his eyes smoldered with restrained rage.

The frisking took nearly two minutes, and near the end of it, she began to worry that he might lash out. He reminded her of a caged beast that the zookeeper had prodded one too many times, teeth bared and hackles raised.

"You next, girlie," the bald man said, and she stepped up to the wall.

As the man's rough, moist hands slid down her back with deliberate slowness, she tensed. His breath smelled like smoke and tooth decay. When he reached her hips, she distracted herself by thinking about Tyler, who had wanted to go along with them but had been swiftly reprimanded by Dr. Miller.

"You're not running around in your condition," Dr. Miller had told him. "Besides, your face is plastered all over the news. Do you want to get shot again?"

It was for the best, but not for the first time, Shannon wondered if Dr. Miller had an ulterior motive for looking after Tyler. Maybe the doctor had more to do with Project Prometheus than she had initially implied. More likely, she just didn't want to be alone with Hades, and preferred Tyler's company. Shannon didn't blame her.

"All clear," the bald man said, taking his hands off her.

She sighed in relief. Her skin crawled with the memory

of the man's sweaty touch. She couldn't wait to get this over with and take a shower.

The dark-haired man zipped the backpack shut and handed it to Hades, but kept the handgun. "We'll hold onto this for you until you're done with Mr. Rosario."

"That's fine," Hades said.

"Follow me," the bald man said and led them through a second door, also requiring a keycard, and down a set of stairs.

"Pretty boy," she said to Hades as they descended. "Can I call you that from now on?"

He shot her a dark look. "Not unless you want to die in your sleep."

The basement room was furnished even more lavishly than the club above, with a marble checkerboard floor and ebony wall paneling. Two black leather couches faced each other, separated by a low glass table between them. Mr. Rosario sat at one of the couches, and as Shannon and Hades entered, he shut the laptop resting on his lap and placed it on the coffee table.

"Patrick, you may leave now," Mr. Rosario said. He was in his mid-thirties, with green eyes and curly blond hair. A scar on one cheek detracted from his otherwise handsome features.

"Yes, sir," the bald man said and shut the door.

"Sit down, sit down." Rosario broke into a bright smile. His dimples added to his charming expression. "Francine told me to expect visitors, but she never mentioned that she was sending over a couple of kids. Are you two even old enough to vote?"

"Age is irrelevant," Hades said.

"Except when it comes to statutory rape!" Rosario said and burst into laughter.

Shannon resisted the urge to groan in disgust. Glancing at Hades, she was surprised to see his mouth firm in a barely perceivable scowl. Wow, did he actually have a moral compass?

After catching his breath, Rosario took a closer look at Hades. "Francine never mentioned having a son, either. She's been keeping secrets from me, apparently."

"I'm not her son," he said, sitting next to Shannon on the other couch.

"Well, you're most certainly not Shannon, so you must be...Hades?"

"Yes."

"An unusual moniker."

"I wasn't the one who chose it," he said flatly.

"I *love* it. It adds a rather theatrical undertone to this encounter. Very atmospheric." Rosario's grin widened. "A god of death visits a dealer of death. I should write a screenplay about that."

"Did Dr. Miller tell you what we need?" Shannon asked.

Rosario turned to her and dipped his chin in a quick nod, looking more like an excited schoolboy than a gunrunner. "She did, and I've already procured it. You're lucky, darling. With a custom order like this, it usually takes me longer than just a week to get everything together. But I have a special spot in my heart for Francine. She saved my life once, you know. I had an unfortunate encounter with the business end of a Civil War–era bayonet. Did she tell you about that?"

"No, she didn't," Shannon said.

"That's too bad. It's a fascinating story. It really is." He stood. "Before we get down to business, how about something to drink? Shannon?"

"Just a water, please," she said, deciding that it would

be rude to refuse their host's offer.

"Hades?"

"No, thank you. I'm not thirsty, sir."

His politeness surprised her, especially since it appeared genuine. Then again, they had both been raised to respect authority figures. It seemed that his lessons in etiquette were more enduring.

Mr. Rosario retrieved two bottles of spring water from a bar fridge built into the wall's wood paneling. He set the drinks on the coffee table.

"I was told that you will be paying in cash," Rosario said.

"That's correct." Hades removed a sealed stack of bills from his bag. He and Shannon had counted it out beforehand. "Ten thousand dollars in twenties and fifties."

"It's a rather curious order, isn't it?" Rosario rested his hands on the sofa top and leaned forward, grinning at the both of them. "Something that can be disguised as a paintball gun. I gave Francine's request some thought, and I think I found a solution to your problem."

Rosario went to the wall at the back of the room and ran his hands along the underside of the millwork. The entire decorative panel slid forward on oiled hinges, revealing a safe built into the wall. He typed a password into the keypad and opened the steel door.

From the otherwise empty compartment, he took out a metal case and a small canvas bag. He carried them over, set the bag on the floor, and laid the gun case on the table.

"It was originally a Mini Uzi," Rosario said proudly, opening the case. "An artist friend of mine helped with the modifications."

Shannon expected a shoddy product, but was shocked by how much the modified submachine gun resembled a paintball marker without the hopper and gas tank. Even just changing its color made a world of difference.

"Anodized aluminum plating," Rosario explained, running an admiring hand over the shiny red-and-silver barrel. "And what you have over here is the collapsible stock. See these little attachments? You'll be able to secure the carbon dioxide tank this way. They're welded in place, so the tank won't fall off if you're running around. As for the hopper, it'll go on the optical mount."

He reached into the bag and pulled out a paintball hopper and CO2 tank. Or at least what resembled a CO2 tank. When Shannon picked it up, she found it incredibly light. She passed the canister to Hades, who regarded it for a brief moment, then set it down again.

Rosario attached the empty hopper to the scope mount, then took the fake CO2 canister and clipped it onto the stock.

"Well?" he asked, displaying the weapon. "What do you think? A nice disguise, isn't it? It's easy to remove and assemble, and it'll fire just fine. God, I love this gun."

"It'll do," Hades said.

"Good, because Francine ordered three of them. And because I like you two, I'm going to throw in some extra magazines as well. I'll have Patrick bring them out to your car." Rosario finished dismantling the gun, then took a small plastic case from within the canvas bag. "Now, these are the electronics Francine ordered. Live-streaming, just like you asked. You'll be able to get a good signal even if you're in the middle of nowhere, and you can stream the video to multiple sites at once. Great audio and video quality, too. This stuff is practically the best on the market. I can help you set it up right now, if that's what you'd like."

"That would be great," Shannon said.

"If you don't mind me asking, what exactly are you going to be filming?" His green eyes twinkled with interest.

"A liberation," Shannon said.

"An execution," Hades said, earning a chuckle of approval from Rosario.

She shot Hades a glare. "In case you forgot, *pretty boy*, we're going to be rescuing people."

"And killing others," he added, returning her scowl with a wicked smirk. Did he really have to be so flippant about it? Was he doing this just to piss her off?

Rosario beamed at them. "Well, whatever you kids decide to call it, I can't wait to tune in."

CASE NOTES 34:

DR. FRANCINE MILLER

Three days before the planned infiltration, Francine Miller drove to five stores before she was able to check all the items off her shopping list. At a hardware store, she purchased bolt cutters and a blowtorch, a wicked device that could shear through solid metal. Black uniforms came from a clothing store, tennis shoes and hiking boots from another. Before going to her next stop, she took a detour to a McDonald's and got a chocolate shake for Caroline, who had begun to whine. At a gun dealer, she purchased a box of 9mm cartridges.

The total came up to over 800 dollars, and Francine paid in cash. A small sacrifice, considering the money wasn't hers. She derived a bitter satisfaction from knowing that Senator Lawrence Hawthorne was unwittingly funding the destruction of the organization that had *dared* try to remove her.

Project Pandora was dead to her now.

After Francine made her last stop, she drove fifteen miles out of the way until she found a workable payphone. She took a scrap of paper from her purse and read the number scribbled across it. She thumbed the gummy buttons, keeping her eyes on the car as the line she dialed began to ring. Then there was just the soft hiss of an open line.

"Hello, Dr. Finch," she said.

"Who is this?" a man asked, his voice just a hoarse whisper.

"Francine Miller."

He chuckled—a dry, rasping sound. "You must have a good reason to call, Francine. It's been far too long."

"It has."

"Is this line being monitored?"

"Not on my end."

"How is your daughter doing?"

"She's doing well," Dr. Miller said. "But I didn't call to talk about her. I found something that belongs to you."

"Is that so?"

"Yes. An item from one of your former experiments."

"I see."

"From Prometheus, actually."

Even across a distance of hundreds if not thousands of miles, Dr. Finch could not conceal his surprise. At the sound of his low gasp, Francine smiled.

"I'm talking about the boy you sent to Dimitri Kosta."

"I don't know what you're talking about."

"If you say so," she said. "Then we have nothing else to discuss. Goodbye—"

"Wait, wait, don't hang up." He cleared his throat. "Can you describe this boy to me?"

She sighed. "He's blond and he has hazel eyes. They're a very striking color, almost amber, in fact. He has a scar on the back of his neck, where something on his skin was surgically removed. If I had to guess, I would say it was a tattoo. Does that sound about right?"

Finch did not respond.

"I'm curious," Francine said. "How exactly did you manage to do it? It couldn't have been easy, getting him out of there."

"Right before transit," Finch said. "The other boy fit his profile closely enough and ended up on the examination table instead. All it took was a pair of hair-clippers and a tattoo gun. I was the one to oversee the vivisection. The others didn't even realize his tattoo was fresh."

"You were always fond of your little pet projects. I know how hard it must have been for you to terminate the Project."

"We had such high hopes. I still see Prometheus as one of my greatest failures."

"Why him?"

"He had no physical or mental defects, or at least none that came to our attention. He was healthy and of above-average intelligence. If I hadn't known any better, I would have assumed that he was part of a control group. How did you find out?"

"Your experiment wasn't a failure, Finch, and that boy's living proof of it. He was shot twice at close range. The second bullet punctured multiple internal organs. The blood loss should have killed him, or he should have died of septic shock. But he's still alive now, and he's doing well. If I didn't know any better, I would call it a miracle of God."

"You can't be serious. Is this some kind of joke you're playing?"

"You're smarter than that, Finch."

Caroline stared at her through the car window. Francine lifted a finger in the universal "one minute" gesture.

"What exactly are we dealing with here?" Finch asked.

"I don't have the proper instruments to assess that,"

she said, "but I can assure you, this is not a bluff."

"Where is he?"

"Somewhere you'll never find him. Without my help, that is."

"Are you proposing an exchange?"

"Yes."

"Why haven't you gone to Charles Warren about this?"

"A schism is forming in the organization, and the Project's cleaning house, Finch. Just like it did with you. I think Charles Warren has finally gone off the deep end and has let his paranoia get the best of him. He thinks there's a conspiracy against him, and I've become a liability to him. I also don't trust him to handle the boy with the same care that you will. Warren will see him as a loose end, not a breakthrough."

"Our friend was never one for the finer points of science," Finch agreed.

"Here are my terms: I want a safe place for myself and my daughter, and whatever you plan to do with this boy, I want to be a part of it."

"How do I know this isn't a trap?"

"It's been six months," she said. "You're water under the bridge by now, Finch. Old news. Charles couldn't care less about finding you when he has far greater matters to worry about."

"Is all this true?"

"Trust me, you'll know when you see him. He's incredible."

"Tell me where you are. I'll send someone over there to pick you three up. How is his condition? Will it be safe to move him?"

"You'll want to take all precautions and prepare appropriate transport. He's also a wanted fugitive, so it will be dangerous to take him across state lines."

"I can handle that," Finch said hastily. "I'll have a medical van equipped, and emergency surgeons on standby."

Francine Miller smiled. The old boy was getting excited.

"I'm going to give you three days to think about it and make preparations," she said. "I have a few more obligations I have to deal with. He will keep until then."

"Wait, let's discuss this first."

"Trust me on this," she said. "If everything goes as planned, by Friday evening Charles Warren will be history and you will be reunited with your precious experiment."

CASE NOTES 35:

ARTEMIS

The night before the infiltration, Shannon couldn't fall asleep. Restless, she crawled out of bed and put on her clothes.

Gathering her hair back, she stepped into the hall and found her way to the boys' room. She expected to find the door locked, but when she tried turning the knob, it opened. She stood in the doorway, waiting for her eyes to adjust.

"Tyler?" She kept her voice at a loud whisper. "Are you awake?"

Nothing moved in the darkness, but her vision acclimated enough that she could make out the outlines of two beds.

Which one was his?

She decided that Hades had chosen the first bed, the one closest to the door. In the event of an emergency, he would have wanted a clear route out, while Tyler would have preferred the bed with the nice view.

She approached the second bed near the window, whose drapes were closed and let in only the faintest predawn glow. She sat down on the edge of the mattress.

It wasn't chilly in the room, but Tyler must have been cold. He slept in a fetal position with the blanket drawn over himself, hooding him. His face was turned away from her, making it difficult to discern his features.

"Tyler," she repeated, reaching out to rub his lower back, far from the healing wounds. He shifted in his sleep, the blanket slid down his shoulders, and her fingers touched a twisted, wiry net of scar tissue where only smooth skin should have been.

She froze, the breath trapped in her lungs.

Wrong bed.

Her common sense screamed at her to get back, but something else rooted her there.

Being careful not to wake Hades, she gently traced his scars with the tips of her fingers. They felt cool, waxy. They crossed through almost every inch of his back.

Who could have done this?

Then a memory slammed down on her full force, and she knew at once how he had received these scars. It had been two years ago, maybe longer, and very late at night. Her entire subset had been awakened and marched into the mess hall. By the time they arrived, the room was already abuzz with life. The entire Academy was there.

Some kids thought that the Leader had died. Others suspected that there had been a murder, or maybe an escape attempt.

"Quiet!" a guard shouted, silencing the conversations.

The doors to the mess hall opened, and the Leader—who she now knew as Charles Warren—strode inside, holding a long, thin rod. Two guards followed behind him, each gripping either arm of the beautiful, dark-haired boy between them.

Not just any boy. A-02, a subject being trained for

a military role like herself, who she sometimes played against during paintball wargames.

A-02's shirt was torn and muddy, and blood seeped from a split lip. His gas-flame blue eyes smoldered with hatred. He stared straight ahead, refusing to look at the crowd that parted around him as he approached the pole in the center of the mess hall. He kept his chin up, his head held high, and his mouth set in a determined line.

The pole was just one of several used to support the structure. A metal ring was bolted to the front of it, and for as long as she could remember, a pair of locked handcuffs had always hung from that ring, soldered into place. A stool stood nearby, for the younger kids who were too short to reach. If a kid was caught stealing food, slacking off, or shirking their duties, the culprit might be handcuffed there all day, forced to stand at attention. A worse crime warranted a dozen hard strikes with a switch or cane, then exhibition for a minimum of twelve hours.

This, apparently, would be a case of the latter. Since it was so late, A-02 would probably be forced to stand there through the night and into tomorrow, his welt-covered back visible to all who passed him.

The guards took him to the pole and locked his hands in place above his head.

"Subject Two of Subset A has committed the grave offense of attempted desertion," Charles Warren drawled, and a collective gasp rippled through the crowd. Escape attempts were rare and unsuccessful, and whenever they occurred, the perpetrators were punished severely. Some of them simply disappeared, and the ones who came back were changed. Terrified and docile, flinching at the smallest sounds or the gentlest touch.

Charles nodded toward one of the guards. The guard

used a utility knife to cut A-02's shirt open, exposing his naked back.

His skin was as pale and unsullied as fresh milk.

It wouldn't be for long.

"This is what happens to deserters." Charles stepped behind A-02 and struck him across the back with the switch. A red welt appeared almost instantly, livid against his smooth white skin.

A-02 tensed, but if he made a sound, it was too soft for her to hear. As the switch came down again, he turned his head one way, then the other. His gaze wandered across the room, in search of someone. Then he looked ahead once more.

A-02 refused to cry out, even when he bled on the fifteenth blow. He stared into the crowd, at a person she couldn't pinpoint, though she tried to. He clenched the pole so tightly, his knuckles blanched, and the tendons in his throat were as rigid as cables.

"Is this punishment not enough for you, Subject Two?" Warren snapped. "Do you remain unrepentant? Is this silence your way of showing everyone that you're too good for the rod? Fine then, let's show them what happens to deserters who refuse to follow orders!"

Charles Warren threw the switch aside and reached down, fumbling with his belt. He pulled free the leather strap and held the buckled end. Then he reconsidered and shifted his grip to the belt's slender tongue.

A-02 wasn't able to see the belt, but he must have heard the click of the buckle. As he bowed his head, the muscles bulged in his back, flexing in anticipation of the blow.

Shannon remembered how the buckle had flashed like a beacon when it caught the light on its way down. In spite of his previous stubbornness, he cried out.

"Stop!" a towheaded girl wailed from the crowd. "Don't do this. You said you would be lenient. You promised me you wouldn't hurt him. You promised!"

The next blow cut him open from his shoulder blade to the small of his back, and that same girl shrieked as if she felt it herself. On the tenth strike of the belt, when he began to sob uncontrollably and beg for mercy, so did the blonde. Then he started screaming.

And he kept screaming until his legs gave out beneath him and he hung there, unconscious, as the blond girl fainted and the belt came down again and again, and blood gushed down his flayed back, blood flowed to the floor, so much blood that Shannon thought he must be dead, dead as Charles Warren grunted from exhaustion or exhilaration, dead as Charles Warren's sweaty face flushed into a ripe tomato-red and his fingers splotched with the spilled blood, and the belt buckle turned from silver to red, and the belt was like a lunging viper, over and over, into silence.

Now, as she looked down at Hades's sleeping face, his eyelashes as dark as soot against his chiseled cheeks, his words echoed in her head: *I want to make one thing absolutely clear. I'm going to kill our beloved leader, Charles Warren.*

She realized then that if he had the chance to carry out his revenge tomorrow evening, she had no intention of stopping him. Let Charles Warren suffer, for he was the last person in the world who deserved forgiveness.

"I'm sorry," Shannon whispered.

He shivered in his sleep. He mumbled wordlessly and drew an arm toward his face. Underneath the devastation of ruts and ropy knots, his muscles flexed against her palm, at the mercy of a dream of his own.

Before she could draw her hand away, he rolled over and seized her wrist. It happened so quickly, she hardly had time to cry out, let alone defend herself. One moment, she was sitting, leaning over him. The next, she found herself on her back with Hades on top of her, an edge of sharp steel pressed against her throat.

"Who are you?" he asked, with none of the sensual softness he usually affected. His voice was hoarse from sleep, and as cold and piercing as the tip of the blade.

Her heart throbbed in the back of her throat. She was afraid that if she spoke, the knife would accidentally cut into her skin, but that if she didn't, Hades would be the one to jam it there. "Let go of me! It's me, Shannon."

A commotion came from the other side of the room—sheets rustling, Tyler's voice: "What's going on?!"

The room flooded with light. Hades loomed above her. His pupils shrunk into pinpricks, which from her vantage point seemed less like a response to the sudden change in lighting than like the way a shark rolled its eyes at the first taste of blood. His lips had curled back from his teeth, not in a smile, but a bared warning.

"Get off her or I'll shoot!" Tyler shouted.

The blade dropped from her throat, and suddenly, the weight rolled off her.

"How dare you attack her," Tyler said as Hades pushed off the bed.

"I was defending myself," he said, holding the kitchen knife loosely in his hand, blade down. Though he was shirtless, he slept with his jeans and shoes on, prepared. "She snuck up on me, and I reacted."

"Bullshit!"

"Tyler, it was just a mistake," Shannon said, hearing a tremor in her voice. "A mistake. I thought he was you. I just wanted to sit and talk with you. It was an accident, okay? It was my fault."

"Did he touch you?" Tyler demanded, looking at her wrinkled pajamas. His dark, gold-flecked eyes blazed with rage, and he held his handgun so tightly that she feared he would try to bludgeon Hades with it, if not shoot him outright.

"No!" she said.

His eyes widened in outrage. "You're bleeding."

As soon as Tyler said it, she became aware of a stinging pain. She touched her neck. The edge of the blade had barely scratched it. From the pinprick of blood she found on her finger, she knew the wound couldn't be any worse than a shaving nick, but the sight of blood incited Tyler.

"You cut her!" Tyler shouted, brandishing the pistol at Hades.

"I didn't realize it was her," he said coolly, but his eyes were wary, darting from her to Tyler to the gun, then to the door. His fingers flexed around the knife handle, tightening then loosening again.

With a jolt of surprise, Shannon realized that he was *afraid*.

"It was dark," Hades said. "I couldn't see. It was dark. There was a threat, and I neutralized it."

"She's half your size, and you think she's a threat? Look at her! I doubt she weighs more than one-ten sopping wet!"

"Tyler, calm down," she said. "It was an accident. It's not that bad. It's not his fault. I shouldn't have come in here. I'm okay, really. It's just a scratch."

"Can't you see it? He doesn't trust us, Shannon! That's the whole reason he's sleeping with a knife in the first place."

"If I wanted to kill her, she would already be dead,"

Hades said flatly.

"He'll turn on us the first opportunity he gets," Tyler said. "That's probably why he wants to go with us tomorrow night—so he can betray us!"

Dropping the knife, Hades pushed past her. He scooped his shirt and jacket off the end table. As he headed toward the door, his back was to her. The scars had been terrible enough in the gloom, when they were barely perceptible. Shining down from above, the lamp harshened them further, showcasing the way his muscles buckled around the pale striations.

"Where do you think you're going?" Tyler demanded. "I'm not finished with you yet."

"I'm going for a walk," Hades said. "Unless you want to shoot me."

Tyler let him pass, but kept the gun trained on him until the door closed. Then he placed the gun on the dresser, went to her, and took her face in his hands.

"Are you all right?" he asked, looking down at her. His face was still tight with rage, but as he stroked her cheek, his expression softened. "You're trembling."

"It's just a scratch and rattled nerves. I'm fine."

Now that her adrenaline rush was dying down, she felt more embarrassed than afraid. She should have known better than to sneak in here in the dead of night. Even worse, she hadn't heeded her common sense and backed away the moment she realized her mistake, but instead had lingered.

How could she have been so foolish? Of course Hades would have panicked when he awoke to find someone looming over his bedside, touching his back. It was the expected response. He had been trained to see threats everywhere.

"I'll kill him," Tyler growled.

"It was my fault."

"No, it wasn't. You shouldn't defend that sicko."

"Tyler…"

He shook his head in disgust and anger. "There's a first aid kit in the bathroom. Let me get it."

"It's really nothing to worry about," she said, but allowed him to lead her into the attached bathroom.

The cabinet under the sink didn't just contain a single first aid kit, but an entire stockpile of medical equipment and toiletries in sealed containers. He searched through them until he found a bottle of peroxide and a box of bandages.

As he cleaned her cut, she stared at his face, searching his hazel eyes for a sign of what lurked behind his vague, troubled smile. She didn't like what she saw.

"Something's bothering you," she said, once he smoothed a band aid over the small nick. "I want to talk about it."

"I'm fine," he said, returning the boxes to the cabinet.

"No. You're not." She grabbed his wrist. "You were shot, Tyler. No one's expecting you to just shrug off something like that. Are you having nightmares? Is that why you've been acting so strange lately? Please, let's talk."

"It's not that."

"Then what is it?"

"It's him," Tyler said and went back into the bedroom. He sat down on the bed, staring at the floor. At first, he curled his fingers over the edge of the mattress, but his hands were restless, going from one place to the next. He kneaded at the blanket, then gripped his knees, and finally clenched his hands together, digging his nails into his skin.

"When we were attacked at Dr. Miller's house, there

was nothing I could do about it," he said, clenching his jaw. "Not a damn thing. I just had to lie there, helpless, and I couldn't stop thinking about what was happening to you. If they killed you, there was nothing I could do about it. Then *he* was the one who saved us, and I hate it so much. Every time I look at his smug, stupid face, that's all I can think about. I was so helpless. I never want to feel that way again."

"It wasn't your fault." Shannon sat down next to him and took his hands in her own. "You didn't have a choice. If you had tried to leave, you would have been shot."

"That still doesn't make it any better." He sighed and shook his head. "I should have tried. I should've done something other than just sit there with my thumb up my ass, waiting to get myself killed."

She rubbed her thumb over the back of his hand. "Anyone would have done the same. Sacrificing yourself would have done you no good. Anyway, you protected Caroline. You saved her."

"How did this happen to us, Shannon?" he murmured, stroking his hand through her hair. "Just how did it come to this?"

"It's not our fault."

"It's just so unfair and senseless. There's been so much violence."

"I know."

"Can I tell you a secret?" Tyler asked as she rested her head on his shoulder. His hand traced her cheek, then slipped down around her shoulder. Against her, he was all heat and muscle. His blond hair hung over his forehead, tousled by sleep. She liked it that way.

"You don't need to ask."

"I am terrified of what I am capable of. I'm so scared that

I'm going to hurt someone, Shannon, even unintentionally. I just can't trust myself anymore."

"Then trust me," she said. "I know you, Tyler. You're not evil. You're probably one of the nicest people I know."

He chuckled, faintly. "You don't know me."

"You *saved* me," she said. "You talked me out of my brainwashing, when you could've just left me for dead."

"Well, now we're even," he said, like it was no big deal.

Maybe that was what he wanted to convince himself, that his actions had no impact. Maybe he didn't believe that he deserved praise, gratitude, or even her affection.

With a sigh, she threw herself down on the mattress, listening to the springs creak. Comfy bed, if only a bit noisy.

"Can I sleep here tonight?" she asked, wrapping the blanket around herself. "We don't have to do anything that the doctor wouldn't approve of."

She wouldn't mind if he just wanted to cuddle. All she wanted was to forget for a moment that this was a world where teenagers were turned into monsters and children were seen as commodities instead of people.

"Dr. Miller can kiss my ass," Tyler said, drawing a laugh from her.

He turned off the light and joined her under the cover. She smiled when his breath tickled her face. Soft lips pressed against hers, and his hands lowered to her waist.

Later, as she drifted off, she heard him murmur, "Whatever happens tomorrow, I swear I'll die before I let them hurt you."

CASE NOTES 36:

APOLLO

Tyler's plans to protect Shannon derailed during breakfast the following morning. He had scarcely cleared his plate before the food returned for an encore and sent him rushing to the sink. With the vomiting came stomach cramps, horrendous, gut-wrenching convulsions that were so painful it was an effort to even reach his bed.

"This isn't good," Dr. Miller said, studying the reading on her thermometer. "You have a high fever."

"How bad is it?" Shannon asked uneasily, waiting in the doorway. Hades was still in the kitchen, apparently unperturbed by the threat of food poisoning. Then again, judging by the amount of food he managed to shovel in at every meal, he probably had a cast-iron stomach.

"103.5." Miller returned the thermometer to her supply bag and took out a stethoscope. "Let me listen to your heartbeat, Tyler."

"I don't feel like I have a fever," he said, only to be struck by another wave of dry retching. He groaned as she pressed the cold stethoscope against his skin, feeling the cramps gnawing away deep inside of him, twisting his guts. "Just give me a minute. I'm feeling better. I think it was the food. Salmonella or something."

"Take a deep breath," Miller ordered, then glanced over her shoulder. "Shannon, will you please get me a glass of ice water? And there should be a bottle in the kitchen cabinet labelled Emetrol."

He inhaled. The sudden influx of air irritated his raw throat, and he began coughing.

"This is serious." Miller returned the stethoscope to her bag and riffled through its contents. "We might be dealing with an infection. Will you lie on your stomach for me? I need to take a look at your wounds."

He pressed his face into the pillow as she examined the bullet holes. They still hurt, of course, but with each day, the pain had decreased. He didn't think he had an infection. He hoped not.

"I was afraid of this," Miller said, reapplying the bandages. "Your wounds are badly infected. You may roll onto your back or side now, but please, don't get up. You don't want to overexert yourself."

Shannon returned with a glass of water. "I couldn't find the medicine you were talking about."

"That's fine," Dr. Miller said brusquely. "I'll look for it myself. Keep an eye on him for me. Don't let him leave that bed. From this moment onward, he's on mandatory bedrest."

"She says it like she thinks I'm going to make a run for it," he said once Miller was out of earshot, and allowed himself to give a weak chuckle. It hurt to laugh.

"She's in doctor mode now." She took a step toward his bedside, then stopped as if worried he would begin projectile vomiting again.

"Afraid to get within the fallout radius?" he asked.

"The what?"

"Blergh," he said and pretended to hurl.

"Don't you dare throw up on me," Hades said, entering the room.

"Wait, come a bit closer, Hades," Tyler said.

Shannon sat down at the edge of his bed. "Is it food poisoning?"

He didn't want to concern her. "She thinks it's a minor infection."

"Oh."

"Listen, you two can't go without me," Tyler said, looking from her to Hades. "We can do it tomorrow night. I'll be better then, I'm sure. It's nothing serious."

Hades laughed. "Right. I see how it is."

"How what is?" Tyler demanded, annoyed at the mocking humor in the other boy's voice.

"Can't pull the martyr act if you're not there. That's how you got those bullets, right? Were you trying to protect someone?"

"Not everyone is a sadistic, selfish asshole," Shannon pointed out drily, resting her hand over Tyler's.

"You have to be a human to be a sadist," Hades said, grinning. "Last time I checked, none of us are. Not even whitebread over here."

"So, what does that make you?" Tyler asked sardonically. "Pumpernickel?"

"More like moldy bread that's only good to be tossed out," Shannon said.

"That hurts," Hades said, crossing his arms. "I was just beginning to think we might be becoming friends."

"We still have a long way to go," Tyler said and was surprised to see a hint of disappointment darken Hades's features.

"Is that so?"

"At least until tomorrow," Tyler said, and turned to Shannon. "Promise you won't go without me."

"All right." Shannon squeezed his hand. "I promise."

Dr. Miller returned with two pills, and Hades left the room as soon as she entered.

"These might make you a little tired, Tyler," Dr. Miller said, "but they should help reduce your fever."

"I really don't feel that bad now," he said.

"Now's not the time to play Superman. A serious infection can cause organ failure." She waggled a finger in his face. "Your body's your fortress; you need to take care of it."

As he swallowed the capsules, Miller watched him like a hawk. He was almost surprised she didn't make him open his mouth afterward to check if he cheeked the pills.

Like a hawk, Tyler thought again as he began to drift off, and at the memory of her piercing blue eyes, he felt a touch of unease.

Hawks were hungry creatures.

They ate their prey raw and trembling.

CASE NOTES 37:

ARTEMIS

"**I** don't like this," Shannon said, catching the pair of motorcycle goggles that Hades tossed at her.

The sun was still high in the sky. If they left now, they would reach the facility by sunset, the perfect time. But she didn't want to leave Tyler alone and asleep, fighting off his infection. It worried her. He had thrown up his lunch, too, and his stomach pains were so severe, he couldn't even make it to the toilet.

"What's there not to like?" Hades asked, turning away. Though his back was to her, she knew he must be smiling.

"I promised Tyler I wouldn't go without him."

Hades shrugged. "Shit happens. Promises don't mean anything, anyway."

"We should at least wait until he gets better."

"He's not going to get better."

"You're such an asshole!" she snapped, stunned at his bluntness.

"Ipecac," he said.

"*What?*"

"That's what she gave him. I found the bottle in the

trash." He glanced over his shoulder. "It's a drug. It causes vomiting."

"Wait, are you telling me that Dr. Miller *poisoned* him?!"

"I'm telling you that he doesn't have an infection or a fever."

"But she gave him antibiotics."

"They were probably just sleeping pills."

"I'm going to kill her," Shannon muttered, furious that Dr. Miller had done this behind her back.

"Listen, you know it as well as I do that Tyler will just get in our way. He has the right intentions, but he's dead weight in his current condition. You know it, I know it, Dr. Miller knows it, and so does he. Now, you can wait all you want until Charles Warren finds us, just so Tyler could feel a little less useless before he kills himself off, but I want to get this over with now, tonight."

"Don't say that," she said, lowering the goggles over her eyes. "Just because you hate him doesn't mean—"

"I don't hate him. I'd like to one day consider him my friend, but that won't work if he's dead. Corpses don't make good friends."

She couldn't tell if he was joking about wanting to be Tyler's friend. She bit her lip and looked back at the house. Whether serious or not, Hades was right about one thing. If they died tonight, at least Tyler would be spared.

"Besides," Hades continued, "do you really want him crawling through a sewage pipe with an open wound? Mine's closed, and she's still making me wear a garbage bag."

"All right, fair point," she said, slinging her backpack over her shoulder. His bag was already tied down to the motorcycle's luggage rack. "Let's go."

As he put his helmet on, the front door swung open and Caroline rushed out. Dr. Miller had isolated her ever since Hades had shown up, but the close quarters made it impossible to separate them entirely. Still, whenever the little girl tried talking to him, he would act aloof, even frigid. Now, he stiffened as Caroline came up to him.

"What is it?" he asked flatly. His mirrored visor made it impossible to see his expression.

"Mom says you're going away, so I made you this," Caroline announced, holding out a sheet of construction paper.

Hades didn't move. Then, slowly, he took the paper from her, and looked down at it. "The hell is this supposed to be?"

"A picture," she said, her smile faltering. "It's for you."

Shannon craned her head to get a closer look. "Oh, it's beautiful," she said, even though she couldn't make much sense of the scrawled stick figures. She elbowed Hades in the ribs. "Isn't it?"

He didn't respond.

"You're a great artist, Caroline," Shannon said, smiling down at the girl. "I'd pay a million bucks for a picture like this."

His fingers clenched around the drawing, crumpling it.

"Thank you," he said, his voice as tight as a noose. "Thank you, Caroline. I like it."

As Hades began to turn away, the little girl did something even Shannon wasn't expecting—she lunged at him and hugged his leg. He flinched, then reached down as if to push the child away, but didn't. He patted her head once and waited patiently for her to disengage herself.

"Caroline Daniella Miller, get inside this instant!" Dr. Miller shouted from the house.

"Good bye," Caroline said. "Come back soon, okay?"

"She says it like we're going on a vacation," Shannon said, once the little girl went inside.

Hades looked down at the drawing, unusually quiet.

"Are you all right?" she asked, trying not to smile. She wished she could see the expression on his face.

"It's ugly," he said, crumpling the paper into a ball. "I hate it. You couldn't pay me to take this."

But when he thought she wasn't looking, he slipped the drawing into his pocket.

Just as they were getting ready to leave, Dr. Miller came out. Hades climbed off the bike and went to Miller, and although Shannon kept her distance, she was close enough to hear their low conversation.

"So, you're going now?" Miller asked.

"Yes."

"May I hug you?"

He stood there stiffly as Dr. Miller wrapped her arms around him. After a moment, he leaned into her embrace and whispered something in her ear. She stiffened and then drew away, the strangest expression on her face.

As Dr. Miller went back inside, Shannon said, "What did you just say to her?"

"That if we get caught and I learn that she betrayed us, I'm going to tell Mr. Warren that she and Dimitri were conspiring to sell project data." Hades glanced at her. "It's not true, but I think I can be pretty convincing. And it will create doubt, which is just enough to get her killed."

"You've given this a lot of thought, haven't you?"

"Unlike your boyfriend, I'm not a blind optimist," he said as he climbed on the bike. "There's a difference between trusting people and working with them."

The first thirty minutes were the worst. He handled

the motorcycle adeptly, but he drove much too fast for her comfort. After an hour, however, she almost began to enjoy herself.

The sun set.

"Just another quarter mile," she called over the wind, consulting the handheld GPS device that Dr. Miller had bought them.

Hades slowed down and pulled along the dirt shoulder. He waited until after she climbed off before getting down himself and rolling the motorcycle deeper into the forest. He stopped once he reached a natural dip in the earth and unstrapped his backpack from the luggage rack. As he eased the motorcycle onto its side, he glanced back at her. "Help me cover this."

They gathered branches and pine boughs from the ground and scattered them over the bike. The black lacquer blended into the night, but the chrome accents proved more difficult to conceal. She eventually dug up handfuls of dark clay and smeared the dirt over the handlebars and spokes. Up close, the camouflage wasn't terribly convincing, but from afar, the motorcycle resembled a flattened shrub.

As Hades laid down the last branch, he said, "Shannon, there's a favor I'd like to ask of you."

She sighed, in no mood for his cryptic riddles, morally bankrupt comments, or gallows humor. Now wasn't the time for that.

"What is it?" she asked, wiping her hands on the seat of her pants.

"If I die, if you could, burn my body." He kept his back to her. One hand retreated into the jacket pocket where he had put Caroline's drawing, and there it remained. "Dispose of the ashes where no one can find them. I don't care where. The forest, maybe, or the sea."

"Did you seriously…" She couldn't finish her question. He always seemed so arrogant, and until now, she had believed he saw himself as immortal. Death incarnate.

"You heard me right," he said, refusing to look at her. "Burn me. I hate…"

He hesitated. She couldn't see his expression, and that relieved her.

"I hate the thought of someone messing with my body after I am dead," he finished. "Cutting me open, putting needles in me."

"Hades…" It troubled her to think that the idea of postmortem desecration bothered him more than death itself. Then she realized that the situation he described was the very definition of helplessness, especially if he feared some part of his consciousness would continue to exist after life itself had failed.

"I know." He turned to look her in the face. "It's a stupid request."

As she stared into his searing blue eyes, she saw a ghost of what he feared most of all: lying on a cold slab, naked and exposed. Absolutely vulnerable, unable to do anything but endure invasive touching, offensive jeers, and the icy kiss of the scalpel.

"No, it's not," she said. "I understand completely."

One corner of his mouth twitched with an agitated tic, and he maintained eye contact longer than was necessary, as if he could stare into the center of her. "I'm serious."

"So am I."

"So you'll do it, if you can?"

"Yeah. Though, to be entirely honest, I have a feeling you'll outlive all of us."

When he realized that she wasn't joking, he smiled in gratitude. His expression was unlike any she'd ever seen him make before. It was genuine, and instead of conflicting with his sharp features, it softened them somehow, smoothing out the cruel lines of his jaw and cheekbones. In his expression, she caught a glimpse of the boy he could have been.

"Thank you, Shannon," he murmured.

She swallowed, struck by the sudden premonition that they would both die tonight. She wondered if their bodies would be burned or buried. Maybe they would be dissected.

"Yeah," she said, forcing a smile. "Sure thing."

He paused to save the motorcycle's coordinates into the GPS, then began walking.

Pine needles crunched beneath her feet as she left the road behind her. The foliage thickened, and the leafy canopy filled in. Pockets of amber light turned into pinpricks, and shadows spread.

They did not talk after the first hundred yards. If there were any microphones, human speech would attract far more attention than their footsteps alone. She didn't mind it very much. The silence was comforting.

Hades moved with a smooth, almost feline grace. He climbed eroded hills with ease and avoided every hole, outstretched root, and jutting rock, as if he belonged to the wilderness. Every so often, he looked over his shoulder or paused to regard the scenery. When he caught her watching him, he smirked as if their previous conversation had never happened.

If he was enjoying himself, she couldn't say the same. Each time a twig broke, she flinched. The cawing of birds startled her, and when a breeze rattled the branches, she ducked down instinctively, reaching for her waist.

After ten minutes, they stopped to consult the GPS

coordinates. The faint glow of the screen was brighter than the dimming daylight.

The moon rose like a silver token. Even though it was a cloudless night, the full moon failed to penetrate the forest canopy sufficiently, and darkness was plentiful.

He was just a shadow now, lithe and powerful, quiet as a panther. She remained at his side so that they wouldn't become separated. When she tripped over a root, he caught her by the arm.

"Don't fall now," he whispered. A vague smirk tugged at his lips, and she sensed that if not for the possibility of hidden microphones, he would have laughed at her clumsiness.

He let go of her, and she stepped back. They regarded each other for a moment, then he turned away and kept walking.

The forest thinned, and the murmur of swaying branches was replaced by the sound of gurgling water. Hades stopped and raised his palm, gesturing for her not to go any further. As soon as she reached his side, she understood why.

The forest floor dropped into a steep sandstone cliff. Stunted shrubs clung to the edge of the bluff, concealing it from view. Even in broad daylight, if a person wasn't paying attention, it would have been easy to walk off the ledge.

There was no manmade route or ladder, but in places, erosion created a narrow, winding path. Gripping the rough sandstone, she edged forward. Sand cascaded down the side of the cliff as her feet slipped in the loose grit. Under the moonlight, the rock was glacial, and bits of mica embedded in the stone walls sparkled like hoarfrost.

Step by step, they descended, holding onto shrubs

and rocks for support. A howl pierced the night, and as Shannon tensed at the prospect of encountering a pack of wolves or coyotes, Hades lifted his head and smiled, clearly delighted.

You'd be right at home with them, she thought. *You both have the same taste for blood.*

The slope petered out into a narrow rocky shelf. When they reached the bottom, they stowed their holstered pistols in the backpacks they each carried. She watched from the corner of her eye as he put Caroline's drawing away as well.

Water sloshed against the sides of the bank in a steady murmur.

He stood there for a moment, staring at the pipe that extended from the wall of the ravine like a hungry maw. Then he set his backpack on the ground and stripped off his shirt and jacket. In the moonlight, his skin was as pale as the sandstone that surrounded him.

From the outer packet of his bag, he removed a roll of duct tape and a folded garbage bag. He glanced back at her and held out the duct tape. "Think you can give me a hand with this?"

"Can't you do it yourself?"

"I need your help."

Warmth spread through her cheeks as she stepped closer. Glad that the darkness hid her blush, Shannon took the roll from him, trying not to pay too much attention to the chiseled lines of his abs and pectorals. He was doing this on purpose, knowing damn well that he could take care of his wound on his own.

"There's something I've been wondering," Hades said as he wrapped the garbage bag around his taut stomach. "Why were you sitting on my bed last night?"

"Uh, because I thought you were Tyler," she said, mortified that he'd brought up this subject now of all times. Couldn't he save it for another time? Like when they weren't about to break into a top-secret facility or crawl through several hundred feet of hellish darkness?

"No. You didn't."

"It was too dark to tell. You had your blanket over your head, and I couldn't see your face."

"You were stroking my back," he said. "I know for a fact that Tyler isn't scarred there. A few inches lower, and you would've cupped my ass."

"I can assure you, your ass is the last thing I'm interested in. Now, just let me do my job." Shannon looked down so that she didn't have to look at him. She picked at the tape with her fingernails, trying to peel off a strip.

This wasn't like him. Why had he suddenly decided to start talking?

"Do my scars make you uncomfortable?" Hades leaned forward, asserting himself into her personal space. He lowered his voice to a seductive purr. "Does the sight of them fill you with disgust? Or is it just the opposite—are you turned on by them?"

"Neither."

"I'll let you touch them if you'd like."

"You're doing it again," she said, taking a step back.

"Doing what?" A taunting smile touched his lips.

"Being purposely intimidating. Invading my personal space. Laughing at me."

"I'm not laughing at you."

"Not out loud, at least, but I know you're enjoying this."

"I will soon."

She had a feeling he wasn't referring to watching her squirm.

"Let's just get this over with." She finally managed to snare the loose end of the roll and peeled off a long strand. She wrapped it around the garbage bag's upper edge, smoothing it down to create a watertight seal. As she worked, he held the plastic sheeting in place.

Hades had cleaned and tested the guns earlier that day, and again just before they left. He still smelled like gunpowder, but she was close enough now that she detected a second aroma altogether. That natural scent of his, like fire and incense.

"Are *you* enjoying this?" he asked, cocking his head.

"Aren't we supposed to be quiet?" she hissed, earning a low chuckle from him.

"The water will cover our voices," he said. "By the way, you have a cute pout when you're embarrassed."

Shannon shook the roll of tape in his face, praying that he couldn't see the flaming blush on hers. "I'm just about ready to hurl this into the pond. Keep talking, and you can get Ebola for all I care."

"You don't mean that."

"Yes, I do," she said.

"You'd be sad if I died."

"But not if you got Ebola," she said, ripping off another strip. Once she had taped down the lower corner of the garbage bag, she sealed shut the edges. As payback, she used more tape than was necessary, knowing that he would have to tear off each strand from his bare skin once they reached the water treatment building.

"I almost died that night, you know," he said, pulling his shirt back on. "The night I got these scars. I remember now. They told me my heart stopped after they took me to the infirmary, and the doctor there had to bring me back."

"Hades, this isn't like you," Shannon said, glancing

around at the surrounding night. Why wouldn't he shut up? Did he want someone to catch them? Even his flirting seemed uncharacteristic, and she sensed that no affection lay behind his empty words. He felt nothing towards her.

"Where we go, there's just darkness." Hades waded into the water, carrying his bag against his chest. It was waterproofed, but he was carrying his handgun and both Mini Uzis, and it would sink if he dropped it. At least he took that part of the plan seriously.

The pipe emerging from the cliffside was wide enough to admit a grown man. Water poured from its steel lip, just a trickle now, but at any moment, it could become a destructive current. The opening of the pipe was covered by a barred grate, locked with a padlock, just as he had said it would.

The pond reached to her waist at its deepest point. She carried her own backpack well above the waterline, and its contents jostled with each step. An underwater current tugged at her legs. She hated to think what might happen if she lost her balance. Water would surely destroy the delicate electronics, ruining their back-up plan along with it.

By the time she reached him, he had already taken out a pair of bolt cutters. The padlock broke easily, with a hard, metallic snap. The groan that the grille made when he lifted it up was quiet in comparison.

Hades pushed his bag into the pipe, then seized the edge, swinging his body upward as if performing a pullup. His fingers slipped, once, and she thought he would fall, but then his grip tightened and his feet touched unyielding metal. As soon as he was inside, he turned around again and took her bag from her.

She struggled to drag herself up. Her days on the track team had strengthened her lower body, but with no foot holds to take advantage of that strength, she could only hang by her hands from the pipe, grunting all the while. The corrugated metal was slick under her fingers, and the edge cut into her palms.

He reached down and seized her by the wrists, pulling her inside. Her shirt rode up, and she scraped her stomach on the sharp metal, drawing blood.

Fantastic. Open wounds, meet raw sewage.

"Thanks," she whispered.

He stared at her, a trace of uncertainty on his face. At first, she didn't understand his confusion. Then she realized that her gratitude was to blame. Had he never been thanked before, or did he mistake her sincerity for sarcasm?

He gave her no time to wonder, just turned and continued deeper in, crawling on his hands and knees, pushing his bag ahead of him.

She followed after him. The stench of sewage filled her nostrils, and in the trickle that oozed from the pipe, she touched something that felt like mud but probably wasn't.

His penlight revealed narrow pipes branching out from the main tunnel, too small to crawl through. Probably for rain runoff or ventilation.

"Blegh," Shannon said. "This is so gross."

He didn't answer.

"I think I'm going to hurl," she said, wiping her hand on the leg of her pants.

Ahead, he was just a shadow.

Even with the glow of his penlight, the darkness was like a grave. The darkness was like Hell. She'd thought that she had prepared herself for this crawl, but there was no preparing for it.

Hades began gasping for breath. His back arched defensively, and he stopped, pressing his hand against his mouth. The flashlight fell from his hand and landed in the muck.

"What's the matter?" she whispered. She tried to touch his shoulder but instead was only able to reach as far as the small of his back. Was he going to vomit?

He struck her hand away with a low moan. "Don't you fucking touch me."

"Sorry."

"Just give me a minute," he choked.

Shocked, she just stared. His chest shook with trembling breaths. The sounds that pushed through the gaps between his fingers sounded almost like the sobs of a terrified child. Not dry-retching at all.

He had seemed at home in the night. She realized it wasn't the darkness that bothered him, but a combination of that and the size of the pipe. No wonder he had been in no rush to leave the open forest. Had his flirting been a subconscious attempt at delaying the inevitable?

The deprivation tank, she thought, remembering his casefile. He must have gone back there again.

His claustrophobia struck a tender chord in her. Even when he stood only inches from her, he always seemed so far away. Every smile was a smokescreen for anger, hatred, or cold humor. Tonight was the first time he had shown his true face around her, and suddenly she realized that no matter who he was now, he had once been like Tyler and her. He hadn't given up his humanity willingly—he'd had it flayed from him until only fragments remained.

If their circumstances had been different, she could have ended up just like him.

"I hate to be touched," he muttered, lowering his hands. Yet he had allowed her to touch his stomach just minutes before.

"I'm sorry. I won't do it again."

"Just don't touch me without my permission," Hades said, his voice flat and lifeless, without emotion. But even as he reinforced his stone-cold facade, Shannon couldn't get his terrified whimpers out of her head.

He picked up the penlight and crawled forward again. As they continued deeper, her fear of drowning in a sudden influx of liquid poop was replaced by a fear of suffocation. The air thickened, and she found herself struggling for breath. She had read once that methane gas could build up in places like this, displacing oxygen, and now she wondered if that might be the case.

Just her imagination, she told herself. Just the stench of mold. It didn't even smell that bad anymore. It was almost over, she only had to survive it for another few minutes.

His penlight glinted off the corroded bars of a ladder. He stopped and rose off his knees. His body disappeared from sight, and from above her, she heard a dull rap as his knuckles struck metal.

"Just like I thought," he said, climbing down again. "Unless they've changed it since, this one's going to be bolted from the other side. Hand me the blowtorch."

She retrieved the safety mask and handheld torch from her bag. The package the industrial torch came in had promised that it would cut through metal, and she didn't doubt it. As soon as she gave it to him, she backed away, keeping her distance in case molten metal dripped.

It suddenly occurred to her that if there was methane gas in this pipe, the blowtorch could trigger a sudden explosion. Hades might get his wish of being cremated after all.

She cleared her throat. "Hey, maybe we shouldn't—"

An eerie bluish light shone from the opening he stood

in, and sparks rained down like fallen stars.

Okay. No methane. Great. She wouldn't be barbequed to death. Now, that left a dozen other violent ends for her to choose from.

"It's working," Hades said. "I almost have it."

Instead of feeling relieved, dread weighed down on her stomach like spent buckshot. Their mission would become only more dangerous from here on out.

A chunk of metal landed next to her hand, steaming once it struck water. She heard the groan of ungreased hinges, and the glow of the torch was lost to darkness.

As they entered the basement, they did not speak to each other. They left the blowtorch and face shield behind.

A red safety lamp offered enough light for them to undress, though the bulb was caked with dust. She kept her back to him as she changed, but couldn't resist looking over her shoulder halfway through, to make sure he wasn't watching.

Sweat shone on his muscular back; in the sullen crimson light, the perspiration resembled a mist of blood. His scars laid a latticework of shadows against his pale skin.

He hadn't had a chance yet to remove the garbage bag. The black plastic blended into the surrounding dimness, producing an unsettling illusion of a man divided into two, like a magic show gone morbid.

As if sensing her gaze, he turned his head. Tear tracks cut through the dirt smeared on his cheeks, but he must not have realized such proof remained, because he smirked at her.

Back in the tunnel, those had been sobs after all.

She felt a piercing urge to clean the filth from his face and comfort him, but when she took another look at him, she realized that his smile was no feint. He almost seemed excited, as if the prospect of death or capture was better than what waited behind them.

He didn't need her pity.

She used the dry areas of her soiled clothing to wipe the muck from her hands and knees. If they were to blend in, they would need to maintain a semblance of cleanliness. The smell, she could do nothing about. Hopefully, no one would draw close enough to catch a whiff of them.

They changed into clean black uniforms and traded their hiking boots for unadorned sneakers. Hades had brought along his bulletproof vest, and as he put it on under his shirt, envy needled away at her. If he got shot in the chest, he would get away with bruised ribs or minor fractures at the worst. She would die.

Shannon touched the hidden pocket sewn into her shirt. From the outside, it was invisible. Unless you felt for it, or took a close look at a certain button, you wouldn't know it was even there. Hades had a similar pocket on his own shirt, but he seemed to view it more as an inconvenience than a bit of death insurance. Seeing her fiddle with her shirt, he touched his own.

"Now?" he asked.

"Now," she said, reaching under her shirt to adjust the object she had hidden there. "We're on."

Sighing, he followed her example.

As Hades assembled the fake paintball guns, she slipped her pistol into a concealed waist holster. Her handgun's magazine held eight rounds, while the Mini Uzi contained twenty.

Why had they thought that this would ever work? It was one thing to escape from this place, but they were walking right into the lion's den with less than sixty rounds of ammunition between them. Pure insanity. Even though they had enough bullets to mow down every guard in the Academy, they were severely outnumbered in terms of manpower.

They discarded their bags and soiled clothing in the sewage pipe, leaving no trace of their presences except for the breach in the manhole and the mud stains on the floor.

The door at the top of the stairs was sealed, but there was a bolt on the inside to prevent people from being locked in. As they stepped into the empty room, she held her Mini Uzi at her side. She kept the barrel angled down but prepared herself to lift it at a moment's notice. All the while, she cursed him for convincing her to take part in this foolish plan. How could she be stupid enough to think it would ever work?

This is what you get for listening to a psychopath, she thought sourly, though she knew in her heart that she was being unfair. No plan was foolproof, and in any possible situation, they would have been severely underpowered. At least they had gotten this far. That had to mean something.

Machines rumbled, and the rhythmic drumming of pistons and pumps echoed in the walls. The room was a maze of steel pipes and boxes, and as she weaved toward the entrance, she rehearsed the plan in her head.

Assuming the security plan hadn't changed in the last couple years, a guard would be patrolling nearby. If they were lucky, they wouldn't encounter him, but she doubted that their mission would go smoothly from here on out.

CASE NOTES 38:

HADES

Hades opened the door of the water treatment building and stepped out into the night. He heard Shannon's footsteps behind him, and he tried not to think about what she had seen and heard in the sewage pipe. Just remembering it made his blood boil and his hands tighten into fists.

He hated that she had witnessed him in that state. He felt humiliated, and every time he looked at her, he wouldn't be able to forget about it.

He looked straight ahead and banished the thoughts from his mind. Now wasn't the time to get distracted. This was just a game. Just a war game, and he needed to focus. Those memories weren't real, anyway. Forget about them. Forget! The present was the only thing that had any substance.

At the thought, he began to feel a little better. Who cared about the past? It meant nothing.

The main building was three hundred feet from the water treatment facility, through thick forest. He hadn't covered even half that distance before a voice barked out: "What do you two think you're doing?"

Hades turned. Twenty feet away, a man stood dressed in blue. He carried a pistol on his belt, along with a stun gun and a pepper spray canister.

"I'm sorry, sir, we were just returning this equipment to the storeroom," Shannon said.

"Practice kept us out late," Hades added.

The guard closed the distance between them until he was just inches away, as if he could intimidate them simply by invading their personal space. Hades was used to having his personal space violated and was unbothered by it. Indeed, it was the guard's own mistake to get so close to him.

"What are your numbers?"

"Subject Seven of Subset D, sir," he said, eying the man's belt. The pistol's holster utilized a strap to secure the weapon in place, so that if someone tried to make a grab for the gun, the guard would have time to respond. However, unsnapping the button would delay him by a second or two. In a struggle, seconds meant everything.

Shannon averted her eyes. "Subject Thirteen of Subset D."

"The rest of your group returned over an hour ago. What kept you out so late?" He sniffed. "Good God, you two smell like shit."

Her face blanched, and a tic formed on the left side of her mouth. "We were just returning equipment."

"If I had a nickel for every time I heard that one, I'd be able to retire now."

Hades bent down. "Just tying my shoe, sir," he said, fiddling with the laces.

"You're the second pair I've caught this week. Oh, well, it's not my problem. Your subset leader will be hearing about this. All right then, let's go back—"

Gagging, he pressed his hands against his throat, trying to hold back the blood that poured from the open gash across his neck. He stared at the short, wicked blade in Hades's hand, then fell on the grass, jerking weakly. He kicked his leg like a dog in a dream, digging the toe of his boot into the dirt. Then he stilled.

"Why did you do that?!" she demanded, seizing his shoulder.

"Shut up." He pushed her hand away and licked his lips. Tasted blood. A little had splattered into his mouth. Ugh. He spat to rid himself of it, then wiped his face with the back of his hand.

"You heard him," he said once he had cleared his mouth. "He would have notified the captain, and we need a keycard. Do you have any better ideas? Did you want me to shoot him instead and draw attention to us?"

"You could have knocked him out. He wasn't even holding his gun."

"He was the enemy," Hades said, wiping the knife off on the guard's shirt. Unlike Shannon, he had entered this situation with the right mindset—that to complete the mission, one must expect bloodshed. It was an inevitable part of combat. Necessary. No war was fought without death.

After he returned the blade to its ankle sheath, he searched the man's pockets. On a lanyard around his throat, he found an ID card.

"Why are you such a cruel, murderous bastard?" she hissed.

"It's how Dimitri made me." The countless hours in the sensory deprivation tank and the voice recordings, the drugs, the electroshock therapy that blotted out his memories bit by bit—he had Dr. Kosta to thank for that.

As far as he was concerned, the dead guard didn't see him as human, only a subject. So why show mercy to someone who would never reciprocate it?

Shaking her head in disgust, Shannon looked down at the body. "We need to get him out of sight."

"No time," Hades said, pocketing the ID card. "We have twenty minutes until the next patrol comes around. Let's go."

"We can't just leave him here."

"Then you deal with him," he said, then kept moving. After a slight hesitation, she caught up to him.

They reached the main building without further confrontation. The guard's keycard unlocked the side door.

Their footsteps echoed on the linoleum floor. White-washed cinderblocks pressed down on either side of them. Here, the cameras were plentiful, and Hades made a conscious effort to keep his movements relaxed and natural. If they ran, they would attract far more attention to themselves.

A nervous thrill shook him to the core. The taste of blood returned, sharp as iron. He licked his lips again, though they weren't dry, and resisted the impulse to reach behind himself and touch the scars.

In winter, the scars ached and burned. Now, though the air-conditioning left the facility at a mild seventy degrees, the old lacerations felt as cold as ice, tight against the surrounding skin. He shivered in excitement.

He was so close. Soon, it would all be over.

Even though it had been more than two years since he had last walked these halls, he quickly found himself familiarized with the layout. There were plastic plaques on the doorframes to lead the way, but as he walked, he relied on them less and less.

Here was the mess hall, deserted at this hour. Rows of collapsed tables were pushed against the walls. That was where he had gotten belted in full view of the entire Academy, chained to one of the poles supporting the structure.

He continued without stopping. Restrooms, class-rooms, storage closets, the sickbay. That night, he had been dragged down this hallway, certain that his death was not far away. In a sense, he had been correct. His future had been taken with the first strike of the belt, and ever since then, he had been lost. But tonight, he would reclaim himself.

He reached an imposing wood door, without a plaque. Beside him, Shannon adjusted her grip on the gun.

He reached out for the knob and turned it. Unlocked. Though he knew it was unlikely, he sensed that once he opened the door, Warren would be waiting for him on the other side, smoking clove cigarettes. Waiting in the dark with one hand on his belt buckle, fondling the sharp, scalloped edge.

Heart pounding in anticipation, Hades eased the door open and stepped inside.

The room was how he remembered it, dominated by a massive oak desk with a polished stone top. Behind the desk, there was a tufted leather chair, an executive's throne, but in front of it, there sat only a backless metal stool. The stool's legs were so short, an adult would feel dwarfed like a child. Even the furniture was designed to intimidate.

"Where is he?" Shannon whispered, shutting the door behind them.

The noise of running water distracted him. There was another door to his left, where the sound came from. He glanced at her, then jerked his head in that direction.

Keeping her submachine gun pointed forward, she took a step toward the door.

As much as Hades liked the idea of ambushing Charles Warren while the man was taking a dump, he decided that it would be better to wait for him to relieve himself first. He positioned himself on one side of the door and removed the fake CO2 tank and paintball hopper from his Mini Uzi. Maintaining their cover was no longer necessary.

The water continued gurgling. Hades grew impatient. He slammed open the bathroom door and leveled the submachine gun.

Water overflowed from the sink and spread across the floor. The room was empty.

"Hades—"

As he began to turn, a pair of sharp barbs embedded in his shoulder. He didn't even have time to cry out before the first blast of electricity hit, sending him crashing to the ground in excruciating convulsions.

He lost his grip on the gun immediately, but it took almost thirty seconds of continuous voltage until he lost consciousness. The last thing he saw before blacking out was Charles Warren, smirking down at him.

CASE NOTES 39:

ARTEMIS

Shannon woke up on her knees, with her arms cuffed behind her back and her body aching. She jerked forward and nearly fell, would have fallen if not for the hands that secured her.

"Let me go!" She bucked against the powerful arms and tried to rise to her feet. Her ankles weren't cuffed, a small mercy. She got one foot off the ground, only to have her leg kicked out from beneath her. As she landed hard on her knees, the impact jarred her all the way to the tailbone. Her teeth clacked together, sending a flash of pain radiating through her jaws.

She whipped her head around, taking in her surroundings. The room she found herself in was much larger than the office, and though it was tiled, too, that was where the resemblance ended. The tiles were just concrete slabs, and collapsed tables formed a barrier along each wall.

In front of her, a pair of handcuffs hung from a steel pole; the bolt that the chain was threaded through had been welded in place, making it impossible to remove the handcuffs. They served as a constant reminder of the cost of disobedience.

Hades lay facedown beside her, his hands cuffed behind his back.

"Hades," she whispered.

He didn't move.

Her heart sank. Was he still breathing?

"Who should we begin with?" a man mused. "Who do you think would make a better example for the children?"

Detecting movement in the corner of her eye, she turned.

Though it had been over a year since she had last seen Charles Warren face to face, he looked exactly as she remembered. He was a tall man with cold, gray eyes and white hair slicked back from his blockish face. His lips were so thin they were practically nonexistent, but he had such a deep philtrum and chin cleft that it appeared as if the grooves had been hewn into his skull with a butcher's cleaver.

"Well?" Charles Warren asked, striding up to her. "What do you think, Subject Five of Subset D?"

He held a belt in his hands, and as he spoke, he stroked the ornate silver buckle.

A heavy lump formed in her throat. She swallowed. "It's Shannon."

"A rose by any other name," Charles said indifferently.

"What about you?" she asked. "Is Charles Warren even your real name?"

"That's really none of your business." He nodded toward someone outside of her vision. "Let's start with Two."

As two guards dragged Hades toward the pole, she tried to rise off her knees again. This time, the man restraining her stomped down on her ankle hard enough to make her cry out in pain. He felt like a freaking elephant!

"Wait!" she said. "You don't need to do this."

"Remove his shirt and vest," Charles said.

"If it's information you want, I can give it to you," she said, flinching at the noise of tearing fabric and Velcro. "We'll cooperate."

The guards cuffed one hand, then the other. Hades hung like a dressed deer, out cold. It was only a matter of time before he regained consciousness, and that was when the real nightmare would begin.

"You're mistaken. This isn't an interrogation. Not yet. That will come later. This is merely a prelude." Charles moistened his lips. "You two will show the children the price of betrayal. First we'll break your bodies, then we'll break your minds. By the time it's over, there will be nothing left of you. We will break you completely."

Shannon began trembling, and try as she might, she couldn't still the shaking in her limbs. She bit her tongue to keep from begging for lenience. It wouldn't do any good. Mercy was dead here.

"Start bringing them in," Charles ordered, looking past her.

Somewhere behind her, a door opened then closed. Hades stirred, awakened. His fingers clenched around the chain, and he found his footing. Grunting and growling like a leashed dog, he yanked at the handcuffs and kicked the pole.

Mercy was dead, but evil was alive and well. And it was staring her in the face, smiling with lips so thin and sinewy, they might as well have been scar tissue.

"Glad to see you're awake, Two," Charles said, circling around to the other side of the pole so that he might look Hades in the eye. "This brings back so many memories, doesn't it?"

She drew her hands against her back. She fingered

the waistband of her pants, searching for the bobby pin threaded through a hole torn in the coarse fabric, just one of several hidden on her person. Had the pin fallen out? Had they found it?

"I see you're still as wild as ever," Charles said, leaning forward. "I never should have sent you to Dimitri Kosta. It was such a waste. Afterwards, I kept thinking, I should have broken you myself. He ruined you, but I could have *transformed* you. I suppose now I'll have a second chance."

"Rot in hell," Hades said, then spat in his face.

"Was that really necessary?" Charles sighed and wiped the ooze of saliva away with the back of his hand. He circled around to the other side of the pole, out of range. Then he stepped back and raised the belt.

"Don't!" Shannon screamed, but her words fell on deaf ears.

The blow cut a fissure through old scar tissue. Hades refused to cry out, but the tension in his muscles and the way he clenched his jaw betrayed him. Blood trickled down his back.

"We'll have to do something about that stubborn tongue of yours... I think we'll save that for the second or third day. What do you think?"

"I think you can go eat my shit!" Hades said, smiling through gritted teeth as the belt came down a second time. The muscles in his throat swelled with a restrained gasp, and his hands went from the chain to the pole itself, his fingernails digging into the unyielding steel.

She found the bobby pin. She had stripped the wire of its plastic coating. With infinite care, she maneuvered the bare tip into the keyhole of her left handcuff and began probing at the lock's inner workings.

There was a guard behind her and another near the

pole, but how many more? Was there someone near the door, lurking just out of her range of vision? Did they have their guns drawn?

"What about you, Five?" Charles asked, glancing over his shoulder. "Should we cut out his tongue tonight?"

Shannon held her own tongue. Calling Charles a sadist or psychopath would only direct his attention to her.

"That reminds me, I found something interesting of yours, Two." Tucking the belt under his armpit, he reached into the pocket of his suit and removed a crumpled sheet of construction paper. He circled around to look Hades in the face.

"'I love you big brother. Dear, Caroline,'" Charles read aloud and tore the drawing into pieces. "How sweet. Looks like you have a little admirer."

"The only admirer you have is your right hand," Hades snarled.

Shannon fumbled with the bobby pin, nearly dropped it. Her fingers were sweaty, clumsy. Careful! Mustn't drop the pin. She kept on prodding.

"Really, you're the last person I'd expect to be sentimental. Then again, you did throw your future away for a foolish girl, so I suppose it's really no surprise at all." Charles's face lit up with a nasty smile. "Would you like to know something interesting, Two? Senator Hawthorne isn't even Nine's biological father, even though he thinks he is. Can you guess who is? Can you see it? The resemblance?"

She couldn't see Hades's expression from where she knelt, but it must have changed in some terrible way, because Charles began laughing.

"Yes, you see it. And you know what? Her death means nothing to me. She was weak, and the weak must be culled."

An inhuman howl pierced Shannon's ears as Hades

went berserk. The handcuff chain scraped and rattled against the steel rung, and though one of his shoes flew off, he never stopped kicking, as if he truly believed he might be able to tear the pole free from its cement foundation. The skin on his wrists split open as the cuffs cut into them, and droplets of blood splattered on the floor.

"I'll kill you!" Hades shrieked. "I'll kill you! You lying bastard, I'll kill you!"

"The children should begin arriving any moment now," Charles said, circling the pole again. "You'll recognize many of them, I'm sure. So many familiar faces. It'll be like a homecoming."

"You're a liar! I'll kill you! I'll kill you! If it's the last thing I do, I'll kill you!" Hades didn't even sound like himself anymore. Gone was his low, velvety timbre—this voice was all harsh, jagged syllables, spat from his lips like shards of broken glass.

She heard a small click and felt the cuff slip from her wrist.

This would be her only chance. She had to react. Disarm the man behind her. No hesitation.

As the mess hall doors opened and people began filing in, Shannon lunged to her feet and swiveled around. She drove a knee into the guard's crotch as he reached for his holster and seized the pistol's handle before he could even touch it. She drew the gun. Hammerless. No need to cock it. Her finger closed around the trigger, pulled it. The pistol lurched in her hand, warm droplets flecked her face, and the guard stumbled back. She didn't see him hit the ground because she was already turning, searching, the gunshot still ringing in her ears, echoing as she shot a second guard in the head. Then she pointed the gun at Charles Warren and screamed: "None of you fucking move or I'll blow his brains out! Drop your weapons and put your hands in the air right now! Put them up now!"

If they obeyed, she couldn't tell for sure. She began to edge toward Charles, keeping the gun trained on him, prepared at any moment to be shot in the back or side. Many voices spoke at once, making no sense at all, and in the corners of her vision, there surged a shifting sea of black uniforms and confused faces.

Shannon didn't think that the other teens would attack her, not outright, without orders. They would see her as one of them from her uniform alone. If she was shot, it might even trigger a sudden uprising.

Charles Warren refused to raise his hands, let alone drop the belt. He maintained his cold self-composure even with a gun pointed in his face.

"You're surrounded. This little act of disobedience will not benefit you, I guarantee." He extended a hand. "Hand me the gun. Now. Before you regret this."

"Listen to me, everyone!" she shouted, hyperaware of the sound of footsteps and voices, even if she couldn't discern the words spoken. Was someone approaching her from behind? She didn't dare turn around.

"Hand me the gun, Shannon." By using her name, Charles had unknowingly revealed that in a single moment, their positions had changed. The scale of power was shifting in her favor.

Hades twisted his head to the side, watching her. His chest rose and fell in rapid, panting breaths. Certainly, he would warn her.

"Listen to me," she repeated. "These people only want to use us. They see us as pawns. They want us to live and die for them, and they don't give a damn what happens to us! There's a whole world out there beyond these walls, and it's wonderful. It's beautiful. I've seen it. You don't need to wait to be given a home or a name or a family, or any of that! You deserve it, and all you need to do is take it! We outnumber them ten to one, so what's stopping you?"

"Touching speech," Charles said sardonically, "but nobody's listening."

"That's where you're wrong," she said. "We're recording."

The impassive line of his mouth bent into a small puzzled frown. "Excuse me?"

"Livestreaming. We're live. The whole world just saw you torture an unarmed teenager." She raised her voice: "Right now, thousands of people across the country are watching this. Even as we speak, the police and FBI are closing in on this place. It's only a matter of time before they get here, whether you shoot me or not!"

The last part was a lie, pure speculation, and she could only hope that when she'd lost consciousness, she hadn't crushed the hidden camera and lavalier microphone sewn into her shirt. The lens, disguised as a button, was present, but since she had disabled the light, she couldn't tell if the Wi-Fi connection had been lost.

Speaking to the crowd, she shouted, "We're nothing to them! They'll kill us one by one for their own personal gain. Are you just going to let them? We don't belong to them!"

The entire mess hall erupted into noisy conversation.

"She's right! They don't own us!"

"Screw them!"

"Kill them!"

"Shut up." Charles looked around wildly. "Just shut up! What are you idiots just standing there for? Shoot her!"

"We're not numbers, we're people," Shannon yelled, and this time was rewarded with an even greater uproar. "It's time we take back what belongs to us!"

Then a gunshot cracked out.

CASE NOTES 40:

CHARLES WARREN

*T*hwack!
　　As Charles Warren came to, he heard a familiar sound.

Thwack!

Hot moisture ran down the side of his head. His skull throbbed, and though the muscles in his arms ached, he couldn't feel his hands.

Thwack!

It was the sound of leather striking against skin.

The first thing Charles saw when he opened his eyes were the bloody lacerations on Subject Two's back, those vertical lines that had oozed and dribbled all the way down to the waistband of his pants. The two wounds were located almost parallel to his shoulder blades, an artistic and unintentional placement, and Charles suddenly thought of the severed wings of a fallen angel.

An angel of death.

Thwack!

As Two turned to him, Charles's feet found purchase on the cement floor, and he hoisted himself up. The handcuffs binding him to the pole rattled, the cuffs tight enough to cut off his circulation. His hands were senseless lumps of flesh, purplish and bloated. His mouth went dry as he discovered that he couldn't move his fingers.

"Glad to see you're awake, Mr. Warren." Two stepped up to the pole, looking him in the eye. He folded the belt in two and snapped it against the palm of his own hand once more. Testing it. "This brings back so many memories, doesn't it?"

Charles began to tremble. Goose bumps rose on his bare back. His guards. Where were his guards? How could this have happened?

As if reading his mind, Two said, "We're all alone. The others have already moved on. Our coup d'état took all of five minutes. When the first guard was shot with his own weapon, the rest of them tried to put up a fight. It didn't last. Most of them are dead now, and the rest will die soon enough. You're lucky. If you hadn't fainted, you would've probably been drawn and quartered."

Damn them all! The children owed him their lives. If not for him, those ungrateful little brats would never have been born in the first place.

"I have to give it to Shannon, I never would've thought to incite a riot," Two said. "I'm impressed. She's looking through your office right now. Soon, everything will be brought into the open."

Open. That's it!

"Pandora's box is opening," Charles said, using the code phrase that Dr. Kosta had created to control his brainwashed subjects.

Subject Two froze, his smile fading. "Olympus is rising," he said, in the numbed voice of an obedient soldier.

Charles smiled. Thank God. Why hadn't it occurred to him to use the code before, back when Five had a gun pointed at his head?

Oh well. That didn't matter. There was still time to turn this disaster around, and there was no pawn more perfect for the task than the boy standing before him.

Even as a fifteen-year-old, Subject Two of Subset A had possessed an exquisite mind for strategy, dominating the wargames the children held against each other. If not for Two's insubordination, he would have made a great military leader. Now, Two's ruthlessness and cunning would give Charles the chance to regain control of the situation.

"Uncuff me," he ordered.

Two's full lips quirked in a smile, and he began to laugh. "Nice try, but that's not going to work. You know, Dimitri never needed to use a code with me. An alternate personality was never created. He just tried destroying the first one."

Damn it! He would have to try a different tactic. Surely the boy was smart enough to see reason.

"L-listen, we're both adults here, Two. Let's discuss this like civilized human beings. Maybe we can come to some sort of a-a-arrangement. Yes, an arrangement. I'm certain there's something that you want. Something that I can provide."

"You talk too much, Mr. Warren."

"You're being hunted by the police, I know. I can ensure your safety. Truly, I can. No one will ever hurt you."

"Maybe I should cut out *your* tongue."

"I have enough money and power to provide for you your whole life. You'll live comfortably, without a care in the world. You'll live like a king."

"You know, I'm a little surprised to see there aren't any scars on your back. I thought you might've done to me what somebody else did to you. But this…it's like a blank canvas, huh? We'll have to change that."

Thwack!

"I regret handing you over to that idiot Kosta," Charles blathered, flinching at the snap of the belt against Two's palm. "It was a waste of your talents. I understand that now. You have a superb tactical mind, and more importantly, you have something that cannot be taught — raw charisma. You could have accomplished so much with the right influence, and you still can. You can become my second in command."

"Oh. Second in command. That's good. I like it. It's quite the promotion."

"Don't do this."

Two continued to circle him like a beast closing in for the kill, gripping the belt strap. He fondled the silver buckle, running his fingers over the polished onyx insets. "Do you know how long I've waited for this?"

Those eyes. Oh God, those eyes.

Thwack!

Closer now.

"Please, what can I do?" Charles asked.

Thwack!

Two was right behind him now. "Bring back Nine."

Charles's mouth went dry.

"I lied," Charles said shrilly. "I'm not her father!"

Thwack!

"Resurrect her."

"P-please forgive me."

Thwack!

"If you can't do that, you can just die."

The buckle end of the belt slammed into Charles's back. He grunted, curling inward on himself.

"Hurts, doesn't it?" Two asked. "I've always been curious, do you enjoy receiving pain as much as you like giving it? Does this get you off, beloved leader?"

"You'll regret this!"

"No, I'm going to enjoy this. Greatly."

CASE NOTES 41:

HADES

He felt nothing.

On the long ride to the Academy and in the days preceding the infiltration, Hades had imagined how the moment might go, how he might feel when the life drained from Warren's eyes. Yet as he walked back into the hall and the mess hall doors swished shut behind him, he felt a sickening emptiness form in his gut. No satisfaction. No thrill at the kill. Just an absence that grew bigger by the moment.

Charles Warren had taken everything from him, had destroyed his future and his very purpose for being. So, why wasn't he glad the bastard was dead? Why had the sight of blood or the man's screams failed to make him feel *something*?

Hades walked into Charles Warren's office and found Shannon standing behind the desk, examining the laptop. When she noticed him, she stopped typing and stared. Presumably at the blood dripping down his bare arms.

Shannon took a deep breath. "I'm not going to ask."

"Are you sure you don't want all the intimate details?" he asked, going to the adjoined bathroom.

"Spare me," she said.

"He suffered." Hades washed his hands at the sink, scrubbing the blood out from under his nails. "But not enough."

Still, although the man had deserved to suffer even more for his crimes, no amount of torture would have made a difference in how Hades felt. Not when the kill had only drained him.

He needed more. He needed to feel, to have his existence reconfirmed somehow. Otherwise, it was like he wasn't even alive at all.

"Are we still recording?" he asked, drying his hands on a towel.

"No," Shannon said. "I'm almost done here. 90 percent of the files have been transferred. I've deleted the files with the code phrases. Apparently, we weren't the only ones they tried to brainwash. We can review the rest with Tyler and Dr. Miller before we leak it, just to make sure there's nothing else that's dangerous."

"I want a copy of the files," Hades said, going to the desk.

She stared at him. "Uh, why?"

"Because I'm not going back there with you." He searched through the drawers until he found a portable hard drive, which he laid on the blotter pad. "This will do."

"Wait. What do you mean you're not going back?"

"This is where we part ways," he said.

"Don't you want to go home to your mother?" she asked, attaching the hard drive to the laptop using a USB cord.

"No."

"I thought..." She hesitated and looked back at the screen as if to avoid meeting his eye.

"That I would kill her?"

Shannon didn't answer.

"She's no longer a concern of mine," Hades said. "She can do what she wants with her life."

His plans were far more ambitious than matricide, and if everything proceeded as he expected, they would occupy him for an indeterminable amount of time. He would have plenty of time to decide what he intended to do about his cell donor, if anything. Maybe the proper punishment would be for her to be a spectator to the consequence of her creation.

"What about Caroline?" Shannon asked.

"What about her?"

"Don't you want to be a brother to her?"

He chuckled. "I'm not brother material, Shannon. I'm not going back to that house to pretend to be something I'm not. Why maintain the charade of a family, when you and I both know that those people aren't my family and never will be?"

"You don't have to run anymore. I'm sure the police will find you innocent, once they learn the whole story. I mean, as soon as they see that video, they'll realize you're a victim."

"I appreciate your optimism, but innocent is the last thing I am," Hades said. "I have no delusions about what I have done or what has been done to me, or how people like you see me. I refuse to spend the rest of my life imprisoned somewhere."

"Even if you don't turn yourself in, it's never too late to start over. You can make amends for the crimes you've done and do good deeds."

Like he was stupid enough to believe that. Did she really think she could guilt trip him into behaving like the common sheeple?

"I thought you hated me," he said, deciding that now wasn't the time to call her out on her clichés.

"I don't," she said. "I think...I can finally count you as a friend."

"A friend, huh?" he said, then smiled. "It's mutual."

"What are you going to do now?"

"You and I are the only people here who've seen the world," Hades said. "For starters, I'm going to talk with the others. I'll tell them what to prepare for, and their options. I figure we have an hour or two before the authorities arrive. That should give us enough time."

"Maybe I should stick around," she said. "Help you with that."

"Just go back. I can deal with it on my own. Besides, your boyfriend's waiting for you."

"Everything's changing." As she turned her palms up and stared down at them, her face clenched in sudden dismay. "It's strange. After I pulled the trigger, I thought my hands would start shaking. But they never did."

Telling her that she was evolving as a murderer would score no brownie points with her, so he chose a more tactful response: "You fired in self-defense. That's why."

"And then I let you do that to him, just walked away..." Tears misted her eyes, and she pressed a hand against her mouth to prevent a sob from escaping. "What's wrong with me?"

Hades wasn't sure how she wanted him to respond. Did she want him to answer or even comfort her?

She flinched when he reached toward her, but allowed him to brush the hair away from her face. He found a patch of moisture on her cheek. Those really were tears. Why cry for someone like Charles Warren or for a guard who stood mutely by as the belt came down? Or was she crying for herself?

"Nothing at all," he said, lowering his hand.

"Take care of yourself," she said at last, removing the hard drive. "Get those cuts checked out. You might need stitches."

"You're concerned about me," Hades said. "That's touching."

"I'd just hate to see you get Ebola." Shannon unplugged the laptop next and wrapped the charger cord into a bundle. She slipped both the laptop and its charger into a leather briefcase she must have found in one of the cabinets or desk drawers.

They walked out to the loading bay together. Cars waited in the dark, and they went up and down the rows until she found the one that matched the key she had taken from Charles Warren's office. As she opened the car door, he reached out and grabbed her wrist.

She looked back.

"I have one last favor to ask of you," he said.

"What it is?"

"Dr. Kosta made me do terrible things, Shannon," Hades said, choosing his words with care. "Detestable things. Worse than anything you two did. The police know my face, and they'll be looking for me. They'll never give up. If you do decide to turn yourselves in, I want you to tell them that I died here. A fire will be set once you leave. It will be a controlled burn. The bodies will be charred, unidentifiable. I don't think the police have my DNA in the system. But they might, so just tell them that I was shot. You couldn't save me, and you were forced to leave me behind. Can you promise me that?"

He knew for a fact that the police had his DNA on

file, or would soon enough, but that didn't matter. This lie would give him a small lead, enough time to do what he needed to do. What was necessary to feel alive.

"I understand." Her fingers closed around his, and she gave his hand a small squeeze. "I promise."

"Thank you."

"Good bye," she said. "Wherever you end up, Hades, I hope you find happiness."

"I'm sure we'll meet again."

Smiling, Hades watched her drive away. Then he stepped back inside the main building. Ten minutes later, he returned to the front yard, where many of the others had gathered to enjoy the spoils of the raid. Some of the teens had already fled, but the majority remained, uncertain of where to go. In need of a leader to guide them.

He carried a garbage bag that he had found in the kitchen. Its contents bumped against his leg. Though the night was cold, he didn't search the barracks for a jacket or shirt. He wanted his audience to have the full view of his back, of those twin banners of clotted blood draped over the scar tissue beneath. His mark would become his rallying cry.

There was a grouping of picnic tables on a concrete slab in the middle of the courtyard. As he stepped onto one, he felt dozens of eyes on him, watching, waiting. The teens had seen his vulnerability, his helplessness. That was unavoidable. It was necessary to remedy their opinion of him. To earn their trust, he would need to show them his power and ruthlessness.

Hades had taken a pistol off one of the dead guards, and now he fired a single shot into the air, silencing the teens' conversations. A few reached for weapons they had stolen from the armory, but no one opened fire upon him. Gunshots were something they were all accustomed to, and they were tame enough to recognize him as an unhostile presence.

He holstered the pistol.

"I was once Subject Two of Subset A, but now I am Hades," he said, raising his voice so that even those near the barracks could hear him. "Two years ago, the Leader told me that I was a weapon, not a person. He told me that I had no right to freedom, and that I was born only for the purpose of dying in servitude. And so that I wouldn't forget, he cut that message into my back."

Now, it was so quiet in the field that he could have heard the drop of a pin.

"That girl lied," Hades said, "when she told you that the outside world is a wonderful place. It isn't. Not for people like us. Once we step through those gates, we will only have each other. The authorities will arrive here soon, and they will treat us just as badly as we have been treated here. We are not human in their eyes. Don't think for an instant that they'll keep you with your own subset— they'll never let any of us see each other again. We will be segregated, imprisoned, exploited, and killed. I know this because I have seen it."

More kids joined the growing crowd, listening in on what he had to say. His confidence swelled, and he found himself stepping back in time, into the commander role he had assumed during wargames. Yes, it was just like that time. These were his soldiers. It was his duty to guide them.

Killing Warren had done nothing to fill the hole inside of him, but maybe this would. The other subjects could hear him, they could see him. He wasn't in danger of fading away as long as he was their leader.

"On the other hand, the pigs who did this to us will be

treated like royalty. They will *never* pay for their crimes. That is not justice." Hades reached into the garbage bag. Knotting his fingers around damp white hair, he pulled out the object housed within and bared it in front of him. "*This* is justice!"

Perseus holding the head of Medusa couldn't have had a greater effect on them. Everyone stared in awed silence, and Charles Warren stared back—one eye filmed over red, the other frozen, askew and sightless.

He threw the decapitated head onto the ground. Not a person, not anymore. Not even a part of one. Just a piece of trash coated in blood and dust.

"Join me," he said. "Help me bring justice. I am the only one here who knows what's outside these gates. I am the only one who can lead you. Who are you going to trust in the end? Adults who've never known true suffering, or one of your own? Well? Who wants justice? Who's with me?"

Affirmative cheers shook the crowd.

Yes. This was how he could prove his existence.

"We're in this together." He raised a fist to the sky. "Let's destroy the Project and everyone who's ever benefited from our suffering."

The other subjects roared in support, stomping their feet and lifting their fists as well.

"We won't stop until they're all gone," Hades shouted. "They will pay for their crimes in blood!"

CASE NOTES 42:

APOLLO

Tyler woke in the night to a presence at his bedside. In the gloom, the person was a silhouette, faceless and indistinguishable.

He tried to sit up, but cool, firm hands pressed him back down.

"Shh," Dr. Miller said, gripping his shoulders. "It's okay. It's just me."

"Something's wrong." He felt separated from his body, like his flesh was a glove that he had partially slipped out from. His movements were sluggish, burdensome. Was this weakness a product of the fever, or an effect of the pills Dr. Miller had given him the last time he had awakened?

"You're okay."

"I feel weird."

"It's just the fever."

"Shannon? Hades?"

"They've left. You don't have to worry about them anymore."

"Wait. Where did they go?"

"Shh. You're very sick." She dissolved into the dimness. Even with the lamp turned on, he struggled to see her as she turned her attention to an object on the nightstand. It was so dark, he could make out only the faintest outline of her profile.

It took him a moment to realize the gloom was a product of his own vision, not reality. The fever or the drugs.

"One moment." Dr. Miller's hands emerged into view, gloved in white latex. In the time it took to blink, a hypodermic syringe appeared in her fingers. She tapped the plastic tube with her fingernail. As she tested the syringe's plunger, a stream of clear liquid shot from the end of the needle.

"What's that?" he asked, finding the strength to sit up. The entire world rotated around him like a midnight carousel.

"Just something to help reduce your fever," she said, taking his arm. As the needle pricked his skin, he noticed a figure standing in the far corner. The lamplight glinted off the round lenses of the man's spectacles.

His confusion accelerated into panic, and he shoved Miller away from him before she could administer the entire dose. By the time the syringe hit the ground, he had already moved out from under the covers.

As he stumbled off the bed, the blanket ensnared his limbs. Dragged off balance, he fell onto his hands and knees.

His gun. Where was his gun? In the dresser, by the man. Shit!

He found his footing and lunged for Hades's bed, praying for once that the boy still kept a knife under his pillow. His hand touched empty space.

Damn it!

Swiveling around, Tyler backed away from the two of them.

"Get away from me," he growled.

"There's nothing to be afraid of," the man said, drawing closer. His shoes were black, but the pants he wore featured a pale houndstooth print. In Tyler's dimming vision, he appeared to float above the ground like a footless specter.

Panic peaked into the purest terror. "Get away."

"You remember me, don't you? It's me. Dr. Finch. I used to take care of you."

"Stay back. Just stay the fuck away from me. Don't come any closer."

"I'm here to take you home now."

Before Dr. Finch could reach him, Tyler turned and fled from the room.

The hallway tilted around him, growing darker by the moment. In his disorientation, he lost all sense of direction. As he stumbled into the kitchen, he encountered two men carrying a gurney between them.

The man facing him let go of the gurney and lunged. Tyler swiveled around and reentered the hallway.

Back door. He needed to find the back door. Where was it?

His thoughts grew muddled, merging, fading as he opened doors with abandon. He stepped into a dark room unfamiliar to him and closed the door behind him. As he searched along the narrow walls for the light switch, his foot met empty air where there should have been solid ground, and he lost his balance and fell.

It was a miracle he didn't break his neck as he tumbled down what turned out to be an incredibly uncomfortable set of stairs. When he landed at the bottom, he lay there, bruised and battered.

His body screamed at him to stay still and let the drug carry him off, but terror won over. He climbed to his feet and groped along the wall, searching blindly. He found the light switch and turned it on.

Concrete floor. Plastic bags of sealed items, metal barrels, boxes of goods, and little else. A window, too small to climb through. No storm windows or window wells. There were two other doors, which he limped to, hoping that one might lead outside. The first led to a closet crammed with pipes and purring machines, which Tyler assumed regulated the home's heat and water systems. The space was too small for someone to walk uninhibited in, let alone hide in, so he hurried to the next door and opened it.

Although the rest of the house was floored in concrete and dark wood, this room was all tile, from one wall to the other. There was nothing aesthetically pleasing about the white ceramic squares, which climbed four feet up the wall, or the bright bulbs that turned on when he flipped the light switch. As for the decor, it consisted of a glass-enclosed shower cubicle and a large refrigerator-like container that was ten feet long by five feet wide.

His gaze sped from the wall to the rectangular box, too large to be a freezer. Its exterior was coated in white enamel or plastic, giving the container a dull, matte depth, like a sea of fog. As he stepped closer, he saw that there was a hatch on one side, sealed tight, with steel safety bars on either side of the door.

It couldn't be.

Caroline's words echoed in his ears: *"I don't want to go back."* At the time, he had assumed she was speaking nonsense, afraid of the dark and in a panic. Now, too late to save even himself, he realized this is what she had been talking about.

The tank door made a soft sucking sound as he opened

it, as the rubber seals were released. Inside, water lapped against the narrow walls. Even with the lamps on, little light reached through the hatch. Once the door was closed, it would be pitch-black in there.

Odors of chlorine and Epsom salt rolled over him, conjuring vague memories of floating in a place so similar, with Dr. Kosta's voice, calm and deep, speaking to him from the darkness: "*Your name is Tyler Bennett. You are a hard-working student, respectful and well-behaved. It is your life's aspiration to join the military. Your name is Tyler Bennett. You are a…*"

Repeated over and over.

This box. This despicable coffin.

It was a sensory deprivation tank.

Had Dr. Miller performed mind control experiments on her own daughter?

His gaze lifted. Over the tank, there was a small window. Probably too small to crawl through, but maybe he could break the glass. Use a jagged shard as a weapon.

Or use it to cut his own throat.

Hearing footsteps, Tyler turned to find the two large men passing through the doorway. Dr. Miller and Dr. Finch waited behind them.

This is it, he thought. *I'm not getting out of this. They're going to take me back there.*

"You're a psychotic bitch," he told Miller as he edged away from the tank. The cogs in his brain churned as he tried to come up with a strategy. "You've been experimenting on your own daughter."

"You're wrong, Tyler," Dr. Miller said. "I've been teaching her how to use her brain to its fullest potential. She will never be saddled with fear, as I once was."

The mother of a monster was a monster herself.

"Get away from me," he said as one of the men advanced toward him.

"There's no need to fight us," Dr. Finch said. "We're not going to hurt you."

"You killed all my friends. You took them to the white ward and they never came back." The words left his mouth before he even realized he had spoken. He felt like he was channeling a different side of himself. Channeling a demon.

"You aren't like them," Finch said. "You're a success."

The man lunged forward, reaching for him. Tyler sidestepped him, only to be seized from behind by the second guy, anchored with one arm folded around his neck.

Ducking his head, he bit into the man's arm, clamping his jaws down like a rabid dog. He tasted blood and sour sweat.

"Ow, the bastard bit me!" the guy screamed and threw him to the ground.

As Tyler rose to his knees, a crushing weight slammed into his spine, forcing him down again. He writhed against the restraining hands, and through an excruciating torsion, managed to flip onto his back.

"Stop struggling!" the man growled, tightening his hold on Tyler's wrists. "You're only making this harder on yourself."

"I hate you," Tyler said as Dr. Finch leaned over him. "I hate all of you. I wish you were dead."

He felt the needle but didn't see it. Within seconds, his remaining strength flowed from his limbs, leaving him numb and senseless.

As the darkness flowed in, a name formed like a prayer on his lips: "Shannon."

"Forget about her," Dr. Miller said, and then there was nothing at all.

CASE NOTES 43:

ARTEMIS

As authorities swarmed the Academy to find it deserted save for a few stragglers, half a dozen torched corpses piled in the yard, and a group of very young children, Shannon drove through the night. She rolled down the window. The wind blew against her face, cold and refreshing, infused with the scent of wet pine. She shocked herself by laughing aloud.

It was finally over. By now, the video would have gone viral. Project Pandora wouldn't be able to bury this.

For the first time in a long time, she felt hopeful, as if she actually had a future to look forward to that didn't involve senseless violence.

On the road up to Dr. Miller's home, Shannon passed a long black car followed by a larger van, like the sort used to refrigerate meats. The road was so narrow, she was forced to pull over to the side and wait for the two-vehicle procession to pass.

All the lights were off in the house. She found the front door ajar.

"Dr. Miller?" she called. "Tyler? We're back."

No one answered. She turned the lights on in the foyer

and the kitchen.

"Dr. Miller? Caroline?"

Silence.

Her confusion honed into panic as she ran from room to room, turning on the lights, searching. At the sight of the sensory deprivation tank in the basement, her stomach plummeted. She realized at once the kind of woman Dr. Miller was. Tyler had been wrong all along.

As she opened the lid of the tank and stared into the empty darkness, she suddenly remembered the cars she had passed on the road up. The vehicles hadn't struck her as unusual at the time, but now the memory of them spurred her up the stairs and out of the house.

She threw open the truck door and leapt inside, pausing only long enough to buckle her seatbelt.

Ten minutes. It had been ten minutes since she had passed the cars.

There was only one route down the mountain, and the other vehicles had been driving at a slow, cautious pace. No doubt because it was dark and they were transporting human cargo. They had to be careful. She could not afford to be careful. If she hurried, she would be able to catch them.

Shannon pressed down on the gas, accelerating. Gravel crunched beneath the truck tires.

Trees formed splintered walls on either side of the road. Although the truck was built for sturdiness, as evidenced by its thick armored exterior, it wouldn't escape a crash unscathed. Neither would she.

Ahead, she spotted red rearview lights. The moment she approached, the van increased its speed.

Her truck's gas tank was less than halfway filled, and Shannon knew she wouldn't be able to maintain a long-distance chase. Besides, there was nothing preventing the van's drivers from calling the police on her. She did not have that same luxury.

She needed to stop them, and she needed to do it now. The road would only get more narrow and treacherous from here on out, with sharp turns and sheer cliffs. This was the safest place to crash.

Shannon increased her speed until she was alongside the van. Her truck's rightmost set of tires spun only inches from the edge of the embankment.

Shannon took a deep breath, then gave a short, sudden jerk of the steering wheel.

As she slammed into the van, she almost lost control. The steering wheel slipped under her fingers, and the truck shuddered in spite of its sturdiness. Her seat belt cut into her chest, as tight as a noose, and her organs jostled sickeningly against her ribcage.

The van careened off the road and struck a tree. Steel crunched, glass shattered. Blood bloomed across the ruined windshield like an inky smog.

She stopped in the middle of the roadside. Ahead, the black car screeched to a halt.

Her hands trembled as she disengaged her seat belt. She reached across the center console for her pistol and touched worn upholstery. Damn it! Where was it?

Steel glinted from the passenger seat's footwell. Leaning over, Shannon groped for the gun. Found cold metal.

The pistol felt surprisingly light, but she didn't realize the reason why until she was out of the car and touched an empty slot where the magazine should have been. When the gun had fallen, the disengage button must have accidentally been pressed.

No time. Couldn't go back. The moment she darted back into the truck, the people in the black car would know that she was unarmed and go in for the kill. They would shoot her through the windshield before she could even reach the magazine.

Shannon stumbled down the shallow embankment, loosening soil and rocks. She reached the van and yanked open the back door.

The interior of the vehicle was outfitted like an ambulance, with containers along one wall and a long bench along the other. Ruts in the floor locked a stretcher in place.

The impact had been violent enough to throw the two men in scrubs against the wall, knocking one into unconsciousness and bloodying the other's nose. But it wasn't powerful enough to dislodge the stretcher, or tear the canvas straps stretched across Tyler's hips, waist, and chest.

She hauled herself into the cab just as the second paramedic began to rise and shoved the pistol into his face. "What did you do to him? Answer me, now!"

"Hey, hey, just put that thing down," the man said, lifting both hands. "He's just sedated. Christ, please don't shoot me. I have a wife and kids."

"Get out."

The paramedic leapt out of the van and stumbled up the embankment. She jumped down from the cab and watched him go. He lost his footing and slid onto his stomach, losing several feet of altitude before he regained his balance. He resorted to crawling the rest of the way, whimpering until he reached the black car. As the paramedic got inside, the driver's window rolled down.

Dr. Miller stared at her, and she stared back.

As the car sped off into the night, Shannon knew one thing: Project Pandora might have been done for, but Project Prometheus was still very much alive.

ACKNOWLEDGMENTS

The Assassin Fall series was my first venture into publishing. As I worked on the series, it fully dawned on me how much of a team effort it is to get a book published. So much goes on behind the scenes in publishing that the book you're reading now wouldn't be possible without the time, help, input, and support of many people.

Liz Pelletier, the CEO and co-founder of Entangled Publishing, has been delightful to work with and has provided invaluable editorial advice for *Project Prometheus*. As well, I would like to thank her assistant editor, Hannah Lindsey, and Heather Riccio, Entangled's assistant publisher, for helping me along the way. All of Entangled Teen's team has been so welcoming and kind, and it has been a pleasure to collaborate with them.

I would also like to thank my critique partners who read this novel in its earlier stages of development: Brenda Smith, Laura Creedle, Diamond Wortham, and Chris Bedell. I feel blessed to have met such fantastic writers, and look forward to reading the stories you send me in the future.

When *Project Pandora* was released in 2017, I was stunned and pleased by the response it received from book bloggers and readers. Thank you to everyone who has read the book and enjoyed it, and I hope that *Project Prometheus* has provided a satisfying continuation to the first book in the Assassin Fall series!

Grab the Entangled Teen releases readers are talking about!

Echoes
by Alice Reeds

They wake on a deserted island. Fiona and Miles, high school enemies now stranded together. No memory of how they got there. Each step forward reveals the mystery behind the forces that abducted them. And soon, the most chilling discovery: something else is on the island. Something that won't let them leave alive.

Unraveled
by Kate Jarvik Birch

Ella isn't anyone's pet anymore, but she's certainly not free. Turns out the government isn't planning mass rehabilitation… they're planning a mass *extermination*. With the help of a small group of rebels, Ella and Penn set out to end this for good. But when they're implicated in a string of bombings, no one is safe. If she can't untangle the web of blackmail and lies, she won't just lose her chance at freedom, she'll lose everyone she loves.

WICKED CHARM
BY AMBER HART

Willow Bell thinks moving to the Okefenokee area isn't half bad, but nothing prepares her for what awaits in the shadows of the bog. Everyone warns Willow to stay away from Beau Cadwell—the bad boy at the top of the suspect list as the serial killer tormenting the small town. Willow questions whether she can trust her instincts…or if they're leading to her own death.

BLACK BIRD OF THE GALLOWS
BY MEG KASSEL

A simple but forgotten truth: Where harbingers of death appear, the morgues will soon be full.

Angie Dovage can tell there's more to Reece Fernandez than just the tall, brooding athlete who has her classmates swooning, but she can't imagine his presence signals a tragedy that will devastate her small town. When something supernatural tries to attack her, Angie is thrown into a battle between good and evil she never saw coming. Right in the center of it is Reece—and he's not human.

What's more, she knows something most don't. That the secrets her town holds could kill them all. But that's only half as dangerous as falling in love with a harbinger of death.

entangled teen

an imprint of Entangled Publishing LLC